What the critics have to say about
Liz Williams:

"Williams has mastered the art of writing clearly and believably about weird, alien worlds." *The Times*

"Williams weaves a rich, complicated tapestry that merges life with afterlife, otherworldly with worldly and human with inhuman." *Publishers Weekly*

"Williams' forte is her depiction of driven characters in richly realised settings." *The Guardian*

"Williams is one of the most original and distinctive voices in British SF." *SFX*

"A cocktail of styles, flavoured by the fruits of an astounding imagination." *SFCrowsnest*

"Adventurous, thought-provoking science fiction." *The Times*

"An author who continually produces intelligent, creative and entertaining stories." *Green Man Review*

"Williams' unique cross-genre voice is a reinvigorating one for SF, fantasy and horror." *Publishers Weekly*

A Glass of Shadow

Liz Williams

NewCon Press
England

First edition, published in the UK July 2011
by NewCon Press

NCP 037 (hardback), NCP 038 (softback)

10 9 8 7 6 5 4 3 2 1

ISBN: 978-1-907069-27-7 (hardback)
978-1-907069-28-4 (softback)

Cover art by Anne Sudworth
cover design by Andy Bigwood

Minimal editorial interference by Ian Whates
Text layout by Storm Constantine

Printed in the UK by MPG Biddles of Kings Lynn

This collection is dedicated to:

Trevor Jones BA (Hons)

The author would also like to thank:

Ian Whates (my lovely editor), The Milford Writers' Workshop, which whipped several of these stories into shape, and Tanith Lee: for being an inspiration.

Contents

A Glass of Shadow

An Introduction

by Tanith Lee

If Liz Williams has a motto, it may well be: *Have Mind, Will Travel.* From the moment you open this collection, you leave the Known behind and enter the brighter, darker, more *actual* possibility that lies just through that door, over that hill, behind the sky.

The ableness of Williams' expeditions to otherwheres is by now well-established. I was lucky enough to learn of her work early in the 2000's, and began with her tremendous *Empire of Bones* (whose organic space-craft, to my mind, have never been rivalled, let alone bettered). She became instantly for me part of that newer, (much) younger battalion of writers who, collectively or individually, give me such glad hopes for the future of speculative, and all imaginative, writing.

Since then, it goes without saying, she has stayed constant to her very high standard, maturing a little, as we all prefer to do, but losing nothing of her flare and immediacy. She also possesses, evidently, a wide library of personal knowledge, not only about peoples and countries to be found on the globe, but the alchemic arts, antique science and astronomy, and the practices and strata of operational Magic, history and its sociologies, humankind et al. Or at least, judging by the authority and logistics of her work, I can only *assume* so! And she is versatile too, something else I personally value very highly – she ventures into all areas of the so-called "Fantastic". Other planets, ancient landscapes – of mind as well as terrain – the far future, the parallel future or past, the delicious, the horrible, the enlightened, and the bitterly sad. Williams is ready to cross genres whenever her material calls for it. As in *Empire of Bones*, where deistic India, and beings from farthest space, meet and mingle like jewels of many colours in a cleverly made casket.

For she is a writer who can encompass both SF and Fantasy, combine knife-edge cool with the sensually romantic, bardic lament with clinical inquiry, the Outside with the In, the insider and the outlawed inside-out. In other words, she is what the genuinely addicted reader prays for: a free-flying innovator still grounded in the roots of a world from which we all derive, whether imaginatively or ancestrally.

To read these stories is to be taken on many journeys. Each is, in its own way – and often geographically – a travelogue through other places, times and parallel Earths so close that their changes, subtle or astonishing, fit like gloves. Williams would seem, physically, to have been everywhere, not excluding the pre-Christian Celtic West, Mars, and Hell. And she has approached every civilisation and culture, earthly or otherwise, with a razor keen eye, yet too with the respect and wonder suitable to all pilgrims. Her discoveries she sets out with the lightest, clearest touch. Her prose, despite the several different voices that speak in these pages, is always spare and concise, though it never lacks exquisitely essential details, nor evocative highlights – red the *colour of a still-beating heart* – snow that falls like *owl feathers*... An understated, innate poetry often infuses the fast-running narratives. These phrases remain with you, just as the plights and triumphs of her characters come back for brooding re-examination.

Williams understands psychology, human or non. They all ring true: ghosts, were-things, heroes and villains, the wise-maiden, the Victorian pragmatist, Goth-girl, hunter, lover, spy. This writer can take a reading from her source as effortlessly it seems, and as accurately – as *legibly* – as any of the cunning machines she has coined. No corners are cut. And though *never* gratuitous or gross, no hard facts are smoothed over. These people and beings *live*, they have brains, hearts – and souls. An exact blend of the mathematical and the spiritual seems to tailor Williams' outlook on worlds. If her supernaturals frequently have their claws firmly on the ground, her science, sometimes, has seen God. I must add too that there is something of the philosopher in Liz Williams. And nor is black humour absent.

But for those of us who like otherwheres, what is paramount here is the fascinating scope of her ideas.

Amongst other exotica you will visit the remains of a drowned London, where a clouded young girl uneasily tends her child, and a future-past Singapore as the latest in hot bands finds access to demons only too simple. You can witness an Eastern Europe lying in the melancholy debt of a sort of mythic Chernobyl or, cast out far from *any*where, discover the real secret of the Egyptian *Book of the Dead*. Why not join the quest after spiteful fey-like spirits on Blackheath, or forbidden desire on the ice, or, within the core of Venice, the outcome of a cure for betrayal-of-the-heart. As for Dracula – let Williams take you to Whitby. You may never think of his kind in quite the same way again.

Best of all, you can trust your guide. Not only marvellous story-telling, but an underplayed and non-judgemental compassion run through the collection. Not every dilemma is solvable. Not every wrong can be righted. And that being the case, an echoing, even beautiful sense of anomaly (reminiscent of Russian literature) lingers across the sequence. A kind of glowing dusk of thought, that stays in the mind long after the last page is turned. A shadow that, like a good wine, provides a haunting *second* taste, once the contents of the glass have been consumed.

Tanith Lee
February 2011

7 Mr De Quincey and the Daughters of Madness

Outside the walls of the cottage, winter snaps at the heels of the fells. The last dose of the drug lies bitter on my tongue, but in a very few moments, this will change. The drug will spread its dark honey through my veins and summer will come. Already, the door is opening with a stealthy caution to let in the night wind. It should be cold, bearing snow on its breath, but instead it warms me: a spice wind, out of the east and the morning, dragon-coiling around the room and sending sparks up the chimney. Beneath it, lies the familiar smell of ancient flesh. I can sense her presence as she comes to stand behind me. I remember the deaths that she has caused, which lie so heavily upon my conscience, and for the first time in years I am able to smile.

"Leave the door open," I say, and without turning round, I tell her "I won't be long. I have a few amendments to make to my manuscript."

She does not answer, but I know that I can rely upon her agreement. Even though it has been many years since we stood in the same room together, our compact was forged in blood and pain and loss. Yet not even those threads are unbreakable: she violated her word many years ago, and there is no reason for me to keep mine. Still, there is a little time, and I have changes to make to my most famous work.

I hope that these amendments will explain matters to you with a sufficient degree of clarity, and that they might perhaps help you to understand the nature of my long and shameful addiction as well as the reasons for it. For the sake of our friendship, I owe you the truth. I do not, you understand, entreat you to publish these alterations. History may judge me as it will; it's of no concern to me now. Let the old manuscript stand as it was originally published.

I first encountered my mistress when I was no more than a youth. As you know, I was obliged to abandon both my studies and what remained of my family as a result of the cruel treatment meted out to me by my guardian. Having either more spirit or a greater gift for folly than my fellows, I resolved to exchange my place of learning for the lessons of London and of life.

My early days in that great city were marked, you will recall, by hunger, cold and the lack of a roof. The latter, at least, was remedied by my move into the house of the person whom I have referred to elsewhere as my benefactor. I have implied that this gentleman was anxious to keep his affairs secret in the eyes of the population at large. I have not, however, said why.

Mr ------- was in truth a friend of my late father. They had been at school together, but had kept in erratic contact once Mr -------- began to travel abroad. I still had the address, however, and it seemed the greatest good fortune that my first visit there coincided with Mr -------'s return to his native shores after many years. My resemblance to my parent was evident, and Mr ------- greeted me with the greatest enthusiasm and expansively invited me to treat the house as my own. This was not quite, perhaps, the munificent gesture which it initially appeared. As I have recounted elsewhere, the house had been abandoned for some considerable time and was inhabited largely by rats and spiders.

It was also the dwelling of a girl even more ragged and forlorn than myself. I have spoken of her in my memoirs, although I fear that I have somewhat rearranged the sequence of events and personalities in order to conceal the true facts of her unhappy fate. She was one of those unfortunates whom society describes as fallen, preferring as ever to blame the victim rather than those who have aided her in her descent. Her name was Ann. Hardship and horror very rarely manifest themselves in generosity of spirit among such women, contrary to the general myth, but Ann was young enough to feel a genuine human kindness towards those as unfortunate as herself. Nothing of a professional nature passed between us, but we became friends. I resolved that, as soon as my fortunes were regained, I would rescue her from the inevitabilities of her life and take her north with me, where we could live out our days in peace and relative prosperity. Needless to say, despite all the romantic impulses of youth, I had no idea how this could be accomplished.

Mr ------- was, ostensibly, a practitioner of law. I have told of how he used one of the rooms of the neglected house as a study. He slept elsewhere, however, leaving the house at nightfall and returning around ten in the morning on the following day. At first, I was of the opinion that his legal practices were conducted principally around the margins of society; his manner was habitually nervous and, on the infrequent occasions when he had a visitor, he would request either myself or Ann to ascertain the guest's identity before admitting them. The room in which he worked was an untidy rat's nest of papers, old law manuals and letters; Ann swore that it was haunted, and would not enter. At first, I assumed that this was no more than a girl's fancy, or some fable told to her by Mr --------- to ensure that no curious fingers interfered with his legal paraphernalia, since he said nothing of the matter to me. Whatever the truth of the matter, Ann would not go near the study after the fall of dusk. Her agitation was such that we were obliged to abandon the floor of the house on which the study lay, and took to sleeping up in one of the attics beneath an old horsehair blanket, our heads pillowed on a mouldering pile of legal manuscripts.

Despite my natural youth and resilience, my health at that time was very poor – a result of starvation and fatigue – and my sleep was habitually interrupted by pain. On one particular night at the beginning of spring it was especially bad, and I was compelled to rise from my makeshift bed and wander around the room. It was a cold night, with the glitter of late frost riming the roofs of the city, but very clear. Standing at the window, wrapped in an ancient blanket, my eyes strayed across the heavens, seeking the stars. The frost imposed a veil of silence over the city: I could, I thought fancifully, hear the stars themselves as they wheeled in their endless course across the sky. And as I listened, I did indeed hear a sound. It came from downstairs: a stealthy, uneasy rustling.

Despite (or perhaps as a result of) the hardships I had suffered, I still retained the confidence of youth, which greets danger without thought to the consequences. I went to the door, peered out into the darkness of the landing, and made my way silently down the stairs. I could still hear the sound, which was coming from the study. It occurred to me that if this was indeed some inimical intruder, I might need something more than my hands and a mouldy blanket with which to meet it. Searching hastily about, I could see nothing which might serve my purpose, so with belated prudence I decided to see what manner of enemy I was dealing with. I put my eye to the crack of the study door, and peered in.

At first, I could see nothing, but gradually a shadow separated itself from the surrounding darkness, gliding silently across the room. Its movement was too regular to be that of an ordinary person, and I felt a prickle of fear shiver down my spine. I also became aware of a peculiar odour: something separate from the usual musty dampness of the house, like an underlay of ancient spice. I remembered uneasily how it was said that the cooks of Turkey and the Indies employed powerful condiments to mask the taste of rotten meat: this was that sort of smell. I must have drawn a breath of revulsion, for the presence halted and turned. A voice whispered something that I did not understand, and my unwilling feet were compelled into the room.

My memories of what next took place are hazed with a sensation uncannily similar to that produced by the drug to which I would later become enslaved. It was as though I lay upon the edge of sleep, and experienced that sense of falling which often occurs before one succumbs to the arms of Morpheus. The dim form standing in the middle of the room was that of a woman. She was dressed in a long shift: pale as bone and dappled with blue shadows. As she turned her head, her hair rippled like rain. Silently, she held out her arms. Had it not been for that pungent odour and its undernote of decay, I'm afraid my natural inclination would have been to rush into them: I was, you must remember, only seventeen, and thus lacked a certain caution that comes – if it comes at all – only in later years. My hesitation did not, however, prove a barrier. I blinked, and found her standing only inches away from me. Reaching up, she put her arms around my neck. It would have seemed a little churlish to force her away. She was shorter than I, and her face seemed to change in the moonlight, becoming first reminiscent of my mother's countenance, then of girls whom I had known in earlier years and who had taken my fancy. I ran my hands down her sides; I felt as though I was drowning.

What should have been a pleasant experience, however, soon turned into something else entirely. To my eyes, the girl still possessed the same slight and elegant form, but my hands told me otherwise. Beneath the soft, pulpiness of her breasts was an arching hollow of bone, as though she had an excessively narrow waist. With an unpleasant sense of fascinated revulsion I ran my fingers along her sides and discovered innumerable ridges of a sinewy substance, which were wet as though slimed with moss. This seemed to please her: she moaned and twisted in my arms, and I felt a sharp tongue run the length of my throat. There was the sudden reek of fresh blood. Someone was calling out the name of the Lord in a loud, hoarse voice: with some surprise, I recognised it as my own. It did no good whatsoever. My seductress was clearly intent upon her purpose, and unlikely to be distracted by the summoning of opposite powers. With a rush of strength that, in my currently debilitated state, amazed me, I twisted a foot around her fragile ankle and we crashed to the floor. Struggling to gain my feet, I heard someone calling my name.

"Tom! Tom! Oh, dear God!"

It was Ann. Overcoming her natural terror, her affection for me had drawn her down the stairs and into the study. My seductress lay beneath me, her head thrown back and her face as devoid of expression as an abandoned doll. It was as though the upper half of her body was nothing more than a disguise: akin to those moths which bear the semblance of an eye upon their wings. A ribbon of steaming flesh ran along my skin; a pocket of gristle encircled a part of my anatomy that, at that particular point, I would rather have left undisturbed. With a dim sense of shame, and more pain than pleasure, I felt myself compelled to discharge within it. Having done so, I was immediately released, with as much finesse as someone ejected from the door of a whorehouse. I found myself standing by the door, in a considerable state of disarray.

Ann's ragged gasps of horror echoed in my ears. My attacker sat up, her head lolling backwards as though her neck was broken. Leaping forward, I seized Ann by the hand and tried to drag her free, but it was too late. A razor-edged flap of flesh seared my wrist and I let her go. With the greatest shame I have ever felt, I confess that I turned and ran. I did not look back until I was standing outside the house, with the sweet spring wind blowing and the dawn coming up over London.

After this, it would be hardly remarkable that I sought the oblivion of opium. Yet my reason for doing so was more than mere fear, as I shall shortly relate. I spent the next night sleeping rough on the streets of the city. The wind from the river seemed laden with ice, and the ground was hard with frost, but it was still preferable to my recent lodgings and after my abandonment of the girl, no more than I deserved. My guilt gnawed at me like rats at the flesh of the damned; eventually, I resolved to return to the house.

With the greatest trepidation, overcome only by my concern, I made my way back to the place that had made so unsettled a home. I am afraid that I took care to visit it in broad daylight.

The house was gloomy, silent, and empty. Motes of dust spun in the shafts of sunlight from the grimy windows, and the mice scuttled in the woodwork, but otherwise there was no sign of movement or life. Swallowing my fear, I looked into the study. Papers littered the desk and floor, and tossed into a corner was a fragment of a scarf, which I immediately recognised. I do not need to tell you to whom it had belonged. Heavy hearted, I walked out of the house and with my last remaining coins caught a stagecoach north.

My life followed an erratic pattern over the years. I befriended many individuals, my chosen companions being artists and poets, since it seemed to me that they had seen something of the realms that lie beyond the world, and might therefore be called upon to advise me when the hour came. For I was certain that it would come; the knowledge that the creature in Mr -------'s study had not finished with me seemed to have sunk deep within my bones. When I heard, through an old friend of the family in London, that Mr ------- had been found dead in the most peculiar circumstances (never fully explained to me) I knew that it would not be long before the demon disgraced me with her presence.

At this time, I lived close to the home of someone whose name has passed into history as one of the leading poets of the age. He and his sister inhabited a cottage high in the Lake District, and we became good friends. There were, I know, hopes that I would one day marry Dorothy Wordsworth, but I knew that this could never be the case. She was an imaginative, fragile soul; such people see too clearly into the edges of the world and it appalled me to think that she might catch a glimpse of what lay there. As soon as I realised what the Wordsworths' expectations were, I took care to disabuse them. I am sure that I hurt her, but I could hardly tell her the truth. Instead, I set up house in a neighbouring valley, attended by a local girl whose powers of imagination extended only to the most material things of life. At length, in an attempt to provide her with the security which my lost Ann would never know, I married her. It was not long, however, before I acquired another, less corporeal, mistress.

It had been a stuffy, muggy summer, and the air lay heavily in the folds of the fells. Though no longer the frail, starving boy I had been, I still suffered from sleepless nights, and on this occasion I relapsed into a kind of fitful doze. My dreams were filled with shifting, queasy colours, and eventually I awoke with the immediate knowledge that there was someone else in the room. My mortal paramour was away, visiting her mother. I knew exactly who my guest was.

She was standing at the end of the bed, grave and still. As soon as she saw that I was awake, she smiled. Soft light seemed to play across her face; she was very lovely, but I could only remember the horror of her beneath my hands.

"Get away from me," I said. To my own ears, my voice sounded thin and old.

Lithely, she stepped around the end of the bed and sat beside me on the covers. Reaching out, she touched my face with a hand that felt damp and dead. I am not ashamed to say that I tried to scream, but found myself abruptly incapable of uttering a sound. She was murmuring to me in some unknown language, and the sounds she was making did not seem to emerge from any human throat. Then she said simply

"Do you want your wife to die?"

She spoke in perfectly good English, but I noticed that the movement of her lips did not match the words. I shook my head.

"Then understand this. It is your choice. In order to live, I need one of two human substances: a woman's blood, or a man's seed. I will not come to you every night, or even often. I will not harm you," her voice changed, to become thick and soft and fond. "How could I?"

I thought of Ann, and of the other girls whose lives had doubtless gone to feed this monster. I thought of my long shame, that I had been too cowardly to save the girl who had been my friend. The demon filled me with revulsion, but I could not face the thought of being the cause of my own wife's death. I made my choice, resolving as I did so that I would endeavour to find a means of ridding myself of the demon.

It was shortly after this that I paid a visit to the local chemist and procured a bottle of laudanum. With the aid of this narcotic, I found that I could dull the senses to such an extent that the visits of my succubus were rendered, if not pleasant, at least bearable. She visited me monthly, during the dark of the moon, and I used the excuse of the drug to sleep alone during those nights. Our arrangement wreaked havoc upon my nerves, however, and I began increasingly to rely upon the drug.

I have made the best of my addiction to opium. Its legacy has been the work that has kept my name in the public eye during the course of this century, and I suppose that I have had much for which to be grateful. I had my friends, throughout the Lakes and beyond, and once I had taken pains to repair the breach between myself and William's family, little Kate Wordsworth became as dear to me as if she had been my own.

During the years, too, I became almost accustomed to my demonic mistress' nocturnal visits; grew almost used to the sensation of changing, unearthly flesh against my own. I grew to regard her as a creature more pitiful than horrifying: trapped within the dictates of her own nature, striving for survival. She kept her promise, and stayed away from my wife.

I used to talk with the demon, and as long as I did not touch her, the illusion of the young and beautiful girl lying by my side served to a certain degree as compensation, especially through the merciful veil of the drug. She would not tell me her name, perhaps because she did not know. She was very old; she remembered nothing of her creation nor her origins, but she came out of the east and it is my belief that she was perhaps generated by some oriental alchemist: an experiment that had failed. She tried to describe where she went to when she was not with me, but here words failed her. I gained the impression of a chaotic place, filled with moving lights.

And then she broke her word. The Wordsworths were staying with me at the time. Slyly, I had told them that I would be journeying to London on the day that my mistress was due to visit, ensuring that they would be away from the house; but when they were due to leave, the child Kate fell ill. It was, very probably, no more than some childish complaint: a fever brought on by the exertions of the day, but William insisted that she should be allowed to rest. Throwing them out of the house was unthinkable; not without trepidation, I pretended to cancel my imaginary journey and let them stay.

That night, I waited for the approach of my mistress, but nothing happened. My nerves were on edge, and I had taken a larger dose of laudanum than usual in order to quiet them. I give this as explanation, not excuse. Gradually, over the course of the next hour or so, it dawned on me that she was not going to manifest, and as irritated as if I had been neglected by a cherished human lover I rose from my bed. It will not come as any surprise as to where I found her.

She was sitting on the edge of Kate's bed, holding the child's hand in her own. Kate was smiling, but the fever burned brightly in her eyes and in the gaze of my unearthly lover I saw an uneasy mingling of guilt and desire.

"We've been talking all night," the child whispered proudly. "All about China, and India, and all sorts of places."

"I'm sure it's been very interesting," I said. "But you really should try and get some rest now," and I held out my hand to the thing sitting on the bed. And as she rose, I saw there was blood on her mouth.

She came with me quietly. I led her into the bedroom and closed the door, but when I turned back, she was gone. In the morning, Kate began to languish further, and that evening she died. The Wordsworths were, of course, distraught, but I was little better. I blamed myself and the drug in equal measure. Memories of Ann returned to haunt me anew, and these two lost children blurred into one another to become one and the same. A

22

month after Kate's death, I lay waiting for the demon to return, but she did not come. One might have thought that I would have been relieved, but on the contrary, I was distraught. Now that our bargain had been broken, the demon was loose in the world, presumably preying on whomsoever she pleased, and it was at this point that I resolved to do all I could to determine how she might be found and slain.

I undertook my spiritual enquiries with renewed vigour, travelling to London to search the libraries for information, but none of the practices I surreptitiously tried had any effect whatsoever. I confided in priests and conjurors and poets, but no one could enlighten me as to where the demon might be found. I even went back to my benefactor's house in London, only to discover that it had been ravaged by fire shortly after his death. Each avenue of exploration seemed to lead nowhere, but I did not yet relinquish hope.

Since it appeared that I had been released from the demon's influence, there was no longer any need to rely upon the illusions of opium. Moreover, the pleasure it brought me was matched by my revulsion at what it had caused me to do. If I had not drugged myself, Kate might still be alive. I resolved to rid myself of the habit, and then I discovered that I could not. My demon lover may have been one of the daughters of madness, but so was opium. In seeking to protect myself, I had merely exchanged one demon for another, and now the drug began to bring new visions, fuelled by guilt and shame and loss.

My quest consumed the remaining years of my life, and at last I was convinced that I had found the way to summon the demon back. I had been studying the practices of Quabbalism for some time, and I made my preparations with considerable care, my aim being to bind our souls together and take the demon from the world in death. It seems that these preparations have worked, for she is here. I find that I cannot hate her, despite all that she has done. Age has brought me a greater understanding of what it means to be alone, and unloved, and to live on the edges of the world, always looking in at the lighted window of other people's lives. Yet she has preyed on this world for too long, and I, too, feel the need to atone for my sins. And now, before we become entirely lost in the long dream of the drug and death, I reach out to take her hand and though she now looks like nothing I could ever have imagined, her fingers in mine feel as human as those of the girl I left to die, so many years ago.

Mr Animation and the Wu Zhiang Zombies

In Singapore Three, séances are always a risky business. Hell lies too close for comfort, and the gods don't protect fools. So I had deep misgivings when Xu Lu Han said that the best way to promote *Chainsaw Killa* would be to summon a spirit at the wetdisc launch. It would make the disc a hit, he said; put the band on the map and ensure that the Zombies would be in demand in every club in town.

I should have protested at the time, but I didn't. The main reason for this was that I was secretly terrified of Xu Lu. True, I thought he was a moron, but I also considered him to be a dangerous one. This was partly a result of his appearance. Xu Lu was bad enough in a good light and the open air, but in the smoky darkness of the Shanxi Club or Juna's, he was nothing short of horrifying. Someone had once told me that he'd been separated at birth from a twin, and at the time I believed this without question since it seemed to explain such a lot, but I later discovered that he'd had his face razored up in a schoolyard fight, and had gone straight to the local skin sculptor to have it remoulded. He was thirteen at the time, from a dirt-poor family, and the results of the remoulding made Xu Lu look as though someone had held him over a flame like a toy soldier, until the flesh had dripped and run. He flaunted his scars in conjunction with a thin mohican that ran like black oil down the centre of his scalp, and a dead-eyed bloodshot stare. He liked to tell people that he'd actually died and been resuscitated, hence the nickname: *Mr Animation*. No one ever called him Xu Lu except me, and then only in the privacy of my own head. It made him a little less like an animé cartoon and a little more like a human being. A little more, but not very much.

It was a shame, really, that I couldn't bring myself to think more highly of *Chainsaw Killa* either, because my younger brother Jhun had written it and it was the first song – indeed, the first thing – that he'd ever managed to achieve. I suppose Jhun and I are polar opposites, in a way. I've always been the studious type (nice retro spectacles, bookpad, NuGap trousers) whereas Jhun was the one to rebel against what he perceived to be maternal strictures. Dad's no longer with us, having skipped up the coast to Hong Kong in search of a fortune. I take after my mum.

Anyway, after the fights and the drug deals (happily nothing more serious than nitromite and soma ore), Jhun's announcement that he was auditioning as a drummer with the Wu Zhiang Zombies seemed like a comparatively positive move. And once he'd actually joined the band, it seemed sensible for me to tag along and keep an eye on him. Heaven knows, I was hardly the archetypal New Century punk, but I did have an exhaustive knowledge of late twentieth century animé and anarchy hardcore house, and this was enough to win me a grudging place on the sidelines of the band. Since the twentieth century was now six years away, Jhun tended to regard my knowledge in the light of ancient history. Xu Lu himself didn't like me, but he'd have lost face in acknowledging my presence, and so he simply ignored me. This suited both of us. My brother Jhun ignored me as well, but I think he was actually rather pleased to have me hanging around. He was, after all, only fifteen, whereas both Xu Lu and myself were twenty, and Jhun knew I'd back him up if things turned nasty. I might wear NuGap clothes, but I still had a black belt under them, metaphorically speaking. Moreover, I lent Jhun a certain amount of credibility as a result of my musical knowledge, and as the irredeemably straight sibling, I made my brother look almost hip. So by the time that Jhun had got it together to write *Chainsaw Killa*, things had attained a certain degree of equilibrium. And then Xu Lu announced that it was time to hold a séance.

I suppose I'd been expecting something like this for some time. Xu Lu had recently split up from his latest girlfriend, which I think had a lot to do with his mood. He'd started shooting a lot of cendra, and his conversation had that unmistakable amphetamine edge. Even when he was quiet you could hear his teeth; grinding on relentlessly like some engine deep in the bowels of the city. The girlfriend had been a dancer at Juna's; a theoretically lovely girl with a permanent collagenic sneer and eyelid tucks. From a distance, she could have passed as a Westerner, and eventually she'd slept with a sufficiently large number of the US Embassy staff to get a visa for the States. I like to think that Xu Lu, despite his psychotic demeanour, was actually secretly something of a romantic; the break-up seemed to hit him hard. He wrote a number of obsessive songs, in which American bitches featured with worrying prominence. Eventually, however, something inside Xu Lu seemed to snap. He called the band together. I wasn't invited, but I went anyway.

The Wu Zhiang Zombies, Xu Lu announced between grinding molars, were losing their edge. If they wanted to promote *Chainsaw Killa* properly, they were going to have to reclaim that darkness of spirit that had got them where they were today. And the way to do that, Xu Lu announced without a trace of irony, would be to summon the hungry ghost of Acid Razor; greatest of all anarchy hardcore rockers, who had been decapitated by his own brother in 2003 as a result of a deal gone wrong. The day on which the séance would be held was the third anniversary of his death.

As soon as Xu Lu made this lunatic proposal, there was a sudden strained silence. I could see Jhun shifting in his seat, trying to look tough, but something was flickering behind his eyes. He was afraid, and I wasn't surprised. The very mention of Hell seemed to bring it closer: shimmering darkly just beyond the edge of vision, as though someone or something was starting to tune in an antique radio. The bass guitarist, a guy named Ho who rarely spoke, shifted in his seat.

"Do you think that's wise, man?"

Xu Lu peeled off his shades and gave Ho an old, cold stare. "Wise? Who the fuck knows what's wise these days? Wisdom's over, man. Dead concept. There are risks, and there are successful risks, is all." He reached into the pocket of his laminated combats and pulled out an ancient digital watch. "We now have seventy seven hours and falling before Hour Zero. Count down, people, and load up."

With that he stalked out of the room, leaving us with the sick realisation that he'd stage-managed the whole thing.

"What do you think I should do?" Jhun asked, as we walked along the waterfront. I was a bit pleased. It was the first time he'd ever asked my advice and I took it as a sign of increasing maturity. I think I had some idea of helping him walk his own path, so to speak, accompanied by my sage guidance. Some kind of Shaolin trip. With this in mind, I said, "What do *you* think you should do?"

"I dunno," Jhun said helplessly, shifting his narc-O-gum from one cheek to another and booting a dead rat into the oily waters of the dock.

"Well," I said. I was enjoying this, in a condescending kind of way. "Let's approach the problem logically. You can participate, or not participate."

"But if I don't go, Xu Lu will think I'm *h'siao shen*."

I wanted to tell him *So what the hell, if that imbecile thinks you've got no balls?* But he wasn't old enough to really run with that.

"And if you go?" I asked. Jhun rolled a nervy eye in my direction.

"Something might happen?" he ventured.

"Something might indeed happen. And what do you think that something might be?"

"Dunno," Jhun echoed. "The séance might – well, it might *work*."

Off the side of the wharf, something surfaced for a moment, then plunged, leaving a spreading coil of ripples. There were few fish in the city's polluted harbour.

"That," I told him, "Is a distinct possibility." As soon as the words were out of my mouth, I knew what I had to do. A vista opened up before me, comprised of new and dangerous possibilities. I saw the chance to get Jhun out from under Xu Lu's thumb once and for all and a long way down in my subconscious, I also glimpsed the opportunity to revenge myself for all Xu Lu's slights and sneering. We would indeed be conjuring a spirit, but not Acid Razor. I had something rather different in mind.

"I think," I said, "that maybe you should go to the séance. Think of it as a rite of passage. A test."

Jhun thought about this laboriously for a few minutes and then he nodded. We looked at one another in the half-light, and then he reached out and gave me a sort of punch on the arm. It wasn't much, from your brother, but it was enough.

I've never been sure, though, whether it really was my persuasion that made Jhun go to the séance. He was too scared of jeopardising his burgeoning rock reputation, and too mortified to countenance Xu Lu's scorn, not to go. And I went with him, of course. I couldn't let him go on his own. Neither of us said anything to mum. We told her we were meeting my friends in the park, for football. It sounded healthy, and she'd never have believed it if I'd told her Jhun had a study evening.

On the evening of the seventh anniversary of Acid Razor's death, Jhun and I headed for the Shanxi Club. Xu Lu wanted to hold the séance before the main performance, in order to summon the required dark energies, but I could hear the band rehearsing as we turned the corner into Shanxi Road. It was a pulsing undercurrent of sound, like the grinding of vast distant teeth. It seemed to travel along the pavement and strike lightning up the spine. Jhun turned to me and for the first time in my life I saw a kind of teary pride in his eyes. He said, "Jesus, they're shit-good, aren't they?"

The band had something, I had to admit. Quite what, remained to be seen.

When Jhun walked through the door, Xu Lu got up from his chair and prowled across the room.

"What's *he* doing here?" he snarled, giving me a baleful look.

Anticipation is the forefront of attack. I said quickly, "You're familiar with this, I'm sure?"

I took Wan Sung's *History of Demonology in Ancient China* out of my pocket and thrust it under his nose. "It's all about séances," I said.

Xu Lu gazed at it with the hauteur of a visiting scholar and muttered, "Yeah, I've seen it."

"As I expected," I replied. "And I'm sure you're also familiar with the chapter on the Summoning of Presences?"

Without wasting any more time, and obviously avoiding the confession that he couldn't remember how to read, Xu Lu snapped, "Like the back of my fucking hand. Explain it to these assholes while I get another drink."

So I did, though not without misgivings which I firmly suppressed. I'm good at explaining things. I did so succinctly and clearly, and by the time Xu Lu returned with a bottle of Scotch, we were all considerably wiser as to the proper procedure of séances.

"I've been telling them that you, naturally, will assume the role of the Summoner," I told him. "Everyone else must generate the necessary dark energies through the reversal of ch'i." Closing my eyes, I took a deep breath. "Reverse breathing. Concentration on the centre. Stillness."

"Blood."

"What?"

"Don't forget blood," Xu Lu grinned, displaying sharp filed teeth. "Did you tell 'em about the sacrifice?"

"One step at a time," I said. *Fuck*, I thought, *what is he planning now?*

"Sacrifice?" said Ho, echoing my own disquiet. "You didn't say anything about a sacrifice."

As if on cue, a small moon-faced girl stepped through the

door of the basement and stood gazing at us solemnly. She couldn't have been more than six; presumably the average age of the city's virgins. Jhun shot me a horrified glance. Ho's mouth hung open. Principles engaged in a fleeting struggle with my fear of Xu Lu and rather to my surprise, principles won. I said, very quietly, "Xu Lu, just what did you have in mind, precisely?"

Xu Lu's shark's smile widened. The little girl said, uncertainly, "I brought your sweets. My brother says you can give him the money tomorrow." With that, she handed over a small package, turned, and ran back out through the door. I've never been so relieved to see anyone leave. Xu Lu opened the package and tipped a half twist of soma ore onto his palm.

"My runner," he explained. "Thinks it's candy." He caught sight of our expressions. "Fuck's sake, you guys. I was kidding about the sacrifice." He fished in his greasy rucksack and extracted a very dead black hen that bore all the hallmarks of roadkill. "Thought we'd use this. Make it look good, you know?" And then he stepped across to me, put his unsavoury face very close to mine, and said in a voice that was almost no voice at all, "So no more shit from you, Professor, okay?"

"Fine with me," I said hastily. I was so pleased that infanticide apparently wasn't on the agenda after all that I'd have agreed to anything at that point. And my plan was still intact. Now that the rest of the band was clued up (and I was pretty sure that Xu Lu had been listening in on my explanation of the séance) I could take a back seat while someone else did the driving. If I had any thoughts of the vehicle veering out of control, I stuffed them down the disposal shaft of my mind.

The idea was that the band would hold the séance at the end of their first set, if one can dignify it with such a term. Xu Lu had ideas about build-up and climax that, even if he did overdo the sexual subtext, were actually sound enough. Somewhere in the course of his benighted life, he'd managed to acquire a sense of theatre. I was given a kind of production role: while the band played, I would be waiting in the wings with the hen (now residing in the bar's fridge) and various other occult accoutrements. Thinking that if we were going to do this at all, we might as well do it properly, I analysed the feng shui of the Shanxi Club to my own satisfaction and sorted out some of the darker aspects. Surreptitiously, I placed *bag gua* mirrors opposite the door and the stage, to reflect any negative ch'i. No one would notice them, and it didn't really matter if they did. Jhun came back late in the afternoon holding a red, heavy piece of material that looked suspiciously like my mum's festive tablecloth.

"Xu Lu says you're to wear it. He says it'll look good," my brother explained, somewhat sheepishly. I opened my mouth to argue, then saw the pleading look on his face. If Xu Lu had asked for it, then it had better be done. This was worse than a wedding. I gritted my teeth, contemplating that after the séance, once I'd made Xu Lu look suitably foolish, I could work on diminishing his influence over my brother. If the plan worked, that shouldn't be too difficult. After all, Xu Lu's idea of raising the ghost of Acid Razor literally did not have a hope in Hell, whereas my idea – well, we'd see. It wasn't a very grandiose plan; no summoning of the Eternal Lords of Night or anything. After all, I was prepared to take a risk, but I wasn't entirely stupid. No, my idea was simply to conjure up a *Ti Hsi*, which according to the book of Demonology is a singularly gruesome apparition that makes the alien in '*Predator*' look like Jennifer Lopez. It is, however, completely harmless. It would caper about for a few minutes before dissolving in the harsh air of the real world, Xu Lu would wet himself, and my brother would lose all respect for him. Such was my plan.

On the day of the disc launch, I duly went down to the nearest remedy maker and purchased a few essential items. I spent the rest of the day writing a respectable essay on the influence of American cartoons on Japanese media, had my tea, and then headed back to the club. Jhun was already there rehearsing, if you can call it that.

The Shanxi Club was, not surprisingly, packed to the doors.

The cream of the city's music industry (or scum, if you prefer) always flocked to disc launches, lured by the prospect of free drugs and alcohol. Xu Lu had hired a few exotic dancers. The management of Hiroshima Records were there in force, which surprised me somewhat. I hadn't thought that the Zombies would attract that kind of executive interest. I wrapped the tablecloth on top of my clothes, retrieved the dead hen, lit the incense burner and waited while the performance got under way. I'd heard the band before, of course, but never at such volume, or from such short range. They were deafening, and I could barely see a thing through the smoke from the incense burner, combined with the drift of dope from the front of the audience. Singapore Three's music press were clearly determined to party hard. At last the music ground to a crashing halt and I looked up in time to see Xu Lu beckoning furiously. I leaped onto the stage, the red cloth trailing about my ankles, and held the hen aloft by its limp wings. I thought I looked ridiculous, but I later learned that what with all the smoke and the flashing lights, my appearance was rather startling.

Xu Lu emitted a roar and stabbed himself in the face. I nearly dropped the hen. He'd done it with a thing like a huge acupuncture needle, and it went right through one cheek and out the other. His eyes rolled back in his head. Blood poured down his neck. He'd have made H.R.Giger proud. I was paralysed. Not for the first time, it occurred to me to wonder what he was on. Xu Lu bawled something, but I couldn't understand him. At first I thought he was miming, and then I realised the truth: I just couldn't hear him through the ringing in my ears. It might have been, "Give me the hen!" so I threw it at him. Xu Lu took a mighty bite, greatly impeded by the bolt through his face, and wrenched off the hen's head with sharp teeth. Even the band was watching him with unmitigated horror. I wondered whether he would in fact be scared by the apparition, or whether he'd just embrace it like a brother. He hurled both bits of hen at his feet, and gestured. I raised the incantation paper and began reading off the litany, still unable to hear what I was saying. I could barely see, either, and it occurred to me later that I might very well have mispronounced something crucial: Cantonese is, after all, a tonal tongue. It would account for what happened next.

Incantations spattered behind me like sparks from a fire cracker. Xu Lu turned. An immense crack was opening up beyond the stage, over the heads of the audience. I could see straight through it, to a place where a hundred heads of demons turned and gaped. I could see something that looked like a bar, and a stage. It was an infernal mirror image of the Shanxi Club. Something leaped down from the stage and bounded through the crack, its tail lashing. I caught a glimpse of crimson fireball eyes, a black leather outfit, and long streaming hair. It seized Xu Lu, threw him over its shoulder, and sprang back through the crack, which closed. There was a sudden surge for the door as the audience recollected its sense of survival, panicked and fled. Xu Lu was gone.

Once the shock of this unexpected event had worn off, I was more than pleased. The séance, wrongly performed and with surprising results, had nevertheless achieved the effect I had hoped for. Xu Lu was off the scene, and my brother was so staggered by my hitherto unsuspected occult bravado that all the respect which had previously gone to Xu Lu now came to me. I abused it thoroughly, demanding constant cups of tea and insisting that Jhun do his homework every day. All was rosy, until we got a letter from Hiroshima Records' lawyers, threatening to sue. I was being held responsible for the disappearance of the band's lead singer, and as such, liable for contractual fees and projected royalties. The sums were astounding. Even if Mum sold the flat and I went into servitude for the rest of my life, we'd never pay it off. I could go to jail, but there was Mum and Jhun to think of and anyway, I didn't want my promising future wrecked by a prison sentence. There was nothing for it. I would have to go to Hell, and get Xu Lu back.

To say that I was not looking forward to this would be

putting it mildly. I'd certainly proved to everyone's satisfaction that it was possible to open a gate between Hell and the world, but I'd never had any intention of actually going there, living or dead. I spent three days spending a fortune on charms and remedies, and then returned to the now-deserted Shanxi Club. Jhun went with me, which alternately terrified me in case anything happened to him, and made me proud. I stood on the stage; Jhun lit the burner and held it up with shaking hands, and I once more recited the ritual. And the gate began to open. Bedecked with charms, and gathering the tatters of my nerves, I ran to the front of the stage and swan-dived through the crack in the air.

I landed heavily on a slimy floor. The place smelled strange and unpleasant, like blood and sour breath. I hauled myself to my feet and looked around. I had been right. This was the Hellish equivalent of the Shanxi Club. There wasn't a lot to choose between the two. No one was around, but a shaft of dusty sunlight filtered through the cracks in a blind. I went over and peered cautiously through.

On Earth, the club was at the top of a hill; so, too, in Hell. I could see all the way down the road, past the torn facades of apparently deserted shop fronts, to where an immense metal spike, its sides gleaming, reared into a boiling crimson sky. Looking in the other direction, I saw more menacing spires, and a huge building shaped like a ziggurat, its summit lost in clouds. Then I let the blind fall, and bolted for the illusory sanctuary of the bar. Someone was coming.

Whoever it was moved swiftly, footsteps reverberating heavily from the floorboards. Someone large, then, and decisive. I cowered beneath the bar, hoping they'd go away. They did not. The footsteps stopped and I hear something snuffling, wetly. Then there was a scrabbling surge of movement, and a shape launched itself around the corner of the bar towards my throat.

The next few moments were confused. I had a shocking image of a great toothed maw, and long clawed fingers.

35

Something rattled and the thing was hauled abruptly back.

"Stop it!" someone roared. And then – "Oh!"

I had been spotted.

"A human!" someone hissed. "Fresh meat for *you*, then, isn't it?"

The creature reared above me onto its hind legs, and snarled. I saw hot yellow eyes, a snaking tail. It was a dog spirit, leashed by a chain around its neck.

"Food!" it bawled, in a slavering kind of voice. Someone reached round, grabbed me by the collar and hauled me up. I looked into a gaze filled with dull, demonic malevolence: the creature's handler.

"You! Into the yard, dog meat!"

"I only came to find my friend!"

"Dog meat, I said!" the demon howled.

"Is that what you did with Xu Lu?" I wailed. The first, stupid thought in my head was that now we'd never pay off the record company. My second was that if I died in Hell, where would my soul go? Clearly, I was about to find out. But then I was abruptly released.

"Xu Lu?" The demon, still clutching the dog spirit's leash, stepped back a pace. "You one of his mates, then?"

A wrong answer could cost me – well, anything was better than dog food. "Yes," I lied.

"You'd better come and see Mr Lu, then," the demon muttered. "Come with me."

Mr Lu? How long had he been here? I followed the demon through a maze of passages, each one more foul-smelling than the last. Eventually we came to a door, on which the demon knocked.

"Go away! I told you I didn't want to be disturbed!"

I knew that voice, anyway.

"Friend of yours to see you, Mr Lu."

"Fuck off!"

"Oh, Xu, why don't you see who it is? Hmm, sweetie?" That

wasn't a voice, it was a purr. The demon shoved me through the door, into a large room swathed with black drapes. Xu Lu was sprawled on a food-stained bed, in the company of the thing with the tail and the teeth that had carried him off in the first place. I have to say, she was even more terrifying on second glance. She gave me the shakes, and not only with terror. It was interesting to see that bondage fashions had penetrated into Hell. Come to think of it, this was probably where they'd originated.

"Oh," Xu said, sourly. "It's you."

"I've come to take you home," I announced, in a voice that even to myself sounded both high and pompous.

"Don't tell me you missed me," Xu Lu grinned.

"Hardly. But we owe Hiroshima Records if you don't come back." The truth will out, they say.

Xu Lu threw back his head and laughed.

"That so? Wear it, then. I'm not coming." He looked at the female demon, and his face changed. If he hadn't been so hideous, I might have called it sweet. I'd been right in supposing him a secret romantic. And the demon simpered back, and gave him a little wave with her taloned fingers. It was nauseating.

"So you can sod off, then, can't you?" Xu snarled.

"Xu..." the demoness drew a claw down his nose. "You know you can only stay if someone returns to Earth in your place. And you know that demons aren't allowed to live in mortal realms. So what are we going to do, darling?"

There was a long, charged silence. I don't know what temporary bond – perhaps one born of mutual desperation – caused both Xu and I to look at one another, and then at the only non-demon in the room. The dog spirit stood, still on its hind legs, panting and drooling, and looking curiously hopeful in that witless way that dogs of all descriptions somehow manage to do.

So that was that, really. Xu's girlfriend sent me back, and the dog spirit came too. I took it along to the record company's offices next day. There was no more talk of costs. Jhun's admiration of his intrepid brother went up by several notches.

The rest of the band kept coming around – I think the dog spirit impressed them. They started talking about doing another wetdisc, perhaps with a more trip-hop ambience: Ho alluded delicately to 'creative differences' with his erstwhile band member, but if they didn't get it together I promised to loan them the dog spirit. It already possessed primitive powers of speech and perhaps, I thought, we could even teach it to sing. After all, it couldn't be any worse than Mr Animation.

Necrochip

"Sure, you can sleep with me," she said, with a small, cool smile: "But only after I'm dead."

I have to admit that this was not precisely the answer I'd been expecting when I made my rather incoherent proposition, and if I hadn't been a bit the worse for wear due to a combination of vodka and spray-on opiates, I doubt whether I'd have had the courage to proposition her in the first place. She was so far out of the league of blokes like me as to be practically out of sight. She was one of those international girls: tall, with skin like suede plastic and a slight crease to her long eyelids that made me suspect Asian ancestry – unless, like so many of the fashion set these days, she'd had her eyelids tucked to give her that essential Pacific Rim mystique. The accent was neutral; anywhere between Sydney and Beijing. It did not occur to me that she might be native to Singapore Three; only the poor remained where they were born these days and the franchise city was full of voyagers. I'd been here for almost eighteen months now, which made me virtually indigenous. I was supposed to be making videos, but I ended up working in a bar in the backstreets of Jiang Min and it was here, fortunately on my night off, that I made my disastrous proposition. I peered at her through the haze.

"Sorry?" I mumbled. "Did you say 'dead'?"

She reached into her Miucci wallet and took out a sliver of something. It had the soft glaze of organic material; like a very thin slice of liver.

"Here," she said, distantly. "This is my necrochip." Her voice took on the sing-song note of a rote lesson. "If you'd like to sleep with me after my death, we can put it on your credit card now and then when I'm dead, you will be notified and can come and visit me." She added in a more normal tone, "I'm due to be placed in one of the franchise facilities in Reikon, so you won't have far to go."

"I'm sorry," I echoed. I felt like a complete idiot; this was obviously some game she enjoyed playing on hapless Westerners. "I'd really rather you were alive when we, um, I mean..." My voice trailed uncomfortably away. She shrugged.

"As you wish."

She slipped the necrochip back into her wallet and stood up to leave. She was wearing a pair of hydraulic Japanese pattens, I remember, and when her weight came down on them I heard a faint hiss. She gained an inch or so in height and stood looking down on me. This wasn't difficult: at that point in the conversation I felt about three feet high.

"Wait," I said. "Why?"

"Why what?"

"Why are you doing this? I mean – hiring out one's corpse for sexual purposes... It's hardly usual, even these days. I just wondered – well, *why*?"

"Isn't it usual?" she said, with vague curiosity.

"Not unless I'm very far behind the times."

"The man at the facility said there'd be plenty of interest," she said. "And you'd be number six – there is a queue, you know." She made it sound as though I'd questioned her desirability.

"Wouldn't you be a bit – well, past it by then?"

Disdainfully, she said

"I'd be perfectly preserved. Quite flexible. I wouldn't want to be involved in something *distasteful*."

"But why are you doing it in the first place?"

"To pay for my treatment."

"Your treatment?"

At that point, a group of similar girls swept in, giving those thin high cries that Japanese women seem to emit at moments of astonishment or pleasure. They clustered around my new friend and gathered her up with them. The last thing that I saw of her was her blonde head at the bar, bobbing over the assembled crowd. She seemed to be laughing, but I wasn't. I drained my drink and left; the alcohol didn't seem to be working any more and the opiates had long since worn away. I scratched absently at the rash they had raised on my skin and shambled out into the street. Before I headed home, I bent down and dropped a couple of cents into the little shrine that stood at the foot of the wall. Inside, the small plastic god stared placidly out and, as I watched, he raised a hand and blessed me. It was only the motion of the coins crossing the infra-red sensor that made him do this, but I felt better, somehow. It was hard not to be superstitious in Singapore Three; ironically, for such a high-tech city, the media was full of talk of magic and demons and it got to me, after a while.

Back at the box I rented on Hsin Tsu Street, I stared out of the minuscule window at the lights of the city. The night sky was a permanent orange glaze, but up the coast, towards the Yellow River estuary, I could see an edge of darkness: a storm coming in over the South China Sea. I shivered, despite the stuffy night heat. I had no wish to spend another steaming summer in Singapore Three, but it wasn't looking as though I had much choice. I was living pretty much hand to mouth in those days, and if I really wanted to get back to Glasgow (which I sometimes doubted), I'd have to find a better-paid job. That night, however, thoughts of home didn't occupy me for long. I couldn't get the girl out of my mind. I've never considered myself a particularly moral individual, but her matter-of-fact acceptance of something so extreme disturbed me. I told myself that it was up to people what they did with their own lives and their own bodies, but my brief conversation with her had given me an insight into the macabre that I didn't feel I could handle. And what had she meant by 'treatment'?

I didn't see her again for a couple of days, and when she

next came into the Azure Dragon I was once again working behind the bar. In between serving drinks, I watched her as she struck up a conversation with some middle-aged businessman. He was wearing one of those heat-sensitive suits that had been all the rage in Beijing the year before last and I could hear the drift of colloquial Mandarin as they talked; the slurring accent like a drift of static above the words. With a disorientating sense of déjà vu, I saw her fish in her bag and take out the necrochip. She handed it to him. The businessman studied it for a moment, then reached into his pocket and took out a credit card. I watched, disbelieving, as she ran it through her pod. He gave a small, curt bow and walked away. It seemed my friend had collected number six. Her face did not change as she replaced the necrochip in her wallet, but remained the same passive mask. She clicked her bag shut and walked towards the unisex restrooms.

On impulse, I put down the glass I was polishing and followed her. I think I had some hazy thought of offering to help her, save her from a life of prostitution – or a death of one, to be more accurate. How I intended to accomplish this, I had no idea. I suppose she appealed to whatever vestiges of romance I still possessed: I saw her as a tragic figure, desperate to be saved. I didn't want to alarm her, so I opened the restroom door quietly. She was leaning over the basin, spitting blood. As she heard my footsteps her head came up and I met her eyes in the mirror. They glittered a crystalline red, like neon in the rain. Her head swivelled around and she hissed. I took a hasty step backwards and fell over a mop that someone had thoughtfully placed by the entrance to the restroom. When I extricated myself, she had gone. The tiny window beneath the ceiling, a good eight feet from the ground, was hanging open. Tottering back into the bar, I told the manager that I was feeling unwell and would have to go home. He acquiesced with a sour nod.

Before I left, however, I went over to the dark booth where Number Six was sitting over his whisky.

"Good evening. Excuse me," I said in my dreadful

Mandarin. "Could I talk to you for a moment?"

Number Six gave me the sort of look that made me wonder briefly whether I'd managed to call him an arsehole rather than bidding him a greeting: tonal languages are full of such pitfalls. I took his stare for invitation and sat down.

"I'm sorry to trouble you," I said. "But I saw you talking to a young lady a while ago."

"Yes. So?"

"Well, it's like this," I improvised hastily. "I'm actually with the, uh, the franchise vice squad, and we have reason to believe that the lady in question is engaged in certain illegal activities."

He looked utterly disbelieving.

"What sort of illegal activities?"

"Well, they're of a varied nature that I'm not at liberty to divulge right now, but I must inform you that if you have completed a transaction of any sort with her, you should contact your bank now and cancel it. I'm also asking you to hand over any information that she gave to you. An address, for instance."

The stare did not waver.

"Do you have identification?"

"No. It would put me at risk, if it were discovered."

He must have thought I was some sort of lunatic.

"You're not a cop," he said in disgust. "I don't know who you are. But I'll give you the address she gave me if it will make you go away. Have you got a pod?"

I slid it across the table and he made a quick copy from his pod to mine.

"Now go away."

Did I really care, I asked myself, if this obnoxious person had some horrible fate awaiting him? I decided that I didn't, and besides, I'd done all I could for now.

"Thank you," I said pompously. "The authorities are grateful." Briefly, I remembered the adverts which littered the city, encouraging people to turn informer. They featured a young man in a pair of stripy pyjamas slumbering peacefully with his glasses on the bedside table, having presumably shopped his mates for a few franchise dollars and the gratitude of the municipal police. 'Sleep well!' the adverts proclaimed. 'You have done the Right Thing!' I wondered whether I'd sleep well that night. Somehow, I doubted it.

I woke up somewhere around five am, with a queasy dawn coming up over the city. Opening the window, I leaned out and inhaled the usual heady blend of chemical fumes, unburned petrol and steam from the city's many restaurants. Almost breakfast time, I decided. Yawning, I dressed and made my way down to the street. I could feel the pod in the pocket of my shirt; the address Number Six had given me seemed to weigh it down. I hadn't even looked at it yet. I took a seat in the noodle bar down the road, among sweat-workers coming off their shifts, and mentally reviewed the range of substances that I had most recently abused. Apart from vodka, hypospray morphine and the occasional handful of tranquillisers, I couldn't think of anything powerful enough to create a hallucination of the magnitude of the one that I'd apparently experienced the night before. I could still see the fragmented sparkle of her eyes in the shadows of the restroom mirror. I was pretty sure that I hadn't imagined the whole thing, and besides, there was the address that the businessman had given me. Absently, I twirled a chopstickful of nasi goreng into my mouth and took out the pod. She had told part of the truth, anyway. The address was somewhere down in Reikon, which meant the waterfront. *All right*, I thought, with a combination of excitement and trepidation: *let's take a look*. I don't know what I thought I was doing. I guess it seemed like an adventure at the time; the sort of thing I'd drifted to Asia in order to experience. I don't think I really believed that anything could happen to me; you don't when you're young. Or stupid.

It took ages to get to Reikon. The trams were running erratically that day, the result of terrorist activity down in the banking district, and the one that I finally managed to catch stopped at every halt. I dozed in my seat as the city lurched by, waking with a start to find that we had reached the docks. The water glistened in the heat, shimmering out towards the silhouette of the islands. I could see a hoverfoil ploughing out beyond the typhoon shelter, bound for Macau and leaving a white furrow in its wake. I watched it go, wishing I was on it. I walked down towards the docks, picking my way over fish wreckage and machine parts. The warehouses were marked, but it was some little time before I located the address that I'd been given. It was one of the new facilities: a smooth high curve of grey plastic some three hundred metres long, tucked away behind a mesh fence. The gates were closed. I could hear the hum of the vibrolock from where I stood, and as I stared at it a short, squat figure bolted out from behind the warehouse and bounded towards the gate. It hurled itself at the wire, barking. The long wedge-shaped head wove from side to side like a cobra; within, I could see a triple row of teeth. Weird women I thought I could handle; sharkhounds definitely not. Even though it was contained behind the wire, I backed off hastily. Well, that was that, I told myself. My little adventure had ended in the usual inconclusive way, but it had been diverting enough at the time. Filled with a kind of pleasantly world-weary ennui, I made my way back to the tram.

After this, life continued in its customary way for about a month. I did not see the girl again, though I kept a sharp eye out for her in the bar. I did not see Number Six again, either, and after a while I found out why. I'd come home in the middle of the afternoon. It was summer by then, and too hot to do anything except melt. The humidity was running at eighty percent and I felt disgusting. I took the fifth shower of the day, donned a sarong and slumped in front of the ancient DTV that I'd inherited from a neighbour. Number Six's face was plastered all over the news. Within the next ten minutes I learned that he was the president of a satellite company in Beijing and a man of quite preposterous wealth. He had apparently gone missing in Singapore Three several days before. It was known that he had a certain taste for the seamier side of life (this was implied in the most delicate manner possible and presented as a charming eccentricity: I suppose they didn't want to be sued), so his family were not unduly concerned until he failed to show up for a board meeting back in Beijing. Then the harbour police found his body, floating in the oily waters of the Reikon typhoon shelter. Police had reason to link the case to a number of unexplained and recent deaths in the area. An exhaustive summary of Number Six's most recent movements then followed; including his visit to the Azure Dragon. The police were apparently eager to interview a young man whom the victim had been seen talking with.

At this point, despite the sultry day, I broke out into a cold sweat. The franchise police were known for their enthusiastic methods of questioning, and had little reserve about applying them to foreigners. I pulled on a t-shirt and sandals and left the flat with unseemly haste. I headed nervously out into the street and caught a tram downtown, intending to lose myself among the crowds. It was undoubtedly an over-active imagination that made me think that everyone was staring at me. I wandered aimlessly through Sheng Mai and New Kowloon until the apricot coloured sky deepened into the soft south China twilight. My steps took me down the familiar alleyway that led to the Azure Dragon. And then I saw her.

At first I wasn't sure if it was really her. She looked different, somehow. Her hair straggled over her shoulders and her shoulders seemed bowed. She looked twice as old as the girl I'd seen in the Azure Dragon, but her dress and the shoes were the same. She was talking to a Korean in a pale suit; as I watched, she reached out and massaged his elbow. It was a curiously intimate, affectionate gesture. Then they parted. She walked slowly along the waterfront on her high shoes, into the twilight. I followed her. She flagged down a taxi, and so did I.

We reached Reikon and the warehouse just as darkness fell. I asked the driver to stop several streets away, and then I ran down to the docks. The lights of distant ships glowed out to sea and the city towered behind. I caught a glimpse of her as she moved through the yards. As she neared the facility, she slipped off her shoes and hobbled barefoot towards the fence. She fumbled with the latch of the gate and as she stepped through she almost fell. She vanished into the shadows, leaving the gate open behind her. The shark-hound was nowhere to be seen. Curiosity got the better of me and I followed her towards the facility. The door stood wide open. Cautiously, I stepped through. I went down a long corridor and paused before a second open door. *Why was the facility so unguarded?* I wondered. It was not reassuring. I could see light coming from a room ahead; a flickering glow unlike the steady gleam of neon. Stealthily, I moved towards it; here, too, the door was ajar. I peered through the crack.

The girl was faltering as she circled the room. She was lighting sticks of incense, and the thick smoke filled the air. She groped her way towards a raised bier in the centre of the room and, as I watched, she collapsed across it. She dragged herself up, until she was lying on her back, and I heard the breath go out of her in a long sigh. Her head lolled to one side, displaying her wan face. At that point, I heard footsteps coming down the corridor. I ducked out of sight around the corner.

After a moment, a man appeared. Like the late lamented Number Six, he was middle aged and wearing a dark, expensive suit. He, too, was Chinese. He paused, briefly, to smooth back his hair before stepping through the door of the room. I could hear him moving about. I returned to the door and glanced through. The businessman was bending over the supine figure of the girl; his fingers touching first her throat and then her wrist. I heard him give a brief hiss of satisfaction. He picked up her arm and let it fall again, and it dropped to the side of the bier like a dead weight. The businessman laughed. He began muttering under his breath, and started to unfasten his shirt. I did not even want to think about what he might be about to do and I certainly had no inclination to watch. It was, I thought, high time to get out of here. Once I was well away, I would phone the police. I could hear the urgent rustle of movement from within the room. I was halfway down the corridor when someone screamed.

It was a high, whistling scream like a boiling kettle. I stood paralysed in the middle of the corridor. The scream abruptly stopped. I am sorry to say that at this point, I turned and ran. I reached the main door and stumbled through into the warm dusk. It felt like the freshest air I had ever tasted. And then I saw her. She was crouched by the outside wall, rocking to and fro on her haunches. I could see her eyes glinting in the shadows. She was panting. As I stared she rose and began prowling around the perimeter fence. She looked nothing like the elegant young woman I had first set eyes on in the Azure Dragon. Her face was distorted with fury like a Japanese theatrical mask and her breasts were mottled with something that looked suspiciously like blood. A long tongue lolled out and licked at it. I fled in the opposite direction but I could hear the scrape of her taloned feet against the concrete as she bolted in pursuit. I ran around the side of the building and there was a howl like a banshee from somewhere in front. For a terrified moment I thought she'd come over the roof ahead of me, but then I saw the cage containing the shark-hound. It must have scented the blood that sprayed her body. The animal hurled itself against the bolted mesh of the cage and I saw my chance. I jumped onto the top of the cage and pulled out the bolt at the moment when she sprang. The shark-hound collided with her in mid-air. They both gave a remarkably similar horrible yell and fell to the ground. I could hear them snarling at each other as they rolled over and over, but I was out of the complex and sprinting alongside the harbour wall, just in time to meet the police as they came in through the main gate.

In the end, it was not the police who charged me. They found a diverting scene back at the facility: a girl and an engineered dog with their teeth locked in one another's throats, and inside, freezer facilities suitable for the storage of meat and a curious, incense-lit tableau, in the middle of which was a thing that the papers described as a husk. I could shed very little light on any of this, beyond telling them about the necrochip, which when found served as some degree of corroboration. The press was rife with speculation; everything from cults to assassination, and I don't think it was ever satisfactorily resolved. But I have lived in Singapore Three for long enough to know that legends still live on even in the mid-twenty first century. It seems to me that if one was a supernatural creature that needed, say, human sperm to bring one back from the dead, then one would necessarily have a problem obtaining it. Perhaps in these decadent times it is easier for demons to survive than in the cautious ages of the past: six customers is not bad going, after all.

I mentioned that it wasn't the police who charged me. Instead, it was the corporation who owned the storage facility, via their insurance company. They sued for breaking and entering, plus damage in transit and the loss of a valuable genetically enhanced guard dog. The bill totalled some twenty thousand franchise dollars, and I can't leave the country until I pay. I have, in these desperate straits, revived the idea of the necrochip. I confess to being startled at its success: there are plenty of people who wouldn't want to sleep with me living, let alone dead, and I don't even want to think about the logistics. But I have been advertising for over a month now, and I already have three customers: one woman and two men. I'm not quite sure, yet, whether I'll be in any position to honour my part of the bargain, but I suppose I'll have to cross that bridge when I come to it.

The Flower of Tekeli

This early in the year, it was very cold, almost twenty below zero. Fairuza huddled in her heavy coat in the back of the car, an old Mercedes of which Arshan was inordinately proud. Fairuza wished that her brother had saved the money and bought a cheaper car, a Yugo perhaps, from some local dealer. She remembered her father, grumbling: *These Western cars, they're not built for Kazakhstan's roads. The tyres are no good; the engines can't take the cold.* Fairuza did not know if this was true, but she did not like the way Arshan drove the vehicle: too fast, skidding around the corners on the high steppe road from Almaty to Taldy-Kurgan. Besides, it was dark and snowing. She leaned forward and tapped Arshan on the shoulder.

"Slow down. You're scaring me!"

In the mirror, she saw her brother grin.

"You want to get home, don't you? If we make it to town before midnight, Mum and Dad will still be up."

"I want to get home in one piece, Arshan."

"Stop nagging, Fairuza." That was Arshan's friend Pavel, in the front seat. "He knows how to drive. He doesn't need a woman telling him what to do."

"I don't like the way he's driving, that's all," Fairuza said. Beside her, Chinghiz patted her hand.

"It's cool, Fairuza."

Fairuza snatched her hand away. She did not like sitting in the back with Chinghiz, either. He kept finding excuses to touch her and it was irritating. She had wanted to sit next to her brother, but Pavel said he preferred the front seat and that had been that.

Part of the problem, she knew, was that Arshan needed to

51

impress his friends. She could not imagine why; it wasn't even as though Pavel and Chinghiz had jobs – and there were plenty of people in *that* boat nowadays, now that the Russian economy had collapsed and taken the Kazakhstani one with it – but Arshan seemed to idolise them. She would never, she thought, understand boys.

"Anyway, what are you going to do – get out and walk?" Pavel continued.

"No," Fairuza muttered.

"Stop complaining, then. Shut up and enjoy the ride."

Fairuza waited for Arshan to say: *don't speak to my sister like that*, but he was silent. Frustrated, she huddled deeper into her coat and forced herself to bite back her angry words. There was no point in quarrelling.

There was little enough to enjoy about this trip. If it had been daylight, and later in the year, Fairuza might have taken some pleasure in the journey: the road over the high steppe was beautiful, with long fronds of grass and wildflowers edging the narrow strip of tarmac. From here, the land swept down all the way to Tekheli, the mountains a blur of indigo shadow at the horizon's edge, merging into the long distances of the Chinese border. But now it was early January, blowing with snow, a long way past the year's best.

Arshan took a sharp turn, heading toward the network of roads that led to the villages and small farms. The Mercedes skidded. Fairuza heard ice crunch under the tyres.

"Arshan! *Slow down!*"

But it was too late. Everything became dreamlike and blurred. She saw the road spinning beneath the car as it wheeled up and over, heard Chinghiz crying out beside her. She felt completely calm. She wondered who was screaming so loudly, why the girl was making such a fuss. Then she was somewhere warm and soft, back in bed in her dad's house and it had all been a dream.

She opened her eyes. The car was resting on its roof, half

buried in the snow. She was lying outside on a bank, curled up in her heavy coat. There was the sharp, unpleasant smell of leaking gas, blackening the snow. It was only when she got up and stumbled down to the car that she realised it was not gas after all, but blood. She did not want to look inside the car. She stood there for what seemed like a long time, with her feet crunching on brittle snow and broken glass as she stamped mechanically up and down. At last, she made herself peer through the window. Chinghiz lay unmoving under the back seat. His mouth and eyes were open. He looked blank, not even surprised. Pavel was half out of the car and when she went around, she saw that his chest had been crushed; the protruding bones were as pale as the snow. Fairuza's hand went to her mouth. Her thoughts were moving very slowly, as though time had started to stop. She thought: *Arshan was in the driver's seat. And there is a hole in the windscreen.* None of them had been wearing seatbelts: the buckles had long since broken. She walked all round the car, looking. Broken glass glittered diamond-bright in the drifts. There was no sign of Arshan. Fairuza went back to the road, somehow surprised to find it still stretching down toward the plain: the skid marks were like writing on the ice.

She could not find Arshan anywhere. She searched and searched until it struck her that it was really very cold, and she should try to call for help. She forced herself to look in the dead boys' pockets and found a mobile phone. She rang her father's number, but she did not know what she said. She thought she heard him answer, but she was very tired and it struck her that by far the best thing to do was to sit down. There was a dim notion at the back of her mind that for some reason this was a bad idea, but she did not care. She sat in the snow, rubbing her eyes. She must have been crying, she thought, because the tears had frozen on her cheeks, but it did not feel cold any longer.

She glanced up and saw that there was a woman standing by the car. The woman was dressed in the traditional manner, with the high white head-dress of an unmarried girl and leather boots.

Fairuza saw a round face, cold as the moon. The woman said, in Kazakh: *I have taken him, just as they took my voice, my words.*

"What do you mean?" Fairuza asked, but the woman was no longer there, lost in a whirling gust of snow.

When she awoke, her grandmother was sitting by the side of the bed, reading a movie magazine. Fairuza opened her mouth, but only a croaking sound came out. Her grandmother dropped the magazine on the floor.

"Oh! You're awake." She clutched at Fairuza with tears in her eyes. "I'll go and get your mama – she's just gone to talk to the doctor."

"It's sunny," Fairuza said. It seemed very strange that it should have been night and winter so little time ago. There was a thorn pricking her hand. She looked down and saw a drip.

"Fairuza, that's the lights, not the sun. You're in the hospital. You've been unconscious for nearly a day. You were in an accident – "

– and it all came rushing back, the road and the night, and the car overturning. She struggled up from the coarse pillow.

"Arshan! Have they found him?"

But she could see from her grandmother's face that they had not.

"Maybe he was hurt, and wandered off," she said. "Maybe he's safe somewhere..."

But the moment she said it, she knew how foolish this was. It had been so cold, and there was no shelter anywhere on the steppe. Then she remembered the woman.

"I saw someone," she said. "A woman, dressed in the old way. She said she'd taken him. Perhaps she lives up there, maybe she took him to a yurt..."

But her grandmother's face was troubled and when Fairuza looked into her eyes, she saw only doubt.

"Just try to rest, dear. Don't you worry about anything."

"But –"

"You mustn't speak. You'll tire yourself out."

And indeed, she was suddenly overwhelmingly weary. She leaned back against the pillow and slept.

When she next woke, her grandmother had gone. The room was dim; she could hear other people mumbling in their sleep and shifting about. There was a single lamp at the end of the ward. A host of tiny shadows skittered up the wall and Fairuza caught her breath, but they were only cockroaches, perhaps drawn by the light. One of the other patients was moving about the ward, shuffling along the floor. Then she turned, and Fairuza saw the woman from the steppe road. She looked exactly the same. She carried with her a breath of cold and snow. She came to stand by Fairuza's bed and stood looking down. Fairuza could see the white owl feathers that decorated her head-dress, to protect the wearer from evil spirits.

"You will not find him," the woman said. She tilted her head back. "He is mine now; he no longer belongs to you."

"Who are you?" Fairuza breathed, but the woman only smiled, and it was a cruel smile.

"They are all mine," she said. "All the young men who took my voice away from me." Then she was gone. A white feather drifted down like a snowflake to rest on the hospital floor. In the morning, Fairuza thought it must have been a dream.

Her classmates were very kind to Fairuza when she went back to college and her language classes. They all told her that Arshan might yet be found; there were herders in the hills, who lived in their yurts in lower pastures even in winter, and maybe one of these people had taken Arshan in. He might have lost his memory: it often happened, they said, to people affected by the cold. Fairuza knew they meant well, but every time she came close to believing them, she remembered the woman and her cold smile.

It was no use pretending that life was normal. Sometimes, she thought it would have been easier if Arshan had actually died, but the thought made her feel so guilty that she stifled it. But if he had died, at least they would *know*: at least they could all stop waiting for the day when her brother might come back, and then, perhaps, her mother might laugh again and her father stop drifting around the house as though he were no more than a ghost himself. She tried to talk to her mother about Arshan, but her mother would not listen and her father told her roughly to be quiet. Later, he apologised, but Fairuza said nothing more about her brother.

When the first thaw of spring came, however, she called the ambulance driver who had rescued her and asked if there was any chance of going back up onto the steppe. Perhaps, and this was a terrible thought, Arshan would be like so many of the people that the locals called 'spring flowers', whose corpses were released by the snow and the ice when winter began to depart.

The ambulance driver said that he would take her there himself. They drove in silence, on a still March morning with the first faintness of green spreading over the lower slopes. Most of the snow was still there on the heights, but when they reached the spot where the car had gone off the road, the drifts had melted. Fairuza got out of the ambulance driver's car and looked around her, shivering. Bare earth and thin edges of grass: no body, no bones.

"He can't just have vanished," she said, for the hundredth time.

"Do you know how long you were unconscious?" the driver, a stocky man named Mikhail Petrovich, asked.

"I've no idea."

"It can't have been very long otherwise, quite frankly, you would have frozen to death. If your brother was thrown clear, perhaps concussed, he couldn't have walked very far before he collapsed." The driver touched her arm. "I'm sorry to be so direct. But it's better that we face the truth."

Fairuza nodded; she agreed, and she was beginning to think that anything was better than this terrible not-knowing. Together, they walked up the slope to the crest of the hill. There was nothing.

"If there was a body, we would see it," Mikhail said. "You said he was wearing a red jacket?"

"Yes, one of those puffy things. But it was red, I remember it clearly. We joked about it, how he was still a Communist. But he didn't have any interest in politics. He wanted to be a businessman." She felt the tears rise in her throat, choking her.

"It's a real mystery. Maybe someone found him on the road."

"But where would they take him? The nearest hospital's the one in Taldy-Kurgan, and he wasn't there. They wouldn't have driven him all the way to Almaty. I wondered whether someone might have taken him to a yurt."

"Not at this time of year, surely. They don't come up as high as this."

"I thought –"

"What would be the point? There's no grazing."

"I suppose not."

They walked along the ridge for a short distance, but found nothing, only a cairn of stones piled high on the rock.

"What's that?" Fairuza said.

"It's a monument. A grave."

"To a khan?" There were plenty of old graves around these parts, Fairuza knew, memorials dating back as far as Genghis's day.

"No, to a poetess. A woman named Gulnara, who wanted to be an *akyn* in the seventeenth century, but the khan at that time was young and arrogant and wouldn't let a woman become a bard. She was supposed to have been very beautiful – they're all beautiful, though, in the old stories, aren't they?" Mikhail laughed. "They called her the Flower of Tekheli. She put a curse on the khan, on all young men, and then she died."

Fairuza thought of the woman, in her old-fashioned dress, and her skin began to crawl.

"Let's go back," she said abruptly, and made her way down the slope to the car.

It was mid-afternoon when they got back to Taldy-Kurgan. Fairuza asked Mikhail to drop her off at the library. Her parents still talked about the days when Kazakhstan had been part of the Soviet Union, but though it was not all that long ago it seemed part of the far past to Fairuza, as distant as the time of khans and poets.

She walked slowly up the cracked stone path that led to the library doors, passing the empty plinth where a statue of Lenin had once stood. When she was a little girl, she remembered asking her mother whether Lenin was the librarian, because he was holding a book. They still teased her about it at home, but the statue had been taken down years ago now and never replaced. As she climbed the library steps, Fairuza could still feel the winter chill in her bones; it was good to get into the warm silence of the building. She went straight to the poetry section.

At first she thought there was nothing. The poetry shelves were filled with traditional works, both Russian and Kazakh. The section was dominated by the poet Abai; it was not a very wide selection. Surely her people had written more than this? Frustrated, Fairuza went in search of the librarian.

"There might be something in one of the collections, but I'm not sure," the woman said. "They didn't write much down in those days – it was an oral tradition."

"Something must have survived, though? Abai's work survived."

"But Abai was translated into Russian from the Kazakh, and he was relatively recent... Let me go and look."

Fairuza sat down on a nearby bench to wait. The librarian took a long time, and she began to feel drowsy. From the corner of her eye, she saw an image begin to form against the institutional green paint of the library wall: it was the woman from the steppe, and this time her face was not arrogant beneath the white head-dress, but sad. Fairuza looked up, but there was nothing there.

The librarian returned, holding a single book.

"It's in here. There's only one poem, and that isn't finished."

"Can I copy it?"

"I don't see any harm in that."

Fairuza handed over the money for the photocopying and found the single page bearing Gulnara's poem. It was a poem to the mountain of Tekheli itself: to the eagle's flight above the waterfalls. The last stanza was incomplete. Fairuza copied the poem, folded it into her pocket, and took it home.

That night, the poetess came to her in a dream.

"You spared me," Fairuza said, standing once more by the cairn on the high ridge. It was winter again, the rocks like black bones under the snow. "I could have died in the accident. But you took my brother. Why? Where is he?"

The poetess was no longer sad, but angry.

"He is young, and a man. It was reason enough. You are a woman, and I cannot kill one of my own kind."

"Why do you *want* to kill?" Fairuza asked. "I know that a young man wronged you, but –"

"Wronged?" The poetess turned on her. "If it had been rape, I could have borne it. Even banishment, I could have borne. But he took my *voice*. He stopped me from telling the poems, the old tales. I could not write – how would I have learned? But the poems, I took from my grandmother, and her grandmother before her. My brothers did not care – all they knew was horses. I would have passed the tales on, but the khan would not let me. And now everything is lost."

"There is one poem," Fairuza faltered. "The poem to Tekheli." But the form of the poetess was breaking up, turning to the intricate curls of words and drifting away into snow. Fairuza woke to an open window and the sounds of morning.

That afternoon, telling no one, she went to the bus station and caught the weekly bus south to Almaty. The bus went up over the high pass, close to the cairn and the site of the accident. Fairuza told the bus driver that she was visiting herder relatives; he let her get down at the edge of the road. With the poem in her pocket, she set off up the ridge toward the cairn. She read the poem over the poetess' grave, taking as much care over the old phrasing as she could, and then she read it again.

When she looked up, the poetess was standing before her. She was a small woman, shorter even than Fairuza, and she was not beautiful. She looked solid, unlike a ghost. She said, grudgingly, "You read that well enough, but the stress was sometimes wrong."

"I'm not a bard. I'm a language student. I've come to make a bargain with you. I've come for my brother."

"I told you. He's mine. I won't let him go."

"Not even if I give you back your voice?"

The poetess grew still.

"How would you do such a thing?"

Fairuza took a deep breath.

"There are no copies of your poems, except this one. But you are known as a bard – people still remember you." She was thinking of the ambulance driver Mikhail. "Times have changed since the Soviet Union collapsed. All the old political figures have gone."

The poetess' face twisted. "What is this to me?"

"They have taken away the statues to Lenin, to Brezhnev. There are only empty plinths left, and so much of Kazakh history has been lost, there aren't enough figures to fill them. If I could ask the town council to erect a statue to you, with this poem inscribed on the base – would that satisfy you?"

The poetess was silent. Then she said, "I will consider it. Go back to the road and wait. There, I will give you your answer."

Fairuza walked down the ridge. When she reached the road, she turned and looked back. The poetess was nowhere to be seen, but there was a figure standing by the cairn: a boy in a red jacket, looking around him, bewildered.

Later that spring, Fairuza walked under the budding oaks to the library. It was warmer now, and the path that led to the library steps was lined with a scattering of flowers. The new statue stood with her back to the building, looking toward Tekheli and the high steppe. Fairuza paused for a moment, gazing up at the statue, then she went into the library and found a quiet corner. Taking the notebook from her bag, she sat down and started to write.

Tycho and the Stargazer

The whole idea is madness, of course, but it's equal folly to tell him so. I should have known he was crazed when I first came here – one look at that miserable tower across the fog-bound bleakness of the river ought to have told me what I'd be letting myself in for – but it's already too late.

I can hear the madman downstairs now, roaring out one of his damned Danish drinking songs, punctuated with snorts through his metal nose as he stamps up and down the icy passages of the castle. He has been feeding aqua vita to the elk again; I can hear it bellowing almost as loudly as its master. He says, grudgingly, that he is 'impressed' by my latest calculations on determining the orbit of Mars; he has written to Maestlin and told him so. But I fear I am simply being used and, moreover, Tycho will not show me his calculations in their entirety. Clearly, he does not trust me.

No, the whole situation is intolerable and if it wasn't for the angel, I'd go straight back to Swabia.

I know I must save the angel, but I do not see how I am to do it. I cannot bear to think of it, squirming beneath the heavy glass jar like a captured moth. And Tycho has such *plans* for the thing: plans that are tantamount to the torture that I will receive if my own soul journeys to Hell, as it surely will. I can feel God looking down upon me, eyebrows raised.

Well, Johannes? What are you going to do about it?

And I hear myself squeak, like the mouse that I am: *Me? What do You expect me to do? I am only little Johannes Kepler, the runt of a bad litter, who studies the stars because he can't bear the sight of his own face in the glass...* But I don't think God is listening, or even cares. After all, I was born under a black star; my father destined for the gallows and my mother for the fire. Their children show the same mark: dead or unlucky, prone to sickness – the fever, worm and mange – and strange accidents. I have studied the stars of my birth: nothing of what they say encourages me. I am not the natural saviour of angels.

I cannot even save myself.

And yet... I suppose I should begin at the beginning.

I was so full of antic hope when I came here to the castle of Benatek. It was the winter of the first year of the new century, this year of our Lord 1600. The Iser had flooded in the January rains and then frozen, so that the castle seemed to float above a wilderness of ice. I thought at first that it was no more than a ruin, and then I realised the truth: the castle was being rebuilt, on Tycho's orders, so that it more closely and conveniently resembled the observatory that he had left behind him on the island of Hveen, not far from Elsinor.

I had heard stories about Tycho Brahe, during his time on Hveen. Everyone had. The whole of Europe, it seemed, knew of his rages, his extortions, his habit of clapping peasants into the observatory's dungeons for no reason other than bowing too shallowly before the great astronomer.

Even the King protested. Tycho ignored him.

I must admit, he was magnificent in his arrogance, but at last a combination of public opinion and royal censure forced him from the island. Accompanied by his wife, his mistress, his numerous children, his dwarf and his elk, Tycho's procession set foot upon the road and after no little wandering throughout Denmark, they at last came here to Bohemia.

Here, deprived of jurisdiction over the local peasantry, Tycho has thrown all his considerable energies into his work, the first stage of which is the remodelling of the castle itself. I am sure that it will be grand when done. At present, however, the place is draughty, cold, and damp with the seeping rains that sweep up the Iser. I have already fallen sick with a fever; it will not be the last.

The observatory itself lies at the top of a tower, in a lofty, echoing space that used to form the attics. There was all manner of junk up here, Tycho told me, but now all that is cleared away and the instruments have been installed. They could not be more precious to me than if they were forged of gold and studded with rubies. I could never have afforded such fine equipment and poor old Maestlin had no more than a few charts to his name. Tycho's great meaty hands are gentle with the instruments; he touches them with a reverence and delicacy that he would never think to expend upon a human being. He claps me on the back with a force sufficient to shatter my bones, clouts his children, pinches his wife – yet he handles the astrolabe and armillary spheres as a woman might hold a wren within her cupped hands. And they excite him, too – not in the way of common lust, but an excitation of the mind that causes him to sweat as he labours over his midnight calculations and charts the course of the stars across the sky. The moisture runs down his forehead and dilutes the glue that holds his metal nose together. Occasionally the nose falls off and Tycho, cursing, is obliged to retrieve the glue pot and stick it back on again. I hear he lost the better part of it in a duel with a fellow student over who was the better mathematician. I do not know who won. I suspect, however, that it may have been his opponent. Tycho, for all his boasting, is not quite the calculator that he pretends – and that is why I am here. For although he treats me as little more than a household pet, we both know the truth: I am the more accomplished astronomer, and Tycho needs me.

But all of these concerns – Tycho, his talents and rages, his inchoate household and the ruin in which we live, my frets and fevers – have been swept away by the arrival of the angel.

Tycho and I witnessed its appearance together. Midnight, and we were up in the tower, making observations of the moon. A chilly, lunar light made the frost glitter on the windowsill and turned the frozen waters of the Iser to silver. My hands were as numb as stumps, but Tycho seemed to give off his own heat, like a great roaring furnace. I did not like to be close to him – even in winter he had a smell that would turn back the Turks – but I found myself scurrying at his heels, writing down the observations that he tossed over his shoulder as a man might toss bones to a dog. Bent as I was over the parchment, in the uncertain light of the candle, it was a moment before I noticed that Tycho had grown silent. When I glanced up, my ears seemed to ring with the uncommon quiet. Tycho, arrested in mid-movement, stood at the centre of the room, mouth open, gazing upwards.

And the angel was gazing down at him. At first, I took it for a trapped bird, or a large moth, for it was no bigger than a pigeon and white as milk. But then I realised my mistake, for it was human in form. Its pale, translucent wings beat to and fro: a maddeningly slow motion to one used to the fluttering of birds. It had a small, cold face, utterly remote; a series of curves and angles in which rested dark eyes without any white – an animal's eyes, I would have said, if not for the spark within. The angel's hands were folded before its breast, and it wore a long robe that did not move with the draught of its wings.

"My God," I breathed, but I heard Tycho say in a low, urgent voice:

"Kepler! Fetch the net."

"What! You cannot plan to capture it," I protested.

Tycho shot me a look of aggrieved aggression. "Why not?"

"It is an angel!"

"And so?" Tycho stepped nimbly to one side and snatched up the net upon a pole with which we used to remove stray birds in case they fouled the delicate equipment. He made a pass at the angel and missed. The angel's face wrinkled in momentary disdain. Tycho swiped once more and the folds of the net fell around the angel. It made no attempt to dart away; the wings continued to beat as best they could within the imprisoning confines of the net. Tycho gave a tug and frowned.

"It lies heavy upon the air, like a toad in a pool. Make a note, Kepler."

I did not inscribe his simile, which was surely blasphemous. I grasped Tycho by the arm.

"Let it go! Do you want the wrath of God to fall upon us?"

Tycho gave me a cold, boiled stare.

"If it's as ineffectual as the wrath of princes, why should I care?" he asked.

It is true that I am not the most devout of men, but this presumption made me take a step backwards, in case God or his angelic messenger chose this moment to make an example of any nearby astronomers.

Tycho dragged the angel down from the ceiling. It came slowly and reluctantly, making no move to escape, though I saw its eyelids flutter with a kind of weary patience. Tycho reached out with a hand like a ham and grasped it. I saw a ripple pass along the angel's smooth throat, but it gave no other sign of distress.

"I had thought," Tycho said, with a wondering air, "That they would be larger."

"The Bible tells us that there are many kinds," I reminded him. "Tycho, you must let it go."

"Don't be a fool, Kepler. It is surely the greatest find of the age. With such a key, we can unlock all manner of secrets, can we not?" He glowered at me. The angel folded its small hands more tightly upon its breast. Swiftly, Tycho carried the tiny figure to the far end of the room and placed it under a glass bell jar, of the kind used for studying insects. The angel lay full length, like a statue upon a tomb. "You see?" Tycho demanded of me. "It does not want to leave. An angel could surely command such powers at its disposal as to level the observatory to the ground, yet it does not do so."

"Did you not think of that when you netted it?" I asked, and then I realised that Tycho did not really care: had little thought for his own life or those of others, but simply wanted to see what would happen next. His was the curiosity of a madman.

I think Tycho was surprised when the angel did not die in the killing jar, nor expire when he carefully pinned it to the board by its bird-winged shoulder. He made me watch and the act sickened me. But I did nothing.

When I first set eyes upon the angel, I do not think that I truly believed what I saw. Since early childhood, I have suffered from shortness of sight and at the same time, a multiplicity of vision that causes the world around me to become a swirling vagueness. I have, as I have said, always believed my face to be turned away from God, and thus I have been driven to study the universe, to seek answers in the stars. It is all theology, but it has comforted me to look to things rather than beings: the regular motion of the planets, the wheel of the constellations.

Stars do not deviate from their course, nor do they curse and strike out. They appear governed by reason, rather than acting from a deity's most singular whim. But now it seemed that a being had sought me out: an impassive one, to be sure, and uncommunicative. Yet I saw in it the seeds of my redemption: the sign of a divine promise in which I had never truly been able to believe.

That evening, leaving Tycho to roar and hoot below, I ascended the stairs to where the angel was held captive. It appeared unconcerned; its face still blank, eyes still closed. But when I peered down at the bell jar, that black, strangely animal gaze snapped open and held my own. I half expected it to speak, but it said nothing, and after a moment the eyes closed once more. I reached out toward the jar. There was a sudden pressure in my head, like the roar of the sea. I stepped back and almost fell, but a hand clasped about my arm and steadied me. I looked up into Tycho's meaty face.

"Examining our captive? Very good, Kepler, very good. I have been following a similar course, down in the library. I have been scrutinising some of the lesser known Kabbalistic texts."

"Oh?" I faltered, "and what have you discovered?"

"A most surprising and worthy tale, of angelic beings and the knowledge they contain."

"Contain?" I echoed, stupidly.

"The knowledge of the universe. The hidden key to the motion of the spheres, the manner in which the primum mobile drives all else."

"You mean that there is a way to question the angel, so that it will divulge secrets?"

"Not question, Kepler." Tycho stared avidly at the angel's prone form, as though it were a piece of candied fruit. "Dissect."

I stared at him in horror. "You cannot dissect an angel. This is a heavenly being."

"Look at the eyes. They are like a dog's. Have you heard it speak? Has it evinced any true understanding of what has befallen it? No, it lies there like a lump, unknowing. I might as well have my elk upon the slab. Moreover, the Kabbalistic text informs me that such beings are of the very lowest orders of Heaven: this is not Gabriel himself, come calling, but the equivalent of some minor imp."

"That still does not entitle you to murder it."

"Kepler. Think of the rewards, man. Think of the *knowledge*."

"But we might be struck dead!"

"What of it?" Tycho said, honestly amazed. "Are we not men of science? Have we not dedicated our lives to astronomy?"

"Our lives, perhaps, but –"

"Consider us, Kepler. You, a mewling weakling from a cursed clan; myself, a noseless drunk with a horde of snotty brats that I can barely feed. You see, I spare no one in my analysis! Our lives are of little consequence compared to the knowledge that lies before us. Anyway," Tycho continued in somewhat less grandiose terms "We might even survive. We will perform the task tomorrow. The key lies in the angel's breast, so the text tells me, and resembles a pearl."

"And if you extract this pearl, what then?"

"Then, it must be dissolved in extract of vitriol and spread upon a parchment, on which the appropriate calculations will subsequently appear."

"Tycho, this is not science," I said. For a moment, the flames that had consumed my mother's body seemed to dance around the walls of the room and reach toward me. "This is magic."

"There is a point at which science and magic meet," Tycho told me.

"And what point is that?"

"Faith," Tycho replied. "Have faith, little Kepler. Not in this being before you, nor in a God which clearly so despises you that he afflicts you on a daily basis with a variety of anguishes, but in knowledge. That is the only pure goal, after all."

I did not disagree. But I also knew that I was too afraid to do as he asked.

"Tycho –"

"And besides," Tycho went on, and now his voice had grown soft as the paws of a mousing cat, "What do you think might befall you, little Kepler, if you refuse to help me? Astronomy is your only chance of distinguishing yourself, is it not? You could, perhaps, become a clerk and slave away in some hovel somewhere, but that's not what you want, is it?"

He terrified me, but I thought of the angel lying beneath the jar, surely even more helpless than I.

"And without me – what?" I heard myself say. "Without me, what hope do you have of comprehending the orbit of Mars? It is too difficult a set of calculations for you; you have hinted as much. You even refuse to show me the whole of your calculations, as if you fear that I am the better astronomer."

Tycho stared at me. For a moment, I thought he was going to strike me, but then he gave a great laugh.

"Some show of spirit, at last! But Kepler, consider this – if I have the secrets of the angel, I do not need *you*, do I?"

"And what of my immortal soul? What of yours?"

"What has God done for you so far, Kepler? Sent your

father to hang and your mother to burn. Afflicted your brothers and sisters – not to mention yourself – with a sequence of poxes and plagues that would try the patience of Job. Do you really think God cares about you and your immortal soul?"

I wanted to say *yes*, but the word died before it reached my breath. Tycho must have seen my doubts in my face, for he said, still softly, "I thought as much. Tomorrow, Kepler. Now go to your chamber."

I did so, but I could not sleep. To distract myself, I took up my pen and wrote down this latest episode in the story of the angel. Then I read again all that I have told you so far. It only made me despise myself anew. I set my notes aside in despair, and lay down upon the bed.

At last, shortly before dawn, I fell into a kind of waking dream in which the ceiling of the chamber evaporated to reveal the open heavens. And beyond the fading stars, I thought I glimpsed a vast, unblinking eye. There was no mercy in it, no kindness, and I felt then that it did not matter what I did, I would still be damned.

I sat up, panting against the bolster. In its wake, the knowledge brought a curious sense of freedom. If it did not matter what I did, then – damned or not – I was free to act. I rose from my bed and crept from the chamber.

No one was awake, except for the rats. I could hear the elk snorting in its sleep in the great hall as I ascended the stairs. A thin light filtered through the cracks in the masonry, sufficient to light my passage to the observatory.

The angel lay still beneath the bell jar, but its eyes were open now, and watching me. I took a breath, reached out, plucked the jar away. Then I withdrew the pin from the angel's shoulder: it came free with difficulty, as though I pulled it from a piece of stone, and the hole that it had made closed instantly, bloodless. The angel watched me, still.

"You are free!" I told it, making flapping motions with my

hands. "You must go, *now*, before he finds that you are no longer confined." Now that I had finally taken action I felt calmer, almost resigned to whatever might follow next. "And then wreak what vengeance you will."

I did not see the angel's lips move, but I heard it speak for the first time.

"Kill me," it said. Its voice was small and musical, remote as a bell far away across the marshes. At first I thought I had misheard it.

"What? I have just freed you."

"The astronomer is right," the angel said. "The knowledge lies within me, within all of my kind. But I cannot reach it, any more than you can see your own heart. You have to release it, Johannes Kepler. You have to take the pearl."

"But if it will mean your death –"

"Do you think that God has sanctioned me?" the angel asked. The question caught me off guard; I stared at it. "Do you think I am here by His will?"

"I supposed –"

"The days of faith are passing, Kepler. You have to step from Eden, to sin in order to bring new knowledge to the world. There can be no change in the order of the Church: the sun must always orbit the Earth, unalterable, forever. But knowledge is not a static force; it must move forward, sideways, back. It cannot be contained. I know this as well as you. Where does it say that an angel cannot be a scientist?"

I looked into its eyes and they were no longer dark and opaque, but as blue as the sky. I took the pin and plunged it into the angel's breast. The angel split apart with soundless force, ribs peeling back and crumbling into stone.

There was no pearl within. There was nothing but powder and ash. I stood looking down at it for a long time, until a draught from beneath the door blew the remains away. Then I went slowly back to my chamber.

The consequences of the angel's disappearance were severe.

Tycho drank for a week. Even the elk went into hiding. When he sobered up sufficiently, I went to see him. I couldn't face telling him the truth, but he accused me of freeing the angel all the same, roaring at me with furnace anger. This time, I stood my ground.

"The angel must surely have been a test. You cannot cheat the universe," I told him. "There are few quick roads in the landscape of science."

He took a step toward me. I moved swiftly back.

"You are a fool, Kepler," he said.

"Am I? Perhaps so," I replied. "But if I am such, then you can easily do without me.' And I turned and walked away.

"Kepler!" – the bellows followed me out of the chamber, out of the castle and across the bridge that led over the Iser. "Johannes, come back!" But I did not once look behind me.

I returned to Prague, feeling lighter of heart all the same and strangely free from fear of God and man. I had discoursed with an angel, a fellow scientist. Even if it had lied to me, or been mistaken, we had been engaged on the same quest, however briefly, and I found that this meant something.

I took work as a humble clerk and continued to develop my calculations in the evenings. I proceeded slowly, hampered by constant sickness, but I worked methodically all the same, and one day I looked down at the charts and the diagrams, and discovered that they made sense. It was, curiously, my notes on the orbit of Mars that had precipitated the breakthrough: the very task that Tycho had set me, and at which – I am sure – he hoped I would fail. My conclusions outraged me, being directly contrary to the Copernican system to which I had always adhered, but I could not argue with the mathematics. I twisted and turned, trying to find fault with the calculations, and could not. At last, I laid down my pen.

The Earth travelled about the sun, and I could prove it. No matter what was to befall me, I had proof.

When I looked up, I was not surprised to see the angel

hovering before me.

"There was no pearl," I told it.

But the angel only smiled at me, before gliding through the door. I followed, to find that it had gone; and for a long while I stood outside in the chilly darkness, watching the spring stars wheel above my head.

Indicating the Awakening of Persons Buried Alive

"But Richard, of course I am entirely sure that she was dead!" my brother Jonathan informed me. "Just like all the others." He twisted his top hat between his hands, crushing it in his agitation. "You surely do not think that I would have sent someone still living to their grave?"

"Isn't there a particular disease that mimics the processes of demise?" I asked. I was vague about such matters: Jonathan was the undertaker, the respectable son who had shouldered the burden of the family business, whereas I was merely a starving poet and, as such, regarded by our aged father with contempt. There was little that I could do to assist my brother in his difficulties, I thought. But the next few moments were to prove me wrong.

"No," Jonathan said, sinking onto the divan. "I have spoken to the doctor. They all died of different illnesses. Simon Anders succumbed to a wasting sickness, Sarah Thorne to pneumonia. And Nathan Lyme died as a result of shock after a dog bit him. Yet all of these people appear to have become revitalised once buried – and these are only the ones who have been exhumed. Indeed, they would have remained below ground had it not been for the need to remove them to the new cemetery. Who knows what other torments might have been taking place beneath the earth? It is putting the wind up my clients, Richard, and one can hardly blame them. Folk are naturally unwilling to commit their loved ones for burial with us if there is a chance that they are not in fact deceased. I shall be ruined! The business is everything to father, to myself."

"I can see how it could be a cause for some apprehension," I remarked. "But a cadaver cannot be kept indefinitely upon a mortuary slab; internment is ultimately necessary." I considered the matter, my imagination reeling from the horror of waking only to find oneself in one's grave clothes, nailed inside a coffin. It would make a good verse – I forced my unruly mind back to the matter in hand.

"One really needs some reliable means of rescue once one is in the ground."

Jonathan regarded me with more respect than he had accorded me for years. "Pray continue," he said.

It was at that point that *The Hugo Patent Device for Indicating the Awakening of Persons Buried Alive* was truly born.

Jonathan set our coffin-maker, one Eben Frame, to work, and a preliminary device was created. Frame threw himself upon the challenge with gusto, but the developmental process was not without its difficulties.

"Observe," he remarked, as we stood in the echoing confines of his warehouse. He made a gesture with one of his crutches. "The lid of the coffin is spring loaded; should you awake in the mortuary and find yourself incarcerated, you merely touch this switch and the lid will open. So!"

He pulled a small string, connected to the coffin's interior. The lid shot forth as if fired from a cannon, immediately felling my unfortunate brother. When we had ascertained that he was not in imminent danger of becoming the coffin's first occupant, and had brought him round with the application of smelling salts and water, Jonathan informed us angrily that the device must undergo modification.

"Besides," he pointed out. "It is useless if one is already buried when one discovers the sorry fact of incarceration. Not even a force sufficient to render a man unconscious can shift six feet of earth."

Eben Frame sighed. "I fear you are right. I suspect that will also be a difficulty with my second patent."

We went to look at the alternative model. This coffin

possessed the addition of a spring-loaded hammer which, when set in motion via a small knob, would smash a glass panel on the front of the coffin, thus allowing the influx of air. The drawbacks were immediately apparent.

"But this is no good either," I protested. "The occupant, in addition to his mental distress, will receive not only a shower of glass into the face, but a forceful blow between the eyes. And again, as you have noted, it is only of use whilst the coffin is still above ground. No, what is needed is a rope, attached to a bell or a whistle. Or a little flag. So that if you woke and found yourself in your coffin, you could pluck the rope and be assured of rescue. Some kind of air hose might also be necessary – after all, one might awake in the middle of the night. I am sure such a device would be popular – set the public mind at rest, so to speak."

A week later, Frame had come up with a third device: a coffin attached to a flag, with a loud electric bell and an air hose running up through the earth to the base of the flagpole. After some trivial modifications, we felt that this was the most effective variant, and production commenced. We placed advertisements in the *Times*, sat back, and waited.

Gradually, orders began to trickle in, and soon they grew to a flood. Jonathan had his practice to run, but he tried to persuade me to take over the business side of the Device. He was somewhat put out when I refused to do so: I did not endure all the hardships of becoming a poet, I told him, merely to take up a post as a salesman.

"But your work –" Jonathan began, then stopped short.

"What of it?"

"The penny papers, monthly poetry journals – it is hardly great literature, Richard. Could you not put your talents to some more lucrative end? Could you not try to be more – well, respectable?"

"A poet lies beyond common society and everyday morality," I replied, stiffly. And Jonathan sighed, but did not say anything more. We hired a keen young gentleman by the name of

Sayers to run the day-to-day dealings of the business, and returned to our respective professions.

There came a week near to the end of November, however, when Richard took to his bed with a filthy chill and Sayers pleaded for a day off. He had an aged mother in Bognor, he said, and he wished to visit her. With extreme reluctance, I agreed to mind the funeral parlour for a day or so. And it was upon that day that I first met Madame Greco.

She was waiting for me, so the housekeeper told me, in the parlour; she had requested it especially, claiming that she felt the cold. When I entered the room, she was sitting in front of the fire with her hands folded in her lap. I had the impression of an elegant figure, clad in the appropriate purple and black of mourning, necklaced with jet. The only curious note was the lily that she wore in her bonnet: it, too, was black and velvety and at first I thought it to be no more than a lifelike ornament, until I realised that the strong sweet perfume that filled the air of the parlour was emanating from its petals.

"I do hope you'll forgive me for imposing upon you," the woman said. She rose, offering me a black-satin hand. "My name is Madame Greco; I have recently become a widow."

Behind the gauzy darkness of her veil her eyes were luminous and huge. It was impossible to tell her age, or her origins; she spoke with something of an accent, but it was not one that I recognised. I was, however, immediately captivated. Something about the timbre of her voice and the almost narcotic fragrance of the lily entranced me. I bent over her hand.

"It is no trouble at all," I said. "I'm so sorry to hear of your loss."

I thought I detected a slight smile beneath the veil.

"Damien died as he lived," she told me. "Ever unexpected."

"And you will be wanting – arrangements?"

She lowered her head and dabbed at her eyes with a handkerchief scented with violets.

"Quite so."

"Then let us discuss the nature of the internment," I murmured.

Madame Greco duly ordered a magnificent coffin and, pressing my hand with a pretty gratitude, left. I did not feel that this was the appropriate time to press talk of the Device upon her. I fully intended to leave a note for Sayers to remind him of this fact, but thinking about Madame Greco brought to mind a number of poetic notions, and I became distracted. In the end, no note was written.

It was shortly before Christmas that I set eyes on Madame Greco once more, as I was walking to our father's house for a party. I disliked these family occasions, which usually involved a series of barbed jibes on my father's part relating to my choice of profession. I thus took the long way through Highgate, past the cemetery, and it was already past twilight when I reached the gates. Upon glancing through the iron tracery, I was vaguely gratified to see in the dim light of the gas-lamps that a number of recent graves – in addition to handsome marble monuments – bore the small red flag and electric bell that signalled the presence of the Device. It was then that I caught sight of Madame Greco.

She was hurrying along the path that led to the edges of the cemetery, past the older mausoleums. She halted in front of an ornate tombstone in the form of a pyramid. These had been fashionable at one time, but had now fallen somewhat out of favour. I saw her run her hand over the marble facade, then move on down the hill to a much fresher patch of earth. She fell to her knees beside the grave and, moved by a pang of pity, I remained to watch her. She scrabbled at the soil.

"James?" I heard her say. "Have you woken? Do you hear me?"

I frowned. I distinctly remembered her remarking that her husband's name was 'Damien.' She paused for a moment, listening, with her ear to the ground. She sighed, rose to her feet, moved on. I watched her as she visited three more graves in turn.

79

Apparently none of them were clients of my brother, for these graves were undecorated by the Device. She scratched and clawed, until the black satin gloves were torn and her hands were bloody.

"Wake!" she whispered, "Why do you not wake?"

Then, with a start of surprise, I saw the earth at the base of the last grave begin to stir. My heart jumped.

"Damien?" I heard her fierce whisper across the silent graveyard. "Damien!"

Next moment, the soil rolled aside like a blanket and a man was standing there. I saw a white face and pale hands, before he was enveloped in a long dark coat that flapped down upon him like a shadow. Madame Greco was speaking to him in a language that I did not recognise. He turned, and I heard him begin to sniff and snuffle, like a hunting dog.

It suddenly occurred to me that I was not in the most suitable location to encounter someone newly risen from the dead. I am not ashamed to note that I turned and ran. That evening, my father's jibes ran over me like water. I remained at his house that night, and I was not sorry to do so.

Next day, I did not wake until past three o'clock. Sitting over tea in the pale winter sunlight, I felt somewhat foolish. I had surely been mistaken, I thought. No doubt I had merely glimpsed a friend stepping out from behind the tomb, in order to comfort poor Madame Greco in her time of need. Perhaps she had become distracted in her grief, had been initially unable to find her husband's burial place. I debated the matter for some time, before resolving to go back to the cemetery and make a few investigations.

When I reached Highgate, it was already close to twilight. I could hear the bell of St Paul's toll out the time, a melancholy note sounding from across the river. My feet crackled on the last dead leaves; the high wall at the edge of the cemetery was half hidden in bramble and the smoky haze of wild clematis. A flock of crows spiralled up from the path as I approached, startling me.

I found the tall point of the pyramid tomb without difficulty. I was somehow unsurprised to note that it bore the name of one Aessia Greco. I took note of the date: she had died at the age of twenty-seven, more than two hundred years before.

I touched the tomb briefly, to reassure myself that it was real, then turned to take my leave. A great dark wing swept across my face. I leaped, stumbling back against the tomb.

"Why, it's Mr Hugo," said a voice behind me. "I'm so sorry. I didn't mean to alarm you."

My vision cleared. It was Madame Greco, still swathed in mourning. Her face was invisible behind a heavier veil.

"No, the fault is mine. A dizzy spell." I said. "Well, delightful to meet you once more, Madame Greco, and now I really must be on my way —"

"Please, let me help you. You're quite faint." She took hold of my arm. Through her thin gloves, her touch was icy cold, with a thread of subtle warmth running through it. I felt a guilty, delicious rush of desire, but I snatched my hand away. She stood like a shadow on the path. The sun had long since fallen below the horizon.

"I suggest some hot tea, Mr Hugo," she said briskly.

"An excellent idea. I shall seek some at once. Now —"

"I think I should accompany you," she said. The thought crept into my mind like a little serpent: what harm was there in that? We would have tea, and then we would climb the stairs to her small attic room and I would raise the veil and she would fall to her knees and – I blinked. Unruly thoughts, of a carnal nature, were flowing into my mind like water, and nothing was standing in their way. I felt myself growing flushed, heard myself stammering something.

The next thing I knew, I was sitting opposite Madame Greco. I had no idea where I might be. The room was shrouded behind curtains of ebony velvet, and lit by a single taper. In the chancy light, Madame Greco's face gleamed like a flame. The room smelled of dust and mould, but the furnishings were rich.

"Where am I?" I asked her.

"At my home," I heard her say. Her voice sounded very distant, as though she spoke from the bottom of a well. She took my hand. I could feel her nails, small and sharp, through the ruined glove, and again that icy touch.

"What are you?" I asked, as if through a dream.

"You are a poet, are you not?"

"Yes, I do my poor best."

"I direct you to Keats, therefore – the poem called *The Lamia*. Are you familiar with it?"

"Yes. It is a poem about a woman who preys on young men."

"Quite so. It is a little like that with my kind. Though I prefer the term 'seduces'. 'Preys' sounds so unlovely." Her grip tightened. "We do our poor best for those we – select. We take what we need, and often they rise to join us. They have life, after all, of a sort."

Dream-like or not, there was a voice struggling at the back of my mind, and it told me that I was in grave danger.

"But I fear you have already seen too much." She leaned closer. I could feel no breath upon my neck. Then, through a roaring in my head, an idea came to me.

"Wait," I said. "Indeed, I have seen too much. I watched you there, searching the graves." This time, it was I who reached for her hand. "Searching, clawing, ruining your hands as you try to wake them. It does not always work, does it? They do not always return."

After a moment, she shook her head.

"Would it not be easier, if you had certain knowledge of when they awoke?"

Her head moved in the fraction of a nod.

"And thus I have a proposal for you," I whispered. I held my breath.

In the dim light, her eyes glittered with a tiny crimson flame.

"I am listening," she said.

Occasionally, when my gaze falls upon the rise of Highgate Hill above the city, and I think of the scarlet flags that flutter within those walls, I wonder if I have behaved quite like a gentleman. I fear I have not. But a poet is, as I have said, beyond the common morality, and as my brother is so fond of reminding me, a business deal is a business deal, no matter with whom – or what – one transacts it.

Voivodoi

It's a long time ago now, but the memories of that last summer with my brother still come to me at night. They unscroll in a series of perfect frozen images before my reluctant inner eye like a dream or a film. I have not seen my brother Roman since I was thirteen. These waking dreams lead me to wonder where he is now, and how much he has changed.

The clearest memories are the most ordinary ones. I remember one particular evening very clearly, even though it was such a usual day. We had finished dinner and Mother and I were still sitting at the table in the kitchen of the stuffy split-level compartment. Dad had bolted his food, furtively, like an animal, before sliding from the table and into the tiny room that he called the office. I think he locked the door. All we could hear was the sound of game shows on the portable TV. My mother didn't say much, but I sensed that she was constantly trying to catch my eye. I could feel her gaze sliding around my own as I stared at the floor. I knew Roman was listening, because there was a sort of suspended silence at the top of the stairs; the sound of someone holding their breath. Andrea, our visiting student, had stayed late at the university and was unlikely to be back before ten.

Before Roman's illness, we'd always eaten at different times; on the run like most families. Then he fell ill and as the days wore on and he became no better my mother insisted that we eat together at least once during the day. Eventually Roman became too unwell to come downstairs and had to have his meals on a tray in his room, but despite his conspicuous absence my parents still tried to deny that anything was wrong. Soon, they said, my cheerful, annoying brother would be sitting opposite me again and kicking me under the table. That was what my mother had said tonight, anyway. Enjoy it while it lasts, she'd told me tartly, but children are only young, not fools, and I was unconvinced. Perhaps my mother knew what I was thinking, and spoke to break my resentful silence.

"I took your brother a tray, Teresa. Maybe you could see if he wants anything else?" her voice trailed away.

"Okay," I said, to fill the gap. The door of Roman's room was closed. Outside, the tray stood on the landing and on it were the meal and Roman's capsules. Both were untouched. He must have had a particularly bad day; it was only then that he refused his medicine. After a moment's thought, I took the warm, slightly glutinous handful to the lavatory and flushed it away. The bathroom window was open, but the screen had not switched itself on. I checked the atmospheric pollution meter and the level wasn't yet high enough to activate the screen, which was unusual in summer.

I was wondering whether Mother might let me go out tonight, but I knew I wouldn't ask her even though it was Friday. I had become a dutiful daughter, thoughtful and considerate since my brother became ill. I knew that Yuliya and Sveta were down at the District Rink that night. Both were comrades in an elaborate plan to entice shy and strutting Bogdan Maretovitch away from the supportive male flock. Yuliya's eye had been on Bogdan for some time, and she had been moving steadily closer for the past couple of months. She understood how things worked, Yuliya. I was dying to see the outcome of her campaign, but I couldn't leave Mother there in the silence to finish the dishes. I didn't have to like it, though, even if it was my own choice. Mother caught my sullen look. Later, she said, "Oh, you know what we're out of? Sugar. And your aunt's coming tomorrow... Could you run down to the co-mart?"

We both knew that the way to the co-mart took me past the Rink. "Don't worry if there's a queue," she called after me. "Take your time."

So I ran down the stairs through the dusty evening silence and out into the last of the light. We were lucky to live here. The woods came up as far as the waste ground at the back of the compartment block, and in summer we could almost believe that we were living in the high ice cream peaks of the Tatras, breathing the clean air and a long way from the Krakow suburbs. It wasn't a bad place at all, Nowa Huta.

The co-mart was in the middle of the industrial estate. You had to go down Wielickza Street, then across Centralny and Tyniec. You could see the gates of the old steelworks in the distance, like the entrance to a municipal park. It's a museum now; a monument to our industrial heritage. Mrs Milosz, my history teacher, used to tell us that we were living in a post industrial age and always added with apologetic irony, "But not round here." Just before the turn-off the road took you past the pyroxin processing plant. When I was little we had a book of folk stories which showed a mill with a waterwheel, and I used to pretend that the plant was really that mill, with the moustachioed miller Potocki inside grinding grain. I could almost see the water weed, greener than grass, dripping into the millpond and the lilies sailing under the wind. Now, as I passed, the evening sky was water-clear above the haze and the black outline of the plant transformed it into the mill again. The monotonous creak of the generators was really the turning of the wheel, and the cooling duct which lay like a moat around the base of the plant became the millpond. In my mind, lilies floated and there was a crescent moon hanging low in the western sky, just like the illustration.

Something broke the water: a round head, mild eyed. It snorted and sank beneath the surface of the cooling duct. In the story, a vodyanoi, one of the old things, lived in the millpond. There was a picture of him scowling, whiskers bristling, with one webbed hand raised irritably among the lily leaves. Voivodoi, as I heard it as a child, is like kikimura, the hen-faced woman who scratches in the barn at night, and the shock-headed person with fiery eyes and a Tartar moustache who is supposed to haunt the cornfield in hot summers. They always looked too sharp to me; I preferred smooth, froglike voivodoi in the millpond. Through the grey evening haze the light was golden and apricot ripples spread through the waters of the processing plant. Voivodoi, or a dog, swimming? I walked on down Tyniec Street.

The co-mart was almost empty. There was no queue, only Mrs Kraszny in a headscarf complaining about the heat. On the way back, I met Yuliya emerging triumphantly from the doors of the Rink. Bogdan was tamed and sheepish in tow. Yuliya grinned; I grinned back at her. "Hiya," she said. "I'll call you, yes? Tomorrow."

"Sure," I said in English. It was hip to talk American again. The previous year we'd all wanted to be Japanese, but cola and distressed matt jackets had been back ever since the WIScomm branch opened. Yuliya waved as she turned down Gdynia Street. I walked back quickly past the dark pond and when I turned the corner to our compartment block there was a light on in the bedroom behind the haze of the screen.

Dad was still in the office, but the TV was on in the kitchen and my mother was knitting, presumably for Natasha's baby. I could hear Roman moving about and the occasional whine of the old lift in the hallway. "Can I watch Shokun Knife?" Mother's eyes rolled, but I *had* come straight back instead of staying at the Rink.

"Don't expect me to watch it," she said. I had wanted to be Keiko Sekura ever since we started getting Shokun Knife. She could high kick, I recall, and she took on the multinats and always won. I wanted a spine-headed Gharenese cat, like Keiko. I remember thinking that my chances of getting one were pretty good, since they were real animals, after all, a gene hatch between an ocelot and a Gharen porcupine. Keiko Sekura had liberated the cat from a gene lab in episode one, and it had been her devoted companion ever since. This was the early twenties, when the gene-trans people were starting to become unpopular and their mistakes were beginning to show, especially in the eastern parts of Europe, and the old ex-Soviet countries. The thought of the gene labs used not to bother me – granddad had worked for one, after all – but now it made me uncomfortable. Perhaps with Roman's illness it brought everything too close to home. I sometimes wonder whether that's why Keiko was such a heroine of mine.

Mother watched the show, too, just as she always did. Then, as we were getting ready for bed, she ran a sneak check on me. It stung. "Don't do that! Ow!" I protested.

"Sorry, Teresa," she said, but she didn't mean it. Every time this happened we said the same things.

"Look, I don't want to know." She ignored me, holding the phial up to the light and watching as the drop of rosy blood grew transparent.

"It's clear, anyway. You want to know that, don't you?" she said.

"I told you, I don't care. I don't want to know," and I turned resentfully away. "I'm going to bed now," I muttered and began to unpack the fold-out bed which stood in the corner of the cramped kitchen.

Normally, Roman and I shared a room, but his snuffling breathing and restless movements at night made it difficult for me to sleep. At last Mother had moved me down to the sofa bed in the kitchen. I slept better there, but I had no privacy and at that age you are beginning to need a quiet place of your own.

I looked in on Roman before I settled down. He was sprawled sleeping across the bed. In sleep he looked younger than seventeen. His legs were covered by the duvet, but he had thrown off the rest of the covers. It was so hot that I bundled them up and put them on the chair, then I stood looking down at him. He didn't look so bad, I thought. In fact, he looked better than he did before it started coming on. He didn't seem so skinny now, I thought hopefully. I think I wanted to turn his illness, and the changes, into an adventure and make them less real and less terrible. Downstairs, I could hear the key in the lock: Andrea coming in. She was always saying how much work she had to do, but she came home late enough. Mother didn't say anything. Andrea was twenty three and old enough to take care of herself, even in a foreign country. She was American, here on an exchange programme and doing some sort of postgraduate degree back in the States. I supposed I liked her, but she was ten years older, the age I am now, and we didn't have much in common. I closed Roman's door before she came up the stairs. Andrea knew he wasn't well, of course, but Roman wouldn't have liked her looking at him and my mother thought it might upset her.

In the morning the phone shrilled. I buried my head in the pillow, but I could still hear Dad answering it. At last he said "When? When are you coming?" and there was a burst of conversation at the other end.

"Who is it?" I mumbled.

"It's only your aunt," he said, and walked out of the kitchen. I caught a glimpse of him as he went through the door, and in the thin light his face looked grey. I could hear him talking to my mother, which made it impossible to sleep, so I got up and put the coffee on.

"What was all that about?" I asked my mother.

"Nothing," she said. "Nothing to worry about."

"Is it Natasha?"

"Teresa," she said, and her voice had that patient note in it. "Take this up to your brother, please."

She handed me his mug. I made sure Andrea wasn't around before I took the coffee in. Roman was still asleep and invisible under the duvet. I put the mug of coffee and the pills down by the side of the bed and shook him awake; I didn't see why he should have a lie-in when the rest of us were up. He muttered something.

"There's your coffee," I said, and closed the door behind me.

My aunt arrived at eleven, bringing the baby with her in a carry bag. "You can hold her if you like, Teresa," she told me, evidently conferring a favour. It would have hurt her feelings if I'd said no, so I took Ludmila on my lap and sat with her while Natasha and my mother talked. Ludmila squalled, and clapped her hands. She was a pretty baby, with fine dark hair and Asian eyes; her dad's Kazak. I took her tiny right hand in mine and waved it for her, and then I put her fingers into the mittens that Mother had been making. They hid the missing little finger and Ludmila stared wide eyed at her hands. She's almost perfect, I thought.

"You hold her for a bit," my mother said, smiling at us. "I want to show your aunty the garden."

The garden was a piece of reclamation to one side of the compartment, where the ground opened out. Our building stood on legs and there was a dark space beneath it, high enough for Dad, but not Mr Polowski, to stand upright. Dad and Mr Polowski were stringing lights across the ceiling, so that we could start growing things. They were hoping that if we got planning permission we could start a hydrogarden, but it was likely to take time. The application for the lights had only just been accepted even though we'd put it in two years previously. The comp committee was clearing back the waste ground and we'd got the first quarter gardened, but we needed to re-hire the breaker for the next bit and there was a waiting list.

As I sat rocking Ludmila, I could hear the voices of my aunt and Mother floating up from the garden. I couldn't hear what they were saying, though, and it was frustrating, so I took the baby up to see Roman. He was pleased, even though he didn't want to show it.

"Hi," he said to Ludmila, and struggled to sit up in bed.

"Say hi to Roman," I told her. She looked at him and laughed. I held her out, but Roman said self-consciously, "I don't know what to do with kids."

"Just take hold of her, Roman, is that such a big deal?"

"Yes," my brother admitted. "Can you turn the light off?" he added, irritably. He twisted his face deeper into the covers.

"Okay, don't be so touchy," I said. "I'll take her back down. Do you want to find your mum?" I asked the baby.

"It's all right," Roman said hastily. "I'll hold her if you like." and gingerly he put Ludmila down on the lumpy covers. In silence we watched her playing with the tassels on the cover of the bedside table. I knew what Roman was thinking, but I couldn't say anything. With any luck they'd find a way to solve the problem before Ludmila was Roman's age.

"What were you up to yesterday?" he asked me.

"Not much. I had so much homework... I spent most of it in front of the computer."

I was lying, because I hadn't been to see him, but I couldn't very well say that I was tired of him being ill. When it first started, I was sympathetic, because I felt so sorry for him, but now it was just dragging on and we were all bored with it. I couldn't say so. The illness wasn't Roman's fault, and Mum had enough to worry about without me complaining. Sitting here like this, with the baby rolling on the blankets between us, it wasn't so bad, and eventually Mother came upstairs with my aunt.

"Hello, Roman," Natasha said, rather coolly. "How are you?"

"I'm okay," he told her, eager to show that everything was normal. "I'm feeling fine."

"Oh, that's good," Natasha said. She was smiling too much, and I remember being glad when Mother took her back down to the kitchen. He was still my brother, after all.

"Natasha doesn't know much," I said to Roman, and after a moment he nodded.

As I came down the stairs I heard my mother saying "And of course it wasn't his fault, but she wasn't used to it, and it just unnerved her. The sanatorium rang this morning; I suppose we should start thinking about it. But it's not as if no-one else has this sort of thing..."

I heard Natasha say, in a low voice, "Yes, but you can't expect people to accept it. Look at Lydia Petrov. When she started to – well, her mother insisted on brazening it out. Took her down to the co-mart and everything. I'm sorry, Vera, but I wasn't the only one who found it disgusting. I mean, you're not having people round here, are you?"

My mother's voice was icy.

"Certainly everyone who used to come here still does. Andrea's still staying with us. All the neighbours drop round, they've been very good. Everyone knows, Natasha. Everyone knows."

Yes, but you might give some thought to, well, Arman and I, for example. I mean, people come up to me in the co-mart and start discussing it. It's just not very nice –"

– and Mother interrupted, winter cold, "No. It isn't."

When I hurriedly pushed the door open, I saw that my aunt at least had the grace to look ashamed.

"I've brought Ludmila down," I said, and put the baby on her mother's lap. Natasha couldn't talk, I thought, and she knew it. Why else did my mother knit mittens, to hide what should not be seen? My aunt did not stay long after that.

A week later, Dad and Mr Polowski had got the lights up. The space underneath the compartment looked like the car park in Mrs Milosz' course texts. It was going to be good if we did get the planning permit; it was a huge area and I imagined the space filled with greenness, like the conservatory in the picture of the Moscow mall. There would be palms and fronds and a pool in the middle for voivodoi and goldfish. That was never going to happen, though, because they planned to give it over to permabeans and small grain rice. I had been helping Dad, holding the skeins of lights as he battened them into the grooves. Mother spent a lot of the day out in the garden strip, weeding and planting. Admittedly, the weather was fine, warm and cloudless, but we all knew we just wanted an excuse to get out of the compartment. I made myself go up to see Roman every evening, and Mother sat with him when I was in school. He kept asking if he could go outside and sit on the steps in the long fold-out chair, but Mother thought it would be better for his lungs if he stayed indoors. The hospital had given us a special AP screen for the window, and it was permanently activated now. Every time I went in there I could smell its faint, chemical odour and the taste lingered on my tongue like paint. At least I didn't have to put up with it all the time, like Roman, but he didn't seem to mind. Whenever I went in, he was lying down, curled on his side with his face away from the door.

Even though I'd heard Mother telling Natasha that everyone knew about Roman, I knew it wasn't true. She had asked me to say nothing at school and I hadn't wanted to talk about it, anyway. I wasn't entirely sure what she had told the neighbours. One afternoon, coming home from class, I met Mrs Tevsky in the hallway. I quite liked Mrs Tevsky, she wore strings of beads and her jackets all had furry collars. She always used to give me a zloty, when I was little and we still had them. However, she was a terrible gossip, and so I was careful what I said to her. She asked after all the family in turn, right down to baby Ludmila, before saying

"And how's your brother?"

"He's okay. As well as can be expected," I said, rather stiffly.

"It's an awful thing, leukaemia," she said. Above the fur collar of her light jacket, her eyes were animal bright; I thought of kikimura scratching about in the hen house. "But they can do so much these days; I've heard they can cure it completely."

"I'm not sure," I said. "We're just hoping, that's all."

"Well, that's all you can do, isn't it?" Mrs Tevsky said. "Bye bye, then." and still unsatisfied, she vanished through her own front door. I repeated this conversation to my mother.

"I don't see why Nina Tevsky should know everything that goes on," she said.

"She said it was leukaemia," I said. "Did you tell her that?" I felt my gaze grow fierce, in case the bitter truth might fall from her mouth, but she only passed a hand over her eyes, rubbing wearily.

"That show's on in a minute," she said.

Mother never minded how much TV I watched, during that time. It meant I was quiet, and not asking questions, but I don't think I would have done anyway. She still did the scans, and said I was fine, but as I told her, I didn't think I wanted answers. As long as you can still ask questions, there's still a chance that the answer may change.

The summer drew on and the school holidays came around. Yuliya's family had a place up in Zakopane, and she suggested that I come and stay for the weekend. It was a beautiful place, lying up among the mountains. There was a cable car snaking up one of the peaks and from the top you could see the smoky blur of Krakow in the distance. Mother thought it was a good idea for me to go and get some fresh air after sitting in a stuffy classroom all year. They were nice, Yuliya's family, and lucky to have the house. It was her grandmother's, and they were allowed to keep it when the property redistribution took place on condition that they let it for part of the year to the unions. I thought that was fair. They got it at Christmas and during the summer, mostly. Yuliya and I were given the run of the place, and we spent a lot of time out in the cornfields, sifting the huge, perfect ears of ripening grain through our fingers. Each grain was larger than my thumbnail and we had endless competitions to find the biggest. The taste of that grain is still with me, how it burst floury in the mouth, like dust. We were allowed to stay up late and in the evening we sat out on the porch and looked up at the sky. It was very clear, so high into the mountains, and the nights were full of stars. Yuliya and I practised looking at the Pleiades; never directly, because then you wouldn't see them properly. Yuliya said that it was something to do with the cones in your eye, but now I think that there are things which forbid too close an examination, too searing for acceptance by the eye or the mind.

We came back on Sunday night. As soon as I came into the hallway I knew something was wrong, because I could hear Andrea all the way down three flights of stairs. Her face was white and crumpled, and she was quite incoherent. Mother was on her knees by Andrea's side, which annoyed me because she was not supposed to bend. Dad was nowhere in sight, and I didn't blame him. "Drink this," my mother kept saying. "You'll feel better." Eventually, Andrea took a sip of whatever was in the glass, choked, coughed and meekly drank the rest. At last there was silence. "Come on, now," Mother said. "Come up with me and we'll put you to bed."

She was a long time. When she came down again, she was wiping her hands on her apron. I couldn't say anything. Mother sat and stared at her hands, twisting her wedding ring. "She met your brother on the landing," she said at last. "It gave her a bit of a start. She's been working very hard."

"Yes," I said.

"I don't know if you've really noticed the... the progress."

"I suppose so," I said. But I don't think I was paying a lot of attention even then to how ill Roman actually was, because he was my brother and I did not want to think about it. It was something else that was not to be seen. Anyway, as I said, we'd all got a bit sick of Roman's illness.

"Look, Teresa," Mother said eventually. "Someone's coming from the hospital tomorrow, just to do a few tests. They called last week. They're bringing the schedule forward." She didn't look at me.

"You've been so good through all of this," she added. "I know how hard it's been." She was trying to make me feel better, so I wouldn't mind about the hospital visit. I reached over and squeezed her hand.

"Thanks," I said.

I went to bed, but I couldn't sleep properly. I kept thinking about the story book, of all things, the pictures of the spirit people, or whatever they were supposed to be. When you're only half awake, things get lodged in your mind and you can't get rid of them. Your thoughts go round and round. At last, I got up and switched the light on. The books were kept in a cabinet on the landing. I took the story book from behind the glass and went back into the kitchen. I hadn't looked at it for years but as I turned the pages I found that it was utterly familiar. There they all were: kikimura who haunts the hen houses, wearing an incongruous apron; the house spirit domovoi, peering from behind the sofa; the dark polevik, pictured among the corn stocks. Then there was voivodoi, vodyanoi, sad-eyed in the middle of the millpond. I sat staring into the empty air with the book open on my lap and thought: they are all there, among us in the world or locked up in the sanatorium where no one can see them. Hundreds of years ago we imagined them, and now we have made them real.

I put the book down and went to look out of the kitchen window. It didn't get really dark; there was too much light from the city and the sky was a blurred orange. It was raining, too, big drops streaming down the window pane. Tomorrow evening, someone would come from the hospital, the special sanatorium, and the car would draw up to where I was staring now and people would climb out and bring Roman downstairs, just as they did with Mrs Petrov's daughter. As quietly as I could, I went upstairs to the bedroom. Andrea's door was locked; the imprint gleamed faintly through the darkness. There was no sound from my parents' room and their door was tightly shut, too. Roman had thrown off the covers again. He really didn't look so bad, not to me. I shook him awake and put a hand over his mouth.

"Roman?"

"What is it?" He looked up at me, frightened and bleary with sleep. "She saw me on the landing," he told me. His voice was hoarse.

"I know. Look, Roman, they're going to take you up to the sanatorium tomorrow. Tell me if you want to go."

"No. No, I don't. I know what they'll do." Under my hand, he was shaking.

"Roman, how far can you walk?"

"I don't know."

"Do you know where you could go?" and after a moment, he nodded.

"Has someone spoken to you?"

"Yes. When you were all in the garden one day last week, a person called. They told me to go to the pyroxin plant, and they'd be there."

"Then that's where we'll go."

It seems so much like a dream, remembering. Roman hauled himself out of bed, and hung onto me. It's a good thing he was always such a skinny kid, because he weighed a ton. It was a wonder no one heard us. When we got out of the front door, he dragged himself over to the old lift and we dropped to the basement with the lift humming on its cables. The door opened out into the space beneath the compartment, and then it wasn't so bad, because we had some time and no one could see us. We ducked out into the summer rain. It tasted of metal, and it was cool, unlike the stinging rain which sometimes fell. There was a drainage ditch which ran along the roadside, and we kept to that. It was revolting, but Roman didn't seem to mind. Maybe it was good for him to be wet. His skin didn't look so puffy, or so raw. We were both panting by the time we got up to the plant.

"Roman," I asked, between gasps. "Can you live there? Like that?"

"I practised in the bath," he said, sheepishly, and for some reason this made me laugh. "I think it'll be okay. Other people do, after all. The ducts all join up to the river." He could no longer talk very well. His mouth looked too small. We were at the side of the cooling duct. Raindrops dappled the surface of the dark water, a round head rose. I crouched by my brother's side.

"Just be all right, Roman," I told him.

His head was level with mine. He started to say something. "I don't want to hear it. Go on, go." He dragged himself to the side of the duct and rolled off the edge, quite gracefully, like a seal. There were more of them in the duct, although it was difficult to see in the rain and the darkness, and one by one they dived. I caught a glimpse of their tapered tails as they plunged and then I was alone by the side of the cooling duct, watching the ripples spread across the water. I must have stayed longer than I thought, for when I turned and walked back home the clouds had cleared and the skies were the colour of pearl. There was a fresh wind blowing out of the grey east, and the smell of rain.

Now, ten years later, Mother and Dad are still there in compartment 3. Nothing much happened after that night. I suppose we all went back to normal. Andrea returned to the States. We got planning permission for the open basement, and I sometimes work in the hydrogarden after college. Eventually, they closed the processing plant down after a third scare. Nothing lives in the cooling duct. Yuliya and I still go up to Zakopane to her grandmother's house, and laze about in the meadows. Sometimes, in the evenings after a very hot day, I catch sight of something moving swiftly through the corn, and wonder how many people were affected. They shut down the big gene projects eight years ago, at least in Europe, but the enquiry totals always vary and the people whom we did not want to see, who should never have been so greatly transformed, are still here. I blame my ancestors, myself, for imagining the form of spirits, the inadvertent marriage of superstition with technology that created voivodoi, and domovoi, and kikimura, the changed and secret people who should only be seen from the corner of the eye, like certain stars.

On Windhover Down

Serena reached the manor road late in the afternoon, with an east wind at her back and the November sun hanging low above Windhover Down. The basket, covered with a cloth, hung on her arm; Serena tried to hold it as far from her as possible, but it was too heavy and she was forced to steady it with her free hand. Blood had seeped through the rushes that lined the bottom of the basket: looking back, she saw an irregular line of ruby specks dotting the cold earth. She prayed that none of it had marked the skirts of her only decent woollen dress.

She hurried along, trying not to look up at the long white figure carved on the hillside. It was said to be bad luck to see the Man from the road to the manor, for then he might choose to walk with you, following close behind, slipping through the twilight. Serena thought of bone-pale shadows, stalking the winter road, following the trail of blood. She kept her gaze on the path ahead, on the light that gleamed in the puddles between the muddy tracks, and the thin hazel wands of the hedges.

Just as she reached the manor, the sun slipped over the edge of the Down and was gone. A blue haze fell across the land. She heard a wren ticking in the hazel, a sudden, sharp warning and there was something behind her: a rustling in the hedge. Serena hurried along, stumbling on the uneven ruts, not looking back. A blackbird shot out of the hazel, calling out, and then she was at the manor gates. They were ajar. Serena slipped through and pushed them firmly shut behind her. It made her feel only a little safer.

The manor stood at the end of a long drive. She could see its turrets, a candle glowing in a pointed window. They said that the manor dated back to the days of the old Queen, but since then it had seen the addition of many wings and outcrops, until very little now remained of the old dark-brick house. Serena thought it was beautiful, though they said that there were many such buildings in London and the north. But Serena had never been beyond the bounds of Sussex, and London to her was as remote as a fairy tale.

Frost glittered in the cropped grass as she walked up the drive. She felt the Long Man at her back, sightlessly watching through the trees that surrounded the manor, and felt a surge of fright and hatred. She was relieved when, at last, she found herself before the kitchen door.

A face looked out at her from the knocker, with the green patina of bronze. Metal leaves curled from its mouth; its eyes were wide and knowing. Serena was surprised to see the old god, here in the door. But he was at the back of the manor, looking toward the woods, rather than facing the new white god who had supplanted him. She reached up to run a hand over the knocker.

I wish we still worshipped you, God of green and growth. The Green Lord of the country: a more ancient figure by far than the one carved across the hillside. But the rule of the Long Man, and all the other gods of the chalk, had lasted over a hundred years now, and they were surely here to stay. The basket seemed to weigh even more heavily in her hands. She put it abruptly down on the step and reached again for the knocker.

A moment later, a broad middle-aged woman stood in the doorway, wearing an apron and dusting flour from her hands.

"You're the girl from the village?"

Serena nodded. "Yes, ma'am. The priest asked me to bring this, for the dinner." She held out the covered basket.

"A bit late in the day, aren't you? The banquet begins at eight."

"I'm sorry, ma'am. I couldn't come before. There were – complications."

"Very well." The cook gave a put-upon sigh. "Place the basket over there, on the flags."

Serena did so. The blood, which by now had soaked the bottom of the basket, pooled over the stone as she set it down. The cook clucked her tongue.

"The new man does not have Father Caius' touch, I see. Now there was a man with a subtle hand! But I suppose we can't be too surprised that he left us for London. He'll be a real find for that Thames-side temple he went to."

"Yes, ma'am." It would not do to say so in front of her betters, Serena knew, but silently she agreed with the cook. Father Caius had been a wonderful priest. Whenever she attended temple and listened to his sermons, Serena felt safe, as though Father Caius truly understood the fears of his flock and the forces that beset them. He knew what it was like, Serena felt, to see the Long Man as nightmare as well as god. He would never have said so, and faced the charge of heresy, but with Father Caius, Serena knew that they were somehow all bound by a common understanding. But the new priest, Father Orme, really did believe in the rightness of his worship, and that made Serena afraid. And he had quizzed her so much, keeping her back after the temple services, asking all sorts of questions: *did she like this or that young man? Was she still a virgin?* The questions had made Serena uncomfortable and she had taken to finding excuses after temple to avoid Father Orme.

The cook twitched aside the crocheted cloth that covered the basket. George Hamp's head stared upward, sightless and bloody. The cook tutted again, sharply as a wren.

"We'll have to tidy him up and no mistake. I wish you'd brought him earlier."

"Yes, ma'am." Serena had not liked George Hamp, but neither had she rejoiced when it became known that he had received this year's mark. No one deserved to go like that, especially someone with a little child. Hamp had become hand-fasted only the previous year, with Marjorie already pregnant. But Serena found herself unable to look away from the head; its mouth was slightly open, as if about to utter accusations. She felt a strange, troubling urge to reach down and pat it, to reassure it as one might comfort a frightened animal. She put her hands firmly behind her back.

"Am I to go now, ma'am?" She did not know what she wanted to hear. The thought of making her way back down the dark road to the village was alarming, but so was the prospect of a night in the manor's kitchens. If only Father Orme had been less dithering, she could have set out in the morning and be back at her mother's fireside by now. At the last, so the goodwives had muttered, even Hamp had begged the priest to get on with the ritual beheading.

"No, you are to stay," the cook said, gazing absently down at the head in the basket. Serena stared at her.

"But my mother will be expecting me."

"Nevertheless, I have spoken with the housekeeper and she says that you are to remain here tonight. It seems this is master's orders. You can come to the hillside with the servants tomorrow, for the rite, and then go to your home. I will ask for a pallet to be prepared for you, and some broth."

"Thank you, ma'am." Silently, Serena cursed. How had the Lord known she was here? Had he seen her, or been told that she was bringing the head? The roaring stove made the kitchen stifling. She could feel her head starting to swim. "May I sit down?"

"You may take your place at the table," the cook said, with the air of one conferring a substantial favour.

To Serena's relief, the head was taken into a pantry, and the flagstones scrubbed by a small, wan boy. Serena tried to talk to him, but he would not reply and only shook his head in a paroxysm of terror. Soon after he had gone, a gaunt, cheerful woman came in.

"You'll be the girl from the village? Lovely, then. Just in time. Cook was starting to fret."

"The – the thing is in the pantry, ma'am," Serena said.

"Lovely. I'm sure cook will see to it." Smiling, she bent to pat Serena's shoulder. "And I have a great treat for you – the master has asked that you visit us upstairs, during the banquet."

"The master?" Serena faltered.

"Saw you from his study as you were crossing the lawn. Such a kind man. 'Bring her upstairs, Ellen,' he told me, 'so that she can see all the pretty things, a reward for bringing the priest's gift to us.' Won't that be nice?"

"Yes, ma'am. Thank you kindly," Serena said, inwardly seething as Ellen disappeared up the stairs. *They have stolen our voices*, she thought. *They have taken our protest.* She should have told the housekeeper that she had no intention of going to see the banquet, but this would have been folly. She had spoken her mind once before, against her mother's advice. She had been no more than thirteen. The scars across her shoulders still burned, on the anniversary of the whipping, and now she took care to say as little as possible to her betters.

No, sir. Yes, ma'am. But at least they could not take her thoughts away from her; not even the Long Man could see inside her head, for otherwise she would surely have been struck down long ago. She thought of simply letting herself out of the back door and running home, but it was fully dark now, and not a good time of year to be out alone. And if she were seen to be slighting the master of the manor... Hugh Sayet was not known to be a cruel man, unlike many lords, but he kept himself to himself and no one in the village seemed to know very much about him. *Go upstairs*, Serena thought, *bob and mumble and duck your head, and hopefully it will be over quickly enough.*

She sat at the table, trying to make herself unobtrusive, as the kitchen became a bustle around her. The cook gave her a pile of turnips to peel, and she did this gladly enough, pleased at having something to do. She even watched with pleasure as the elaborate sugar confections were brought out: an elegant sparkling swan, a tiny horned horse, all made from confectionery. It reminded her of the tales her grandmother had told, of the old Queen's court and the marvellous feast she had once attended as a serving maid.

The old Queen kept Them in order, and no mistake. Oh, They weren't as powerful then as They are now – folk gave Them Their due, to be sure, brought flowers and fruit and other gifts at the right times of the year, but the real honour – the blood honour – went to the Green Man in those days. That's how you summon all of Them, no matter what their nature. I remember going up to the Lamptown Wyrm, white as the moon on Salisbury hill, and I passed the Horse of Uffington many a time as a girl, when we lived near there. Carved in chalk, they were, to keep the land safe and conjure the spirits out from the hollow hills. But then the new young king made a bargain with Them, so it's said, to keep back the French from the south of the country. And now it's all Lords and their Figures-in-the Chalk, and we just have to do what they say.

Her grandmother's voice echoed inside her head, drowning out the noise of the kitchens. Serena kept her gaze on the table when the pantry door was opened. She knew the head was being taken upstairs, for there was a great cheer: perhaps cook had demonstrated some particular artistry with the thing. *Poor George,* she thought. *At least you'll have one night of glory, even if you are no more.*

The summons came halfway through the evening, just as the clock had struck nine.

"They'll see you in a few minutes," the housekeeper said. Clad in her black finery, hollow-faced, she was nonetheless beaming. Serena found her cheerfulness disconcerting. She fussed over Serena's hair, unpinning it and fanning the blonde coils over Serena's shoulders. "What pretty hair you have. So pale, almost white."

"Yes, ma'am." Serena bobbed her head as dutifully as she could manage. "My mother came from the north."

"A York lass, perhaps? There. You look very nice. Follow me up to the dining room; don't speak until you're spoken to. But I'm sure you're a good girl."

If she said, *yes, ma'am,* once more, she would choke, Serena thought. But she followed Ellen nevertheless, up the steep stone stairs to the hallway. Here, it was dim and quiet. The only light came from sconces on the wall, but she could hear the sound of voices and laughter coming from a room to the left. Ellen led her to a pair of oak doors, carved with acanthus curling from the mouth of a man. Serena looked once more at the familiar face of the Green Man. Ellen pushed open the doors, splitting the face in two, and led her inside.

The dining room was filled with a long table and lit with candles. Light chased shadows around the room, warring with the flickering fires of the hearth, casting ruby sparks in the depths of wineglasses and from the jewels of the women. The master of the house sat at the top of the table. Serena glimpsed a melancholy countenance, sad dark eyes. George Hamp's head took pride of place in the centre of the dining table, curls of vines spreading from the dead boiled mouth. His eyelids had been sewn tightly together. Serena thought of the image on the doors and shuddered. George Hamp's head symbolised the death of the old order. Tomorrow, they would be worshipping the new lords of the land.

Ellen passed swiftly to the top of the table, skirts rustling, and whispered in the master's ear. He looked up, saw Serena, became still. He beckoned, a short sharp motion of the hand. She did not want to go, but it was as though he had hooked a line to her body; she felt a thread of warmth, uncoiling within. The guests all looked at her as she walked the length of the table, and one by one, fell silent.

"Sit by me," the master said, indicating a footstool by his side. Serena did so. Gradually, the conversation resumed. The master turned to a woman on his left and began a long, fretful account of a hound's illness. Serena sat still, half-relaxed, wondering if it would be no more than this. Perhaps the master just wanted a pretty face at which to glance from time to time; the guests were plain enough. But the nobility were rarely so simple. She wondered, with a creeping unease, whether she would be spending the night in the kitchens after all. She remembered Father Orme's questions with a shiver.

At last, the meal drew to a close. The confectionery swans were brought in, sailing on golden platters, and then the port. Serena started to rise, to follow the women out, but the master put out an absent-minded hand and pushed her down again.

"My dear, you may stay." Serena swallowed hard and remained where she was, gripping the velvet edges of the footstool. Seven of the men were still present, she saw, including the master, and two other women, both of middle age. She did not know who they were. They studied her as dispassionately as they might consider a prize heifer.

"Come with me," Hugh Sayet said, and took her hand. She considered trying to run, but his grip was too tight and in any case, where would she go? Out into the darkness? But as they passed the table, she saw her chance and slipped one of the little gold knives into her sleeve.

Sayet led her into a side chamber, followed by the remaining guests. Here, it was almost dark, apart from a single candle. She saw panelled walls hung with tapestries, a stone floor.

"Sit," Sayet said again.

"Forgive me, sir, but I would rather stand," Serena said.

To her surprise, he nodded. "As you please."

The guests formed a ring around the room, with Serena at its centre. She thought of Hamp's head, splendid in the middle of the dining table. Was Hamp to be the only sacrifice that night? She knew she had taken Sayet's fancy, but as what? She slid the little knife down her sleeve into her palm.

"Now," Sayet said, to one of the guests. The woman handed him a lump of something that glowed pale in the candlelight. To Serena, he said, "Just watch. Don't be afraid."

The guest nearest to the door was a woman. If she had to, Serena thought, she could make a run for it, shove the woman aside: the guest was a small person, bird-boned. But what of the others?

The woman was staring at her, a sharp, black-eyed gaze. "Why the girl, Hugh?" she said.

Sayet took a strand of Serena's hair and drew it absently through his fingers.

"Have you ever seen anything so pale? He'll like that, don't you think? Perhaps more than some peasant's head? And when he likes something, he can be very generous..."

Serena drew away and Sayet smiled. He knelt to inscribe a circle upon the stone floor. The thing handed to him by the woman had been a piece of chalk, Serena realised.

Within the circle, he sketched a swift figure: the image of a man, faceless, holding two staves. It was as familiar to Serena as the moon or the sun: it was the Long Man of Windhover Down. The guests joined hands, began to chant the prayer to the Lords of Earth.

"May the Dragon of the Dales be our Protector..."

and the room grew suddenly furnace hot, the walls glowing russet –

"May the Scarab of the Tor be our Initiator"

something clicking in the wainscoting, a spiny shadow above her head –

"May the Lamptown Wyrm guide our feet upon the land" –

and her hands were coated with slime, a cold chill on her brow –

"and may the Long Man ever watch over us, according to the terms of our King's bargain..."

– and Serena was standing on the hillside, high on Windhover Down. The Long Man towered above her, rising from the side of the hill, no longer a flat chalk image but bone grinding on bone, the jaw teeth-filled. Something filled her mouth, a dry, schoolroom odour. She spat, tasting chalk, and looked up to see a staff sweeping through the air like a scythe.

Serena did not stay to meet it. She darted forward, between skeletal legs, and cannoned into something warm and yielding. A woman's voice cried out, and Serena realised that she was still in the small chamber, surrounded by the master and his guests. She pushed the woman aside and tugged at the door. It opened, and she fell through into the dining room. The candles were burning down and the table had been emptied of everything except the platter that carried the head. The vines still coiled from its mouth; her grandmother's voice echoed in her mind:

The real honour – the blood honour – went to the Green Man. That's how you summon all of Them, no matter what their nature.

Serena ran to the table. Bones clattered behind her. She took the small gold knife, and held out her hand.

"Here!" she cried. "You can't be any worse than Them!" and she sliced the knife across her wrist.

Blood spattered across the severed head of George Hamp. Vines curled into sudden green life and the sewn-shut eyes flew open. Light poured through them, sealing the door of the chamber behind her. She looked back, to see Hugh Sayet and the guests trapped like flies in amber. And the head spoke.

"Do you think they have not tried to bring me back?" it said. It was not Hamp's voice, but a furred, thick speech.

"I thought –" Serena's wrist burned; she clasped a hand to it.

"You thought it would be simple. It is. The charm is an old one: a virgin, dying willingly for the land, the Sovereign Queen. The simple folk could not find one such, the last time this was tried. For the key is willingness."

"If I die, willingly, will the power of the Figures fade?"

"It will change," the head said. Serena risked a glance behind her. The light was beginning to break down; she could see Sayet starting to move again, sluggish and slow. She thought of the life ahead of her, of her mother. She thought of the people taken, one every year from all the villages around, from all the towns of the southern counties, of the nightmare voices in the head as the ancient spirits that lay behind the Figures whispered to their victims. She thought of Hamp's infant son, who would, perhaps, go the way of his father if the mark fell on him.

"Then I will do it," she said. She brought the knife down

again, opening up the arm. It did not hurt as much as she had expected. She stood, watching the blood flow until she fell. She heard a bony footstep behind her, but it was too late. There was a skeletal rattle as something slunk back into the ground; others followed it. She heard nothing more.

Serena awoke. She was lying on frosty grass, with a bitter wind blowing from the east, yet she was not cold. There was no sign of Sayet, or the guests, or the head. She could see the manor lying in the valley below, wreathed in the early morning mists. She must have found her way here after escaping, and fallen unconscious. But when she tried to rise, she could not. She looked down at herself.

She had no body any longer. There was only the outline of a chalk figure in the grass: a woman's form, wreathed in spirals of pale hair. But she could feel the land around her like her own self, stretching as far as the sea and the distant hills, and so she knew when the first visitors arrived, carrying gifts of crimson leaves, and apples, and the fruits of the season.

She could see the maze from the summit of the hill and it flickered like fire in the last of the light. Beyond, across the lawns – deep emerald now, the colour of poison – the windows of the manor caught the dying sun and flared up into brief blank gold. Then the sun went down into the cloudbank and the great house fell dark, as if it had closed its eyes. Now, the maze was no more than a mass of shadow.

It was time to be going home. Em snapped the birch twig that she carried, rounding up the straggling geese into a shuffling, bickering line. She drove the birds down the hill into the back yard, trying not to look to where the manor lay. She'd seen it all her life, of course; it was hardly unfamiliar. But now, so close to sixteen, the building had taken on a new significance.

She'd known this time would come, but it was never spoken about, one of those things that never are. She'd heard whispers, hushed conversations behind hands in the corners of barns and byres, mention of the maze. And when she had passed her twelfth birthday, her mother had taken her to one side, told her a little of what was to come, but not what lay at the heart of it, although she must have known. She'd run the maze herself as a girl, come out of the other side of the black, impenetrable yew trees and out beyond the walls of the manor forever. That had been in the old king's day, and now there was a queen on the throne: had been for the whole of Em's life. There were times when her mother seemed impossibly old. Em had felt her eyes and her mouth fill with questions and her mother had looked warning back: *don't ask, it's forbidden, I cannot tell you.* But some shadow of the thing she had seen remained, a haunt within her face, and that more than anything else had dried Em's questions inside her mouth, forever unspoken.

And soon she would find out for herself.

By the time she reached the cottage, it was quite dark and a thin crescent moon had slid up between the branches of the elms, now almost bare of leaves. It was very cold, with a scatter of stars burning across the sky and a bite against the skin. Three days to the Solstice, and the maze-running. Em hoped she'd still be here for Yule and the hope rose up in her throat and made her choke with longing: on Yule Eve she'd go out with her father and Will, fetch in the boughs of the green, holly and ivy and sacred mistle from the apple trees in the orchard, string it all up along the mantle and the doorways so that it glowed in the lamplight… Familiar things.

If she lived.

She herded the geese into their pen and bolted the gate firmly against wandering foxes. A vixen's yip from the direction of the woods lent sense to her actions and she gave a sudden shiver against the cold. Inside the door, she unwound woollen layers with relief and sought the fire.

"All's well with the geese?" Her mother handed her a cup of milk.

"All's well. I saw Edward Ruthen on the road, he says he'll take one for the Solstice. *She'd* like one at the manor, says he mentioned it in September." Her voice nearly faltered when she spoke of the manor and its mistress and she gritted her teeth at thought of it.

Her mother nodded. "He did so. Miss Treharn always takes a goose from us. Well, you can take one up when you go, can't you?"

As if this was an everyday thing, and not the making or the breaking of you. Em stared at her mother sidelong, but her mother's profile was unrevealing: long nose, small chin, a calm, concealing face.

"Is Da back?"

"Not yet. Still chopping wood. Wanted to get ahead of himself, so he said." Her mother smiled. Em, looking around the little parlour, thought that some folk might think them poor: whitewashed walls, worn upholstery, rushes on the stone flags. In Thamesis, so she'd heard, the streets were paved with gold and coins showered from the air like apple blossom. All the boats that sailed along the great river had sails of silk and when the Queen walked out from her palace, the breezes were perfumed with sandalwood. She wasn't sure she believed all that, but she'd never been to the city, so who was she to say? But here at the cottage, the rushes were fresh and the few copper pans were polished to a fiery gleam. She would like to see the city one day, Em thought, just to say she'd been, but she wasn't sure a person needed all that. She'd be happy enough to stay here and be wed and have her own pans, her own daughter tend the geese.

If she lived. Everything kept coming back to that.

Because sometimes, Em was only too aware, they didn't. Not last year, but the year before that, and then again the previous year. It had been a bad time, the villagers had whispered, with one gone at midwinter and another taken in the summer's heat, the longest day. Not a good thing, to have two in six months like that. A winter funeral and a summer one, two empty coffins borne up to the little chapel behind the manor, two graves in the red earth. Ellen Grant and Hugh Fole, both sixteen. Might have married if they'd lived, but they hadn't and now you could see their graves in the chapel yard, under the quiet yews: the same stretch of woodland from which the maze had been grown.

That maze: a Troytown, her father called it, the old word for a labyrinth. *Comes from Greece, you see, and Troy, the old city that is no more.*

"Em?" her mother said now. "You're very quiet." Their eyes met over the cup of milk and Em knew that her mother understood.

"Just thinking," Em said, and they left it at that.

The next few days went quickly and then it was Solstice Eve. They went to service in the chapel, her mother bringing a candle for the Lady, and Em knew what that was for, too. Her mother usually took a candle up: a little hummock of wax taken from their own hives, but this was different – tall and slender and pale, like a bone, and with a delicate scent. Em saw Will looking at the candle and she wasn't sure if he realised quite what it meant: he was still a little too young for all this to be more than a strange game. Em's mother clasped her hand tightly when they knelt to prayer and Em clasped back. Tomorrow evening, at this time…

And no supper. Something else not to look forward to. They said it was best to eat white food only throughout the course of the day: milk and curds and oats, as an honour to the moon. Em had no idea whether this would really work – Ellen had eaten porridge for a week and she'd still been taken – but it was tradition and, as such, you had to keep to it. Her mother nudged her and dutifully Em bent her head in prayer and tried not to think about tomorrow.

The next day, she woke to a white hard frost and the promise of snow in the air. The clouds massed heavy over the silent fields and the distant edge of the fells. Em forced down some curds, but had little appetite. Her father did not go out to the fields that day, but hung about the byre with Will at his heels. Neither of her parents had much to say and when the sun started to go down, in a sudden blaze of crimson, Em bundled herself into her woollens and hugged her Da goodbye. A mother takes the daughters, a father takes the sons.

"Till later, then," her father said gruffly. Em tried to echo him but she could only nod against the roughness of his jacket. Her mother was silent all the way to the manor. When they reached the tall iron gates, her mother turned to her and put her hands on Em's shoulders.

"You'll know what to do, Em. You're a sensible girl. I have faith in you." But there was a desperate worry in her voice, all the same.

"I'll try," Em said. It was a squeak. The gates were open a crack. She slipped inside and made herself not look back. She could feel the weight of her mother's gaze on her all the same, as she walked up the drive.

She had never been in the manor before, only stood outside for the Yule and the May carolling, when the ritual alms were given. Miss Treharn had been there, a shadowy figure in the background, as her housekeeper distributed the coins, and Em knew that she had been there, too, when Em's mother had been a girl. Perhaps she had always been there; she was surely old enough.

But this time, as her footsteps rang out on the steps of the manor, Miss Treharn herself opened the massive oak door.

"Em Silver?"

"Good evening, Miss Treharn," Em said.

"Annet's daughter? You look very like her, don't you?" Miss Treharn reached out and took a curl of Em's hair. "Dark hair, like your grandmother, too."

"She died when I was little," Em said.

"Well," Miss Treharn replied. "You'll want to get on with it, I suppose." She opened the door wider and beckoned Em inside, and it was only now, in the circle of lamplight, that Em could see her clearly: white hair, piled high on her head, and a sad, delicate face, nothing like the witch they said she was. There was something foreign about the curve of her black eyes, the heaviness of her brows. But she was already ushering Em onward into the hallway.

Dust, and silence. It lay on the manor like a lid. Em walked past opulent tapestries, unicorns and prancing dogs and small lions. She walked past carved chests of black oak, and a glimpse of her own reflection in a tall stained mirror made her start. Miss Treharn nudged her gently on, through a parlour and towards a pair of high glass doors.

"Out again, and down the steps. Mind your footing – it's icy tonight. But you'll have the moon to guide you. See the maze?"

Em could not miss the maze. It lay at the far end of the lawns, beyond the terraces with their Grecian urns and the dead twists of roses. The yew walls looked like those of a citadel, impenetrable, black. She hesitated in the doorway as Miss Treharn's hand reached out and opened the doors. The house had seemed cold, but the air outside smacked her like a fist. She took a deep breath and stepped forwards, a tottering puppet walking down the steps, careful on the slick stone, then boots crunching on the frosty grass, all the way down the lawns to where the maze was waiting.

She reached it more quickly than she had expected. It rose up in front of her, a wall of fronded yew. The berries were silver in the slight light of the moon, rather than waxy scarlet, winking in tiny sparks. She took one last look back, to where a single lamp shone in the downstairs of the manor, casting a warm glimmer out across the grass. Then she stepped into the maze.

Neither Miss Treharn nor her mother had told her what to expect. She knew she was to follow the maze to its heart, and then to the other side. The younger children had always told stories about what was in there, but the ones who had gone through never spoke of it and so it remained as stories only: the Dark Lord, some said, or lions, or ghosts. Something that killed, anyway. The fronds of yew brushed against Em's skin as she walked, hastening now, eager to get this over with even if she didn't come out again. She thought of her mother, her father, of Will, of the green-and-flame of Yule, and of Candlemass when the snowdrops would come and this would be over.

Behind me, and I will be here.

The yew was soft against Em's face and smelled of old growing things, of leaf mould, of frost. She looked up and saw with a pang that the stars were not visible, although they should have been. The sky above the maze was perfectly black, without a moon, but the yew berries still sparked silver in the hedge. Em swallowed fright and walked on. The thought of the churchyard hovered close; she wished it was yesterday, with herself kneeling beside her mother, or tomorrow, safe at home with what kind of new understanding?

And then, ahead of her in the maze, something moved.

Em stopped dead. She couldn't see what it had been, only that it was big, larger than a man. Shadows shifted. She'd been walking for some little time and the maze was not large. She must be nearing its heart. She could not stay where she was and she could not go back: they'd told her that much. She had to go on. She bunched her fists in her pockets and forced her feet forwards.

This was the heart. The yews opened out to reveal a small building like a summerhouse, with a peaked roof. Frost glittered on the tiles. The door stood ajar. Em came closer. She couldn't see what was within the summerhouse, but she thought she could hear something breathing. A breeze got up at her back, herding her in.

Inside, it took her eyes a moment to adjust. There had been no sign of light outside the summerhouse, but within it, a lamp was guttering and the faint smell of hot fat filled the air. The summerhouse was much bigger than it should have been, a vast low room like a cavern, with two rows of columns in front of walls that had been plastered red. Beneath Em's boots, the floor, too, was red: paved in tiles that were so polished they looked wet.

At the far end, something moved. Em had a glimpse of horns, high against the red wall, a massive, swinging head. Then the thing was loping along the farther row of columns, so swiftly that she could not see it clearly. Its shadow swung and veered across the room and Em heard herself give a high, thin scream, abruptly silenced as she clapped a hand over her mouth. Where was it? What was it? The horns had been those of a bull, sharp-pointed. She turned, searching for the door, but it was no longer there. She ran, panicking, to the far end of the room and stopped.

There was another little door, set in the wall. She heard a soft, heavy tread behind her, did not look around. She made for the door but, as she did so, the configuration of the room changed. She was in a chamber that contained a throne. The door was still there, and the walls were the same ochre-red. It was stiflingly hot, making it difficult to think after the chill of the maze itself. Once more, Em made for the door.

There was something sitting on the throne. She only saw it as she hurried by, from the corner of her eye: a huge dark shape, with a glint beneath the heavy, inhuman brows. She glimpsed a thick hand. The door was suddenly very far away and she was still close to the throne, the shadow of the thing falling upon her. She was so afraid that she thought she might faint and then the thought followed: *if you do, you won't wake up*. The fear was so great that it swallowed itself. Em turned to face the thing on the throne.

Moth-eaten velvet covered the bull's head. The horns were ivory, and dulled in death. A shapeless mass of rags formed the body and the eyes were glass. Only its shadow moved, shifting around the room in a dance of lamplight. Em stood and stared for a long time at the bull puppet, thinking of graves in a quiet churchyard, and then she turned and walked slowly to the door.

Outside, the bite of the air was welcome. She looked back. The summerhouse stood behind her, no more than a few feet across. Em walked around it, just to make sure, and when she came back to her starting point, Miss Treharn was standing there, holding a lantern. A welcome warmth of light pooled around her black figure.

"Annet's child. I thought you'd be one who came back." There was a distinct satisfaction in her voice.

"It's nothing at all, is it?" Em's own voice sounded loud in the winter hush, and not a little indignant. "Just make believe."

"It is the fear of your death," the old lady said. "Some never turn to face it and it comes upon them; they conjure it for themselves. I am just the guardian."

"The summerhouse," Em said, "is much bigger inside than out."

"So it is."

They looked at one another. Then Miss Treharn turned and made her way through the maze, Em following, towards the green-and-fire of Yule, and candlelight, and the future waiting.

Woewater

I wear the skins of the things I have slain, for my mistress told me long ago that it would be my only protection against their spirits, and the cold. The hood that hides my face is sewn from the spotted pelt of a lynx; my collar is made of marten's fur, and the long coat that keeps out the bite of the snow is that of a white leopard, from the lands far to the east of this island of Albion. I am not one of those men who hunts for food, nor for gold or pleasure, but from necessity: to prevent the spread of evil. And when I falter, thinking how soft and comfortable it would be to settle down in some small walled village with herbwife or merchant's daughter, I remember the death of the white leopard whose skin I wear: how it looked at me with human eyes at the last, and with its final breath hissed my name. There are animals in this world, but there are also beasts.

That winter, late in 1792, I had come north, up through the dark forests of Gwalia to the lake country, to seek such a beast. It was not long before the depth of the cold, and the Solstice – a festival I mark more than the Christian's Christmas. The Hunter, my own constellation, span overhead with his hound running at his heels, a star as blue as the eye of a god. I paused at the crest of a ridge, seeing the pines march away before me into the frosty dark. Strapping the snowshoes more securely to my feet, I glided swiftly on. The old man, the one who had sent me on this quest, had given me a name and a place in the last moments of his life: Minerva Vow, and a house named Woewater.

That house now lay below me, on the still shore of a long lake. The gleam of a crimson lamp shone in an upstairs window, patterning a bloody square onto the snow. The house was tall, with pointed gables, and iron gates. I tried to picture it in sunlight and summer, and failed. As I neared the gate, I slipped the coat from my shoulders, reversing it so that the fur was on the inside and it was once more dark and anonymous. I took the hood and stuffed it into a pocket. I did not want to bear the signs of my hunter's calling; I feared that they might already be too evident to one such as Minerva Vow. Pausing for a moment before the gate, I touched the sigil that hung on a chain around my neck: the symbol of Cybele, lady of beasts. As a hunter of her creatures, I was myself bound to her, and must placate her when necessary. The sigil was warm with my own warmth, but I knew how quickly it could grow cold when one of the beasts was near. To my surprise, the gate was not locked: ones such as Mistress Vow are often justly fearful of visitors. The latched gate spoke of unnatural confidence. I walked down the path to the oak door and reaching up, pulled the chain of the bell. I did not hear it ring, and was about to reach for the chain again when the door opened.

A woman stood before me on the step. I am used to the nature of the *were*; their haughtiness, their bravado, but Minerva Vow – if this was she – looked only alarmed. I had an impression of dark eyes in a pale face, a cloud of light brown hair, and then she drew back into the shadows.

"Who are you? How did you get inside the gate?" she asked, breathlessly. "I locked it not an hour before."

"It was open."

"Open?" The white oval of her face tilted up, as if seeking an answer in the heavens. "I was certain it was locked. Who are you?"

"My name is Leopold Dee. I am a traveller in medicines. I fear I am lost." The name was true, at least, though it was not the one by which I have become most usually known.

"And I am Minerva Vow. Where are you headed for?"

"For the Scotland road. But I lost my path, and it was dark and cold – I wondered whether I might seek your hospitality?"

She paused for a moment, uncertainly.

"I am here alone. I do not think –"

"Then where is the nearest inn?" I asked, to call her bluff.

"Amble, ten miles away." She looked up at the sky once more, to where the snow clouds were massing over the pines. The Hunter was gone now, but beneath the edge of the clouds I could see the hard light of a winter's moon, two days from the full. I was certain she would let me in, despite her dissembling. Why hunt the wild wet woods, when you can stay by your own fire and feast in peace? I have learned this of beasts: they are ruthless, but they are also lazy.

She seemed to make up her mind, as I had known she would. "Very well, then. You may stay, but only until the sky clears in the morning." No doubt this was designed to put me at my ease. She stepped aside, and I followed her into the house.

Within, the hallway was panelled and shadowy. She led me into a small parlour, with a fire smouldering in the grate. Had I indeed been the traveller I claimed, I did not think that I would have been too appreciative of the hospitality offered: the house was barely warmer than the woods, despite the fire, and almost as dark. Beneath the resinous smoulder of the logs, and the smell of damp and age, I thought I detected something more pungent: the scent of old meat, or fresh blood. The homes of beasts are rarely to human taste, or human comfort. Woewater served only to confirm my suspicions about the nature of my hostess, but looking covertly at her now, I was unsure as to which of her kind she might be. Something little and quick, perhaps, that relies on a snap to the throat. Not wolfkind; she was too frail for that, too unassuming, and she lacked the sensuality that one finds so often in the great cats. I thought once again of the snow leopard, and inside my sleeve my fingers curled into soft, dead fur. Then she turned, and I saw her sharp profile against the firelit wall: the hook of a small nose, the eyes, the brown hair like dappled feathers. I thought I had my answer, then.

"There are rooms upstairs," she said. "You may use one of those."

"You live alone, then? You have no family? No servants?" No honest young woman would have let me into her household, should she live alone.

A short, quick shake of the head. "None living."

Beneath the cloth and the fur of my coat, my sgian dhu, the hunter's black dagger, rested comfortingly against my thigh. I reached down, and touched its topaz hilt. *None living.* The presence of the dagger reassured me, a little. I followed Minerva Vow up the stairs. Her long skirts drifted like a ghost's. She opened a door and motioned me inside.

"Here."

The room was small and damp, and dominated by an ornate bed. The posts that held it up were carved in the form of trees, entwined with ivy in a different wood, and at the top the spread wings of oaken owls supported the curtains. There was no fire, but there were fresh sheets on the bed and a cover, the mottled skin of an animal that I did not immediately recognise. It was only after Minerva had quietly withdrawn, leaving me with the candle, that I realised it was not one skin, but many: the little hides of mice and voles and shrews, painstakingly stitched together. My suspicions fell into place. Minerva was not a beast, she was a bird. I would have little enough to fear from an ordinary bird of prey, but the *were* were larger than the original form, perhaps from some need to conserve physical substance, and like all their brethren indisposed to human kind. It seemed to me that I could hear a shrieking in the dark.

There was a basin filled with water on the dresser, but I had to break the skin of ice before I could wash the journey from me. I did so hastily, then crawled beneath the musty cover, with the sgian dhu clasped in my hand. I fell into the hunter's light sleep, more trance than unconsciousness. Figures moved in the darkness behind my eyes: the long body of a wolf, a seal with a woman's tearful eyes and sharper bite, the glistening coat of a fox against the shadows of the pines. All dead by my own hand, and no one but a hunter knows how greatly to mourn the passing of something beautiful and dangerous. Beasts do not have the limitations of animals; their hunger is human, and wholly mad, like a maw at the world's heart, but for the sake of my own soul, they must be slain when they have taken their animal form. Dreaming, I remembered the curves of Minerva's face; its lunar crescent, now on the wax, now on the wane. Two days and the moon would be full. *You may stay, but only until the sky clears in the morning.* And beasts are liars, like all humankind. I did not sleep soundly until dawn.

When I awoke, it was to grey light and snowfall. Peering through the casement, I saw with grim and distant satisfaction that the flakes were coming down so heavily that the ridge of the pines beyond the house was invisible. The sill was icy to the touch, and skeins of cold curdled water had formed in the basin. I gathered my coat around me, and went downstairs.

Minerva was sitting at the fireside, her brow furrowed as she stared into the flames. I said, "It's snowing hard, now." I startled her; she jumped like a hare and her hand went to her throat. Her kind often grow nervous, as the moon swells.

"Yes," she said, faintly. "Yes, it's a blizzard."

"Perhaps you would not mind so greatly if I stayed?" Both hunter and prey can toy with words, like cats with mice, but she said, sounding strangely worried, "I think you will have to. But by tomorrow, I'm afraid you must be gone. I am expecting – company."

I smiled. "I doubt if it will prove troublesome."

She frowned, as if teasing out meaning, then rose swiftly to her feet.

"I have to see to the porridge."

The game was ended in so prosaic a manner that I stared at her as she went out of the room. Her feathery hair was bound up into a coil; she looked like a fierce, but secretly shy, school mistress. She brought me my breakfast in silence, and the day passed. Fortunately for my patience, there were many books. We spent the time companionably enough, in front of the meagre warmth of the fire. We spoke little. Once I said, "It seems a cold house, and a large one. Would you not be more comfortable in a cottage?"

"This was my family's house," she answered. "I inherited it when my father died. He had no other children."

"Could you not sell it? I'm sure some fashionable person would pay good money for such a rural retreat."

"It is not for sale," Minerva said firmly, then added, "But I would love to live elsewhere."

She gazed wistfully into the fire and the corners of her mouth turned down. I felt a brief pity for her: of course she could not move. They would put her to death after the first full moon. Here, she had solitude and probably victims enough. A bird would be able to cover a larger area than an animal form, and would be less traceable. Any experienced tracker can follow footprints, after all, but there can be no mark left on the sky. She fell silent after that, brooding, like a hawk that longs to be flown.

That night, I looked once more out of the casement window. The snow was still drifting down, but I could see the gleam of stars to the east, and then the disc of the moon slipping up between the treetops, only a sliver away from the full. I placed a chair against the door that night, and again clasped the black dagger close to me. Transformation is an unchancy thing, and some of the more powerful beasts could summon up their form before the full of the moon. Indeed, I once met a hunter from the east who had slain a tiger at twilight, when the moon was new. I drew the dagger from its sheath and held the blade before me. The topaz at its hilt glinted in the candlelight, like a fierce, cold eye. I do not remember falling into slumber, but I must have slept, for I awoke with a start to find the candle had gone out. It felt like that still, silent darkness just before dawn, when the night is at its deepest. There was something in the room. I heard it rustling. The dagger's hilt was cold in my fingers. I lay still, breathing the slow, calm breath of sleep. It was at this time that the snow leopard had come for me, slinking in through the flap of the tent. I had woken with its breath on my face, and that breath had been as cold as a grave. I heard nothing more, but the room seemed filled with a clammy dampness. I peered beneath my eyelids, but could see nothing. Then a hard, curved claw curled around my wrist. I struck out with the dagger, and felt it bite home. The claw was snatched back. I rolled from the bed, the dagger held before me.

"Do not touch me," I hissed. "I know what you are!" I stumbled across the room and tripped over the chair wedged beneath the door handle. How had she got into the room? Perhaps through the casement, closing it softly behind her. With my back against the wall, I fumbled for the candle and lit it. Light flared up. The room was empty. I searched but found nothing. I sat on the bed until dawn, clutching the dagger.

That morning, at breakfast, Minerva Vow was pale and withdrawn. Surreptitiously, I glanced at her arm for some sign of injury, but the voluminous sleeves would have concealed even a thick bandage. Yet she seemed dispirited, and I thought I knew why. Her attempt on my life had failed. She peered anxiously out of the window and said, "I thought the snow would have stopped by now, but it's worse than ever. The drifts have piled up against the gates."

"Reluctant though I am to partake further of your hospitality," I said, with some sincerity, "I fear I must do so for a further night. I cannot travel in this."

"Then you must stay," she replied, with an uneasy glance in my direction. "May I ask one thing? It is a strange request, I know. But will you leave your door unlocked tonight? It – it was a custom in our family, on Solstice Eve, so that the luck would not become trapped in the house."

"I think I might manage that," I said, with a smile. I had no intention of doing as she asked. Tonight, I planned to wedge the bed against the door, and to sleep as much as possible during the day so that I would not have to do so at night.

I spent some of that day reading, and a couple of hours

exploring the house. It was a huge, rambling place, but much of it seemed uncared for and neglected. The kitchen was neat and clean, but the main room – a once-handsome, panelled affair hung with what I presumed to be family portraits – was filled with dust. I studied some of the portraits, and saw that the crest of the Vow clan was indeed an owl. So many of the aristocracy had taken on the power of the *were*; literally feeding off the peasantry. Yet so many of them could not help but betray themselves: the crests, the coats of arms, even sometimes the names... as though they almost craved the recognition which would be their downfall.

In one of the bedrooms leading from the first floor landing, I discovered yet more evidence. In this room, the rusty smell of ancient blood was strong, and there were stains on the floor and skirting board. Some of the more refined *were*-clans occasionally boasted a killing room, to bring their victims back to the security of their own homes and dispatch them at leisure. The thought, and the room itself, conjured a deep unease in me. I felt as though there were eyes on my back, and when I whipped around, I found Minerva staring at me.

"What are you doing?" she asked.

"I do beg your pardon. I was bored. I was exploring. It was rude of me, I know."

"It was – inadvisable," she said, coldly. "Parts of the house are unsafe; I do not have the money to effect repairs." We stared at one another in silence. Her chin was lifted, and the dark eyes were opaque with anger. With mock meekness, I followed her back down the stairs.

Night came quickly; tomorrow would, after all, be the shortest day of the year. The house fell into a muffled twilight, with blue shadows hazing the snow before Minerva rose abruptly and drew the heavy, stifling curtains.

"You said you were expecting company," I said. "Friends?"

"They won't get through the snow, I'm sure," she said, quickly. "They're from a village twenty miles away. It will be quite snowed in by now."

"A pity," I said, slyly. She shot me a startled, nervous glance and I realised I had frightened her. It should have made me glad, but I found myself suddenly sorry for her. Why this should be I did not know – the *were* bring their fate upon themselves through the darkest of magics, for greed and for power, but at that moment she looked like a human girl and nothing more. I wanted to say, "Don't be afraid of me. I won't hurt you," but it wasn't true and we both knew it. Tonight was the full moon. By morning, one of us would be dead.

"I – I have things to do in the kitchen," she said, and bolted.

We ate a meagre dinner in silence. I was wary of the food, wondering whether she might not poison me, but that is not the way of the *were*. They prefer to eat what they have killed, and she could not poison me without condemning herself. That evening we both retired early.

On the landing she said, anxiously, "You won't forget, will you? About not locking the door?" In the candlelight her face looked pinched and drawn. I wondered whether the change was already beginning.

"I won't forget," I said. That, at least, was the truth. When I reached the illusory sanctuary of my own bedchamber, I secured the casement from the inside with a length of wire, twisting it around so that it could be opened only with difficulty. Then I pushed the heavy bed across the room, so that it partly, but not entirely, obscured the door. I would wait until I heard her trying to get in, exhausting even her unnatural strength, and then I would move the bed aside and slay her. It occurred to me that she might hunt elsewhere, try other prey, but there would be few creatures abroad in this snow and besides, I was sure now that she knew me for her enemy. She would do all she could to see me dispatched. I placed a chair by the window, so that I could see not only the room but the soft, cold darkness beyond, drew the dagger, and waited.

As the early part of the night passed, the full moon rose

above the pines, casting an icy light across the snow. Once, I started at the beat of wings, only to see a great tawny owl drifting across the garden towards the trees. I wondered, then, but it did not return. From the direction of the woods I heard a vixen's sharp cry, then silence. The moon cleared the treetops and sailed up into a starry vault; the snow clouds had finally gone. Then a shadow swooped down from above, enveloping me. Cursing, I struck out with the dagger, but caught only the loose, soft folds of drapery. It was then that I realised that the heavy curtain had fallen from the window on top of me. I struggled free, but it was too late. Claws snapped shut around my wrist as I raised my hand. I turned, lashed out with the dagger, and connected. The claws once more retreated into the darkness. Frantically, I spun this way and that, seeking Minerva's changed form. The door thudded open and reverberated against the bed. I stumbled forwards, but my ankle was torn and bleeding, and I caught my foot in the folds of the fallen curtain and fell. A high, panicky voice cried my name.

"Mr Dee!"

I struggled to my feet, glancing wildly about me, but the claws once more grabbed at me and I went down. As I fell, I realised two things: the snatching claws were inside the room, but the voice had come from outside. And as I stared up towards the ceiling, I saw in the lamplight from the half open door that one of the owls on the pillars that supported the bed bore a thin, ugly scar of newly exposed wood. The wall at my back creaked, and moved. The carved ivy that ornamented the bed twined out, lashing itself around the doorframe so that the gap between the bed and the door was filled with a mass of snarled foliage. A further strand snaked forth and wrapped itself securely around my leg, pulling me towards the wall which, as I watched in horror, began to open up, revealing a great dark hole.

"Mr Dee!" Minerva cried again. "Guard your face!"

I froze for a moment, then covered my head with my arms. There was a rush of light behind my eyes as the flame of the thrown lamp touched the curling ivy. It went up with a roar. The frond encircling my foot was abruptly withdrawn. Scrambling to my feet, I saw that the fire had spread to the bed and licked the fur coverlet. It flared up like a torch. I was trapped. I could not reach the door without passing through the fire, and the wall was still gaping open behind me. The stench of old meat poured from it.

"Minerva!" I shouted. "I'm going through the window!" Stepping back a few paces, I threw myself against the pane, and the window shattered. Cold, fresh air streamed past me as I fell.

I landed in the snow bank below the window. Fire billowed out through the shattered pane and the lacerations on my hands stung in the cold. Then the front door was jerked open and Minerva Vow rushed out into the garden. She threw herself to her knees beside me, in the snow.

"Are you hurt?"

"No." I blinked. The snow had cushioned my fall. "And you?"

She grimaced. "I bruised my shoulder against the door. I told you to keep it unlocked." She pulled me to my feet and we made for the gate, then beyond, to the comparative safety of the pines. I could hear the fire gaining strength as we staggered through the snow.

"It isn't you who becomes a *were* at full moon, is it? It's the house." A fresh shower of sparks hissed into the snow, as if to add emphasis to my words. She nodded, wearily.

"Woewater has been in my family for generations. It – seduces you, Mr Dee. If you are born in the house, as I was, then you can never escape. It whispers to you in the night, it shows you wonderful dreams and visions. But at the full moon, it summons things in. Sometimes just rats, or foxes. Sometimes people – though not for some years, now. I would have warned you, but I was not sure and, besides, you could not have made your way through the snow. It was a choice of two evils. I waited until you had gone to bed, and then I kept vigil in the hallway. I thought if – if anything happened, I could hurry you outside."

"But you must have known that I might tell folk of what I'd seen, if I lived."

"I thought I could pass it off as an accident – a collapsing ceiling in an old house, if anyone came. But this place has an evil reputation. A deserved one."

"Then why did you not burn it years ago?"

"I had nowhere else to go. And the house – I told you. It held me." She paused, chafing her hands against the chill, and I could see the shock in her face. "And will you, Mr Dee? Tell folk of what you've seen?"

I looked at her. Her hair was trailing across her face, and her brow was smudged with soot. The dark eyes were anxious, but there seemed to be a light behind them. I wondered how much of her nature I had imagined, and how much might yet be real.

I said, "No. We've both gained our lives and our freedom, tonight. I won't tell."

In the woods, I once more heard the vixen bark. Full moon, and we were outside.

"We should find shelter," I said. "And I'll help you to find a place, when we leave."

Minerva looked at me, doubtfully. "There's a boathouse down on the lake. Now that the snow has stopped, we can make our way to the village when dawn comes."

I took her hand. It felt as small and cold as a claw. Together we made our difficult way through the snow towards the lake, and behind us, Woewater burned.

Blackthorn and Nettles

I have thrown the little dark thing over the lip of the cauldron and now I stand and watch as it falls, twisting through thickets of starlight, past pools of moons, spiralling down. The cauldron's rim is cold bronze beneath my hands, sticky as ice. Arian once told me, with that I-know-something-that-you-do-not tilt of her head, that it was cold between the stars, but I do not know why she believes this.

At last the little dark thing has fallen so fast and so far that I can't see it any longer. I peel my hands away from the cauldron and go to the window to push the hanging aside. Now, toward the end of the year, it is frosty first thing in the morning. The snow has begun to glide back down the slopes of Yr Wyddfa and the woods around Nantlleu Lake are a haze of fading gold. There are anemones growing around the foot of the fort and the world seems too fair for me to feel such hate, but it rises in me like boiling sap, welling out in thick tears as though drawn up by the failing sun.

But this is the last time I will ever look out of this window. Once twilight has fallen, I will slip out into the frosty dark and head for the coast and my father's lands. I do not think anyone will see me go. There is to be no feast tonight: the fortress hums like a hive, aghast, all except me. For I am filled with hate and rejoicing, so bitter and sweet that I can taste it on my tongue like new wine.

A year ago, I foresaw none of this. I knew nothing of the land of Gwynedd, nor of Math and his shaman nephews, save that which I had heard in stories. But stories are always growing and changing, acquiring more and more stitches with each telling until you can no longer see the weave beneath. When my father sent me north, I did not know what to expect, only that it was a great honour to serve as the foot-holder of Math, and a great danger, too. I was to be the Land Maiden, who anchors the lord to the world and saves him from the veil of Annwn. That is, my father spoke of it as an honour, but I had heard the whispers: of what had happened to Math's last foot-holder at the hands of his nephew Gilfaethwy.

"You need not worry," my father told me. "The rapist has been sent away now, raiding to the west across the sea. You will not have to see him. Math had them punished – the rapist and his brother Gwydion both."

But I was to learn that punishment and Gwydion did not stick; it ran from him like rain, leaving only a faint bitter residue behind, and little learning. Given the fate of the previous foot-holder, I resolved to be wary of Gwydion, to keep my guard up. I pictured a dour, brutal man, like so many of these northern lords, but he was also a shaman and I did not understand, then, that Gwydion could slide around one's guard as subtly as sunlight, so softly that one did not even realise that The Danger had been invited in, until it was far too late.

Before I left for the north, I went to the woods and sought out the oak-wife of our tribe. She had trained me, since the day my courses came, and I had learned much. Surely, I thought, no northern magic-man was a match for our oak-wife.

I found her in a sacred task, cutting the mistletoe that gathers in the branches while the snow fell around her like owl-feathers. Neither of us spoke. I watched her, and she gave no sign that she had seen me, but I was certain that she knew I was there. When she had finished, and climbed down the tree, she gestured with a nod and I followed her small limping figure into the wood to her cave. There, underneath the twist of ice that would soon thaw to become a waterfall, she spoke at last.

"Remember what I have told you about your *nemeton*, your shadow-shield. How it lies around you, unseen, protective, an armour of air."

Obediently, I closed my eyes and felt the *nemeton* draw up around me, an invisible snail-shell of air, woven from the spirit of snow and the iron-hard ground. I felt it encase me, just as leather armour encases a warrior.

"Good," the oak-wife said. "Use what is around you for your own protection. Use the land – the woods and sea and sky, thorn and bramble and briar. Weave yourself into the web of the world, until you are part of its warp and its weft, and no one can work ill upon you without tearing the world apart. Now go, and remember what I have told you."

I remembered, and at winter's end I was sent north.

I had been at Math's fortress, that stone tower on the shores of Nantlleu lake, for almost a month before Gwydion returned. I spent the day in an agitation that it was difficult to conceal. When Gwydion's presence was announced at the feast that night, the air in the chamber seemed to crackle and hiss like the air before a storm. I sat with Math's feet in my lap and stared straight ahead.

Gwydion was smaller than I had imagined, but then, heroes often are. He was not the hulking warrior that men consider impressive, but a slight man with a quick dark gaze. When he stepped into the torchlight, I saw that his hair had a red gleam to it, like the coat of a stoat or a fox. But later I learned that his totem was the crow, and he made no secret of it: he had taken on the aspect of the bird, the shadows that it cast. And something in those shadows spoke to me. I could feel his gaze upon me as I sat with Math's feet in my woollen lap, and it drew me as a lure draws a hunting hawk. I do not know what he saw when he looked at me. I thought, perhaps, that he smiled. Math's voice, and those of the other men, retreated to a sound like the distant sea. I forgot the *nemeton* around me, but the walls of the fort seemed as insubstantial. I heard nothing except Gwydion's quiet voice. When I was once more alone in my own little chamber, I cursed myself for a fool of the world.

That night, with the crescent moon rising over Yr Wyddfa's

white shoulder, there was a soft knock at my door. I thought I might be imagining it, and I was also afraid. I did not open the door. But next day, he came to find me as I worked among the herbs. I crouched with my fingers buried in the soft black earth and would not look at him, and kept my voice cold when I replied to his greeting. I felt, rather than saw, him crouch down beside me.

"Look at me," he said, and against my will I looked up into crow-black eyes. "That's better. You are Creirwy, are you not? Daughter of Gwilym of the red-earth country? May I call you Crei?"

"If you wish, my lord."

"Oh," he said. "You do not have to call me that."

His gaze was half-mockery, half challenge. I could see little in it of desire. He wore a thong around his neck with a bone hanging from it, pale against paler skin, and at first I thought it was the bone of a bird. But then he moved, shifting position a little, and the bone changed, broadening and flattening like a human finger. My eyes must have widened. At last I remembered my *nemeton* and drew it up around me, out of the sun-warmed earth and the nearby briars.

"I have to go inside," I told him, and rising, I left him there among the herbs.

But that night, I woke and Gwydion was standing by my pallet. I felt his shadow over me, feather-soft.

"How did you -?"

"Hush," he said. The bone around his throat seemed to glow with its own light.

"Lord," I said, shaking. "You understand that -"

"The foot-holder must be a virgin. Yes, I know." Once more, he crouched down beside me. His voice was still light, still mocking. "After last time, how could I not know? Do you know what my uncle Math did to my brother and I?" Without waiting for an answer, he went on, "He ran us through the changes of the world. Hare and hound, stag and doe. He made us mate with each other, in vengeance for the girl. But still," – a faint shrug – "It was worth it, for the knowledge gained. Gilfaethwy doesn't think so, but then, my brother always was a fool. I know you have to stay a virgin. Don't worry. I'll keep you as one."

He reached out a hand and I took it. The snow whirled in, hiding him from my sight. I could feel his hand warm in mine, but all of a sudden it felt like a claw. I pulled away, but he held me tight. There were feathers all around us and then blossom, sweet as May. We were no longer in my chamber, but on the shores of Nantlleu, deep in the alder groves which march down to the shingle.

He did not lie to me. Virgin I remained, though I learned of other pleasures. After that first time, I feared that he might boast about it to the other warriors, but the manner of all toward me stayed unchanged and the gossip among the slaves was that Gwydion had always expressed disapproval of loose women. I do not know how he reconciled this with his connivance in the actions of his brother, but then, Gwydion always could believe two contradictory things at the same time. I see now that it is a property of a shaman, a fluidity that helps them to slip through the small cracks of the world's weave, to change form as easily as I might change my gown.

"My brother has no restraint," he said, when I asked him about it. I lay with my head against his arm, staring at my own black hair as it fanned across his pale, freckled flesh. He had the muscles of a scholar rather than a warrior, but he was stronger than he looked. "What he wants, he takes."

"It seems to me that so do you."

"Me?" he said. "Do you think so?" He always spoke in this way, as though nothing really mattered, but it was light as some swords are light, with a sharp edge. "I never want anything."

It seemed strange to me that he should say this, when he found so many excuses to seek me out, but I was in love and I told myself that it was better than he did not lie, tell me that he loved me only to cast me aside when he grew bored. He seemed to want to talk as much as to make love, and that was flattering.

And so it went, as the spring grew on and Wind-month turned to Seed-month and the green grew over the land. I was just beginning to think a little beyond the next day, and to let my closed heart open with the sun, when Gwydion told me that Arian was coming home.

"I will welcome your sister," I said, and meant it. But after a pause, he said as if I had not spoken, "Of course, you'll say nothing of what has passed between us."

"I have no intention of letting her know that we are lovers. Do you take me for a fool?"

"No, but I mean that there must be no hint that I am even – interested – in you."

"Why not?" There had already been some rumour in Math's court. There was no reason why we should not eventually wed: I was high-born enough, and Math could always find another foot-holder.

"She is – possessive – of me."

"She is your sister. I'm sure she wishes you well, is concerned for you." But something in the way he said it, the bright sword-edge under the words, made me sit up amid the rushes and look at him. And I saw the truth in his eyes, before he turned his head away and the truth slipped and slid. I said nothing more. We were not as the followers of the new god, who believe – or so I hear – that incest is a great sin. But it still dismayed me.

"But Arian is married, is she not?"

"Yes. For some years now, to a man from the east named Constantine."

"Does her husband know?"

"Of course not. She and I were not raised together, Crei. Gilfaethwy and I were fostered to a war-tribe on Mon. When Arian and I met, we were grown and there was – something."

"But has there been no one else for you?"

He laughed. "Of course. I was even supposed to be wed, once. A girl from Dyfed. Arian arranged it."

"But if she arranged that, why should she be jealous of me? And if she herself is married..."

"She changed her mind. Became hysterical, threatened curses. She has some knowledge of that kind of thing. It is not, I will tell you now, safe to antagonise her. Anyway, it suits me well enough. If she threatened to put Constantine aside, as she could do under law – well, let's say I should not be happy with that. But there has never been any real threat of it, and if there had, our association would never have lasted so long. She likes the status that her husband gives her, and the comfort of his wealth. You have nothing to fear – as long as you keep quiet."

I did not know what to do. My own position was fragile: Gwydion could ruin me with a word if he chose. I remembered the words of the oak-wife, spoken to me long ago. *Girls should be as mountains. Fertile slopes, but snow-cold at the summit behind the clouds that they draw.* And so I told myself that I would indeed stay as chill as the snows of Yr Wyddfa, and as silent. I even tried to withdraw from Gwydion, but he would not have it. He seemed genuinely bewildered that I should wish to, and a little amused.

"If you leave me, I'll be angry," he said, smiling as he said it.

"But if you tell me now that you love her, Gwydion, then I will walk away."

"Ah," he said, and smiled again, and said nothing more. I tried to find reassurance in that, but the words flowed like water, and their meaning drifted away like blossoms on the spring wind.

I did one thing well. I remembered the words of the oak-wife, and worked on the conjuring of my *nemeton*: drawing it up through frustration and love and hurt, and a great growing rage. I conjured it from blackthorn and nettles, from bramble and briar, from the wood-wife's tree and the serpent's sting, burn-green and sharp-tooth, protecting myself through the world's will.

When Arian arrived, amid much confusion and fuss, she was not as I expected. I had imagined someone tall and pale, like the new moon. But Arian was small, with hair the colour of oak bark. Her totem, whose emblem she wore, was the polecat and she reminded me of one: little and brindled and greedy and quick, with a swift snapping bite. And like her totem she was clearly jealous of her territory. She can have known little enough of me, but her cold brown gaze summed me up quickly enough. She knew that something was going on. She gripped her brother's arm with tight possessiveness and made sure she sat next to him at the evening's feast. She wore red, I remember, the colour of danger and blood, flying the war-banner, as women do. Around her neck she wore a great pearl on a silver thread, pale as the moon, and, when I deemed it polite to admire this, she looked a challenge into my face and said that it had been a gift from her brother. "My husband was a little put out," she said, lifting her chin with pride at the trouble she had managed to cause, "But I told him not to be so foolish. He bought me something just as beautiful, after all." The message was clear. But she had to tilt her head to look me in the eye and I did not think she liked that at all. I am sure the men thought we were getting along wonderfully.

And after this, we were well enough together, though wary, like two cats in the same small room. Her husband was usually with her, a quiet shadow of a man who rarely spoke, but perhaps this was due to the fact that the Cymric was not his native tongue. He was no longer a warrior, having sustained an injury in battle, and now he was responsible for the provisioning of Math's war-tribe and I found that he was well-respected.

Arian divided her time between her husband and her brother: one sometimes came upon her and Gwydion in corners, and it was the only time I saw her laugh. She had a wit like a fish-hook and I admired it against my will. Every time, it filled me with fury and despair. But Gwydion continued to seek me out, two or three times a day, and there were also times when he would sit across the table at the feasts, staring at me, and then she would grow quietly frantic, plucking at his sleeve and talking in too-loud a voice. This enraged me, but I could not help feeling a little pity for us both. At such times Gwydion would take on the air of a man who has fought himself into a corner, and he even spoke to me of it, with a faintly injured note in his voice, as though the situation were my fault, and my task to provide the unguent of sympathy. He did not get it. But I was careful when I spoke to Arian, except once when I came into the hall to find them all a little drunk. Gwydion was not there, but Arian was sitting in the middle of a group of admiring warriors. I would have liked to have been able to say that it was due to her position alone and the favours she could confer, but honesty made me admit that she would probably have been popular anyway, at least among the men.

"Here's Crei," she cried. "She'll sing you a song, won't you, Crei?"

I was unprepared, but something rose hard and cold in me and I took up the harp and sang the story of Bright-hand betrayed by Blodeuwedd the Fair, so pointedly that now, sixty years later, the story has become linked with Gwydion and Arian, and her own son, whose name was Lleu. As I sang, Arian stared into her lap the whole time and said nothing when the others complimented me.

And still her brother took me to the woods in a shower of flowers, all that summer and on into Leaf-fall-month, when the rowan berries grew red and withered. One morning Yr Wyddfa was white against a white sky, pale as a bone upon skin, and both Gwydion and Arian's husband were sent south in one of the last raids of that year. On the morning that they left, Arian clung dry-eyed and white-faced to her husband and her brother in turn and when they had gone she shut herself in her chamber and did not emerge for the rest of the day.

I kept my hollowed heart to myself and tried to keep busy in the kitchen. I even polished the great cauldron that Math's own oak-wife had left behind her when she passed into the Wheel. When Arian came down, she immediately began taking inventory of the kitchen supplies. There was much to be done – slaughtering and skinning and bottling and spinning, and Arian and I suddenly found that we were glad of one another's presence. For her, everything had to be perfect. She ran the slaves ragged, but she and I got along better in the absence of the men, and we took to cooking together in the evenings. I did not speak of her brother: on the few occasions I had reason to mention his name, I saw her face grow pinched and sour, though she herself talked of him often, harping on their closeness. Within me, fury grew, and with it a strange unwilling affection for Arian herself. Once, she wrote a song for the pleasure of the other women, about a girl whose lover leaves her for the sea, over and over again, and I could see that she had talent.

One day, late in Slaughter-month when the leaves were hanging yellow on the trees, the sister of Math's dead oak-wife came to visit, bringing simples and charms with her. Arian and myself were engaged in spinning in the tower room. The oak-wife's sister watched us for a while, and remarked that it was good to see two women who were close friends, adding acidly that it was surely one of the Three Lost Blessings. I met Arian's gaze for a long minute, and neither of us spoke, but I knew what we were thinking. For we were not friends, but close enemies, and I wondered, then as now, whether there is so great a difference, at the end.

Later the oak-wife's sister asked to speak to Arian alone. I did not find out until years later that she had approached Arian as matchmaker between myself and Gwydion. It seemed talk about us had broken loose after all, and the match was considered to be a good one. Arian, of course, said nothing of it to me. I do not know what excuse she made to the oak-wife's sister, but she was bitter-faced and pale all the rest of that day, and snapped her polecat teeth at me. She got her words flung back at her, but I stopped short of the conversation that we should not have and spent the evening bunching herbs in the cauldron room. I felt as though it was looking at me, a great dark eye behind my back.

At autumn's end, shortly before Samhuin and the New Year, the men came home, leading their captured pigs and cattle before them. That night a sudden shower of rain pattered against the hanging at my window, from a clear cold sky, and Gwydion was there. In the days that followed, we fell into our old pattern: sleeping together every few days, talking always. And so I was happy for a time. Arian and I settled back into our cart-track of comfortable hate and so the winter wore by: up at dawn, to bed at dusk, the same stories told over and over until the captured pigs became the great boar of the otherlands, snatched from the depths of Annwn rather than the hills of Dyfed.

Then, one morning, I went down to the council chamber to find the place with a hive-hum. Math's face was cold and set, though he spoke gently enough to me. Gwydion was standing in the shadows, his gaze haunted, not looking at me.

"Bring her in," Math commanded. The guards left, to return with Arian, her hands bound, her hair dishevelled. Her husband Constantine followed, his saturnine face more closed than ever.

"So," Math said to Constantine. "You say that she is with child, and it is none of your begetting?"

"It cannot be. I was in the south when it was conceived."

"Then who do you accuse?"

"One who can come and go as he pleases. One to whom a journey of many thousand *llath* is no more than a step through a door of air." He did not look at Gwydion, but everyone knew who he meant.

"He didn't -" Arian cried, and, very strangely, I believed her. Math looked at me.

"You were here with her, in this fort, all the while. Did you see anyone come and go?"

"My lord, I did not." I would have loved to have set her life alight, but it was not the truth. Arian flashed me an unreadable glance.

"Let her step over the branch and see the truth of it," Math commanded. One of the guards hastened away and came back bearing a branch of blackthorn, curled and gnarled by ivy, the ancient wife-of-the-wood, the witches' tree.

"No!" Arian cried, but the guards seized her arms and forced her forward, over the branch. She looked frantically at her husband and her brother, but both of them lowered their gaze.

At first, nothing happened, and Arian gave a triumphant smile, but then the hem of her skirts twitched and something small and dark, as quick as a polecat, darted out. It hissed at all of us, then fled behind a tapestry and was gone. I listened in silence as Math condemned his niece to exile and her brother's charge.

"Wait!" Gwydion began, but Math silenced him with a look. Behind my walls of air, weaving my *nemeton*, I could feel him seeking my gaze, but I would not give it. When Math ordered Gwydion out of the chamber, I would not look up, beyond blackthorn, beyond nettles. I would not look up, either, as they led his sister shrieking away.

But that night, in the hollow silence that follows disaster, I went down the stairs to the council chamber, pausing only to collect a falconer's glove. When I looked behind the tapestry, the small dark thing was still there. It squirmed and spat when I picked it up and sank sharp teeth into the glove, but it no longer had the power to do me harm and we both knew it. the creature looked a little like a polecat, but black and hairless, with small human hands and watery red eyes. I think it tried to speak, but its thick tongue could not manage the spirals of the Cymric and I did not want to hear whatever it might have to say to me. I took the thing, mewling and glaring, to the oak-wife's cauldron and then I closed my eyes and let myself drift away into blackthorn blossom and nettle flower. When I opened my eyes again, the cauldron was filled with dark and starlight, and it was then that I dropped the thing I had, the thing that Arian had been carrying inside her for so many months, the child that was no child at all, but simply her hate for me. I dropped it over the cauldron's lip and watched it fall.

That night, I left Math's fort and made my way south to my father's lands. There, the oak-wife welcomed me and asked no questions, then or ever. It was through her that I learned, months later, that Arian had gone alone to the coast and shut herself up in a sea-tower that had once belonged to her mother, and would see no one, including her brother. But I had left her hate behind and cared nothing for this news – or so I thought.

For the cauldron of starlight is within us, within all women, and whatever one casts into it finds form. The hateful thing that I believed to be gone from me had taken root. At Lughnasadh, I gave birth to a son, a child as swift as a polecat and as dark as a crow, and together we waited among the blackthorn and the nettles, for his father to come.

The Water Cure

I suppose that I would never have set foot in the spa town of Avern had I not been struck repeatedly by lightning. At the time of which I write, it had occurred on no less than seven occasions, each more serious than the last.

On the first occurrence, I had been in the process if unfolding an umbrella, that new-fangled invention, outside St Martin in the Fields, when I became aware of a tingling across my scalp and a ringing in my ears. Next moment, I was flat upon my back with a river of rain pouring down my collar and a concerned passer-by bending over me. I had, he informed me, been felled by a thunderbolt.

Not unnaturally, I considered that I had enjoyed a lucky escape; considered – also not unnaturally – that such an occurrence was unlikely to happen again.

The second occasion took place during a walking holiday in Wales, halfway up the slopes of Plynlimon. The day was balmy and the sky clear, and I do not even remember the clap of thunder, nor the sudden fiery strike that followed. I awoke two days later, to a strong odour of singed hair, in the bedroom of the remote farmhouse to which my friends had carried me.

On the third occasion, which took place on a ferry crossing over the Irish Sea, I was incapacitated for almost a week, lying insensible in a public house in Fishguard. By this time, I had developed a morbid fear of weather and was reluctant to venture out into even the lightest shower. I took to traversing the streets only when the weather was clement, but this did not prevent the unhappy repetition of these previous events, a further four times.

After the final occurrence, the turbulent heavens left me alone for several months, but my health was quite ruined. Never before a man of nervous disposition, I discovered that I had developed a tremor in the hands that made it impossible to hold so much as a teacup without spilling the liquid within, a stammer that eroded my small reputation as a wit in polite society, and a lamentable tendency to sit bolt upright out of sleep, several times a night. I had, in short, become a nervous wreck. Concentrating upon my legal work proved an impossibility and eventually my fiancée, though a most long-suffering young woman, suggested with some force that I take a cure.

"You used to be such a vital man, Ronald," she said sadly. "Perhaps if you went to Italy for a month or so... It is, after all, the native country of your dear late father."

"I cannot afford Italy."

"Somewhere nearer home, then. Perhaps a spa? You could visit Avern and take the waters. Dear Mrs Addison did so, you will recall, and found herself quite restored to her former strength."

Conceding that this was so, I made the appropriate arrangements, and thus, on a frost-rimmed day in late September, found myself alighting shakily out onto Avern station. It was already late, so I made my way to the hotel without seeing a great deal of the town.

Next morning, however, I prevailed upon myself to undertake a little exploring, eyeing the sky warily as I stepped through the door of the hotel. The principal spa was, at that time, housed in a building some distance above the town, amid the hills for which the region is justly famous. Avern itself proved to be a pleasing, if steep, place, prosperous enough to judge from some of the horses and carriages. I hastened up the High Street, passing a handsome church and a churchyard full of cedars, and found myself in a long, low park. Water poured through the open mouth of a woman, an unusual form of statuary. Her hair flowed in spiral stone coils along the edges of the rock and her eyes were wide and blank. An ornate sign proclaimed this to be the route to the spa: St Avern's Well.

I duly followed the sign, keeping an uneasy eye upon the heavens, and wandered up a winding path through beechwoods. There was a sensation of silence and age: some of the trees were so old that the earth around their roots had worn away, exposing the grey bark to the open air. It looked as hard and polished as stone.

The famous spring itself lay in a dip between the hills. I could see the rise of a low peak before me, blazing with heather and bracken. Pausing briefly for breath, I hurried on. I was by no means the only walker. The path was filled with strolling couples, elderly folk in bath chairs being shoved precariously up the path, a few hollow-eyed children. I began to feel a little less of a victim when I saw some of the patient, weary faces that surrounded me. At last, unscathed by the elements, I reached the well itself.

The spa was housed in a small building rather like a cottage, with a tiled roof that rose to a point. On this, sat a weathervane in the shape of a leafless tree: an unusual conceit, and to my mind rather a pretty one. Now that I neared the spa, I could hear the water running and gushing within. When a gap in the crowd allowed me to do so, I stepped through the doorway into a low room with a tiled floor. The water from the spring was channelled up into a large marble basin, decorated with the head of a lion. Rather than being confined, the water was permitted to run freely over the sides of the basin and onto the floor, creating a curiously unreal effect, as though basin and lion's head floated above a small lake.

I waited my turn, then stepped forwards to drink. The water was very cold, and tasted of rust: this must, then, be a chalybeate spring. The chill of it numbed my teeth and went straight to my head: I felt momentarily dizzy. And, just for a fleeting instant, it seemed to me that I could see a woman's face looking up from the swimming surface of the floor: lips parted, hair streaming out like weed. I must have started, for the cup fell from my hands and plunged into the basin. Fortunately, it did not break.

Still feeling unsteady, I went outside and sat down on a

149

nearby bench, breathing in the cold autumn air with a gasp. Leaning back, I raised my head to the clear sky and saw, with distant horror, a black cloud rolling over the edge of the hill. I do not remember anything more.

When I came round, it was to see a cracked plaster ceiling floating above me. I had no idea where I was, or how much time had passed. Though I could recall nothing of what had occurred, it seemed reasonable to assume that it had been the same disaster that had so dogged my life in recent months. The displeasing odour of scorched hair appeared to corroborate this theory. I struggled to sit up.

"Lie still," said a low female voice. "You will only feel worse if you try to rise."

I did as I was told. I felt something cold and wet touch my brow: it was wonderfully soothing. The owner of the voice leaned over me then, and I found myself looking up into an oddly familiar face. She was young, with unbound pale hair and jet black eyes. She smiled at me.

"You were struck by lightning," she said.

"I know," I informed her. "Not for the first time, either."

Her near-invisible eyebrows rose. "It has happened before?"

"As far as I can recall, this is no less than the eighth time."

"That is indeed unfortunate," the girl said, with what I felt to be considerable understatement. "Well, you should rest now. I'll come back later, but do call if you need anything."

Only once she had left did two things occur to me. One, that it was odd that such a young woman should be instructed to tend to a male stranger with no hint of a chaperone, and second, that hers was surely the face I had seen gazing up at me, from the watery surface of the well-house floor. Blinking, I struggled up against the pillows. A few minutes passed before I could bring myself to rise, conscious only of the need to get out of there and return to the guest house. It did not occur to me to wonder why I was so desperate to vacate a comfortable enough bed, and a charming enough nurse: I only knew that I must leave.

One look at the sky beyond the windows was, however, sufficient to dissuade me. The heavens were thunderous. From this height, I could see clear across the flat expanse of the Vale to the distant hills. Lightning crackled and spat along the Herith Edge, and with a shudder I turned from the window.

The girl was standing immediately behind me. Her shift drifted out in the draught from the window frame and her eyes reflected the lightning, twin bolts that glittered for a moment and then were gone. She said, rather diffidently, "I've brought you some brandy, from my father's medicine chest. I am averse to strong liquor, but they say it is good for the health..."

I took a sip. She was still standing very close and I moved uneasily back against the window. I could almost feel the lightning, as one might sense a great hound casting about for one's scent. Next moment, I thought I had been struck, but it was only the brandy: searing down my throat and, it seemed, through my veins. It tasted like no cognac I had ever drunk. Rather, it was more closely akin to mead: a flowery, pungent honey-taste that filled the room with the scent of summer. I took another sip, and then another. I felt instantly restored.

"You've been most kind, Miss -"

"My name is Sabrina," she said. "Like the river that flows through the Vale."

"Very pretty. And now I really must be going..."

"Sit for a moment," Sabrina said. Suddenly, I was down in the chair, and the glass was full again. I must have drunk it, I think, because when I next awoke, it was quite dark.

I was still seated in the chair, but the empty glass had been taken from my hands. I had none of the unpleasantly lingering effects that normally follow intoxication. Rather, I felt light and floating, a vessel to be filled. But by now, I really should be back at the guest house with some decent food inside me. I rose and went to the door. It was locked.

I rattled the handle, but to no avail.

"Sabrina!" I cried. "Sabrina! Let me out!" But there was no

sound from beyond the door.

I looked through the window, hoping to juggle with the catch. It was not, after all, so very far from the ground. After a few minutes' work, I managed to open the catch. I leaned out. If I swung down from the windowsill by my hands, it would not be so very great a drop... A difficult, strained moment later and I was on the ground.

Sidling through the shadows, I made my way around the side of the building and soon discovered that I had been in the upper rooms of the well house itself. The tree-vane upon its roof creaked in a wind that I did not feel, and span around. A flurry of leaves rose up as I turned the corner, momentarily blinding me, and rain dashed against my face. I think I cried out, fearing another attack of the lightning, but then I realised that I was standing in the well house, at the point where the spring bubbled up through the lion's head, and it was the splash of the water that I had felt. I stood shaking in the damp shadows, needing to take flight down the hill, and too unnerved to move. There was the distant mutter of thunder in the distance.

I felt, though I could not say how, that the next bolt would be the cause of my death. Lord only knew how I had survived so much, for so long. There was a flicker of rosy fire across the far hills. The storm rumbled closer. I saw the glint of lightning on water as yet another flicker flared over the Vale. And now the thunder was almost overhead. I stood paralysed. A bolt hit an oak at the foot of the lane that led to the Well: I saw it explode in a shower of sparks and acorns. The lightning was questing over the ground, sending the dead leaves into a scatter of flame. I had never seen it behave in such a way. I knew that it was looking for me.

But just as that great fiery arm reached the open doorway of the well house, the water rose up in a curling wave, breaking over my head and dragging me downward. I felt a strange, cool sensation as my body passed through marble, as smoothly as if it were nothing more than air. I landed on bare earth with a jarring thud, water filling my eyes and mouth. I spat.

Sabrina was rising above me, her body curdling out of the water-drops. I could still see the lightning in her eyes, or perhaps it was only a lingering image, burned upon my own.

"What are you?" I cried. Rolling over, I crawled from her as swiftly as I could, fetching up with my back against the wall.

"I am the well," she replied. "Riverwater and rain, all that forms the spring."

"You're a *nymph*?"

She looked a little put out. "Undine, actually."

"You saved my life," I said. "How can I ever repay you?" It seemed the thing to say, at the time. She looked down at me. Her eyes were as cold and hard as ice.

"I'm sure we'll think of something," she said. I did not see the blow coming. It hit me like a wave, and once more, I went under.

When next I awoke, I found that I could not move. Squinting to one side, I could see stone walls and a slitted window, but to my horror, the chamber was open to the rainy sky. I lay upon my back. My ankles and wrists were strapped to a strange contraption, like a leather bed. Above me, protruding from the wall, was a curved dome like the upper part of a bell. Sabrina, human again in her shift, was padding about the chamber.

"What are you doing?" I whispered. My mouth was dry as summer dust. She did not answer, but continued with her preparations. She seemed to be doing something with a bundle of what looked like hair, but which I then recognised as copper wire.

"What is that?"

"Power," she said.

"What do you mean?"

"What does your word 'nymph' mean to you?"

I thought about it. The charming spirits of poetry and song, fluttering about Arcadian hills... I said as much.

"Precisely," she answered. "Pretty, weak, ineffectual... Nymphs and undines do not have the power of sea or storm, of earthquake or hurricane. We are supposed to keep to our little pools and wells, enticing young men who stroll by. It was as much as I could to do to render you, one man, unconscious. I have kept to these hills, this well, for long enough. We are in a more modern day, now. And I am sick and tired of *all these people.*" Her face contorted, spitting. "They come here, and they bring their sickness with them, and they leave it behind when they bathe in the waters. It sours the ground. I taste it constantly. It saps what power I have and leaves me a poor, pale thing." She gestured to the dome. "That leads to a generator in the ancient vaults beneath the chamber. Once I have harnessed your ability to attract lightning, I will use it to power a thing that I have devised: a web of wire that will protect the well from people for ever more."

"You are mad," I whispered.

"And why do you think that is?" the undine hissed. "I told you – I am sick of all these damned *people!*"

She touched a dial. I heard a humming sound deep beneath the earth, underneath me. Above the roofless chamber, the clouds began to gather.

"You're summoning a storm! You'll get me killed!"

"No," I heard her say. "You are the one who is summoning it. Don't you know what you are, what your lineage must be? There aren't just water elementals, you know."

The generator was whining into life. Above me, the clouds were massing. But her words echoed in my ears. I felt a sizzling in the earth, as though a spark had ignited. And this time, it was as though I reached out my hand toward it.

"Now!" the undine cried. She threw the switch and I threw lightning, as it arced through the chamber. There was an immense bang and a flash, so bright that it seared my eyes. It was a moment before I could see again. I clapped my hands to my face, realising a moment later that they were free. The chains that had held them had melted. I sat up, rubbing my eyes.

The dome lay on the floor, blasted from the wall by the

explosion. Of Sabrina, there was no sign, only a small pair of pale, soot-rimmed feet, still smouldering. I stared at them in horror. As I watched, they began to melt, like icicles in the sun. When they were quite gone I scrambled up from the bed and threw myself at the door. It opened easily enough and I charged down the hill through the dripping bracken to the hotel, where I locked myself in my room with a bottle of brandy for the next three days.

I think I must have been somewhat delirious. Strange, dream-like images chased themselves through my head, of flames and forges, dancing wildfire, salamanders amid sparks. When I thought of the earth under me, I could sense sparks within it, like fiery seeds. I conjured none of them up, but I could still taste the fire in my mouth, an ashy bitterness which, I realised, I was coming to crave.

On the morning of the fourth day I wrote a long letter to my poor fiancée, saying that I had discovered that I was suffering from a terminal illness and therefore released her from her engagement. Then, I returned to London, where I purchased a one-way packet ticket to Italy and made arrangements to visit Etna. I did not know quite what I would do when I got there, but I had the feeling that something might present itself.

It was raining on the morning of my departure, but this time the lightning did not find me. I stayed below deck as the boat steamed out of Dover, however. I had never before suffered from seasickness, but I seemed to be developing a distinct aversion to water.

All Fish and Dracula

The girl slipped across the cobbles, black lace trailing over rain-wet stone. The two women were walking a short distance ahead: elderly, bowed down with shopping bags, headscarves keeping out the worst of the October drizzle. In one bag, the girl could see the wet golden skin of an escaping onion. The women were talking together in low voices, the soft Yorkshire accent running the words together.

She shied from the threat of her reflection in a shop window, bouncing back the lights above the rows of jet jewellery. She already knew what she looked like: all lace and velvet beneath the billowing leather coat, lips the colour of what else, hair slicked back from a high pale forehead. Her hands clicked with silver.

As she drew closer to the two women, she thought: *it would be so easy.* But then she spied the others at the end of the street: her vampire clan. She hurried toward them.

As she passed the old women, she wondered how she must appear: alarming, sinister, a vision out of dark. She smiled to herself, a little. She was a few yards in front of them when one of the women spoke.

"Ee, Mary," she said. "In't it nice to see so many young people taking care of their clothes?"

"WHITBY WELCOMES THE GOTHS"

The banner was huge, taking up most of an advertising hoarding at the entrance to the main street. Around the letters, someone had painted bats with little smiling faces.

"Look at that," Lily said, disgusted. But it made Katya smile. Julian twisted around in his seat to look at them, flicking back a black lock of hair.

"What, you were expecting them to meet us with pitchforks and stakes? They love Goth Weekend up here. No one getting pissed and throwing up in their gardens. We're polite. We keep ourselves to ourselves."

"We spend loads of money," Katya murmured. She waved a jet-and-silver decked hand. "What's not to love?"

"Precisely."

But Lily's mouth turned downward, like a child who would not be comforted. Katya sighed. Lily had been in a mood ever since they left Leeds and she was beginning to regret ever accepting Julian's offer of a lift up to Whitby. She didn't know them very well – they were friends of a friend – and even though they were all Goths, she could not help wishing that Lily and Julian were a little less... well, Gothic. Lily sulked and pouted, and Julian hadn't stopped talking since they had started, in a superior, educating-the-young kind of way. He was four years older, it was true, twenty-two to Katya's eighteen, but even so... She supposed that he did know more about the bands, but she would rather see them for herself and make her own mind up. But she was too polite, or too *something*, to say so.

"Where's the guest house?" she asked, longing now for the journey to be at an end so that she could go and find Damian and the others. As they turned the corner, she saw a huge group of young men, all frock coats and knee boots. She wondered, with an odd stab of disloyalty, how many of them might be called Damian. Or Julian, come to that. Or Katy, with an extra 'a'.

"Not far now," Julian said, quite kindly, as if reassuring someone very small.

"Oh good."

She spoke more sourly than she had intended, and Lily gave her a glance of surprise, as though she were the one to have a monopoly on sulleness.

"I'll drop you two off and park," Julian said. They were climbing, now, high into the town. Craning back, Katya saw a thin line of estuary through the rainy haze, banked by black harbour walls. The town stepped down to meet it and beyond lay the chilly expanse of the North Sea. A boat, tiny from this height, was setting out from the harbour mouth.

"Herring." Julian said, with authority.

"I'm sorry?"

"That's what they fish for here," Julian amplified. "And cod."

"I thought cod was all fished out?" Katya ventured. She wasn't sure about herring, either. Julian frowned, clearly preferring not to be questioned.

"Is it?"

"Yes. Everything was over-fished up here. There's barely anything left in the North Sea."

"Well, that shouldn't matter much to you, should it? As long as they don't run out of nut roast."

"Don't you even eat fish?" Lily asked.

"No," Katya said. "I'm not that sort of vegetarian. I've never eaten fish or meat. I'm vegan, actually. My mum's a bit of an old hippy. She brought us up that way. It's just the way I am. I don't bang on about it."

She saw Julian's lip curl. "It's natural to eat flesh. We're predators, hunters. We need the protein."

"Beans have protein."

"You can't be a vampire and eat beans."

"I'm not a vampire, am I? I'm just a Goth."

"Anyway," Lily said, suddenly animated. "That's not cod."

Katya peered through the car window in the direction of her pointing finger. Right at the top of the cliff, by the roadside, stood a wishbone gateway: white against the storm-dark sky.

"That's a whale's jawbone," Julian said.

"Big, isn't it?" Katya remarked, and wished she hadn't made such an obvious remark. Of course it was big. It belonged to a whale. She thought of her sister Jess, who had a job in an estate agent and read Cosmopolitan.

"I don't know what you want to go to Whitby for at this time of the year. Whitby's boring. All fish and Dracula. Why don't you book a week in Malaga?"

"Here we are." Julian pulled up at the kerb.

The guesthouse, set on the wind-driven cliff, had lemon-coloured gables and a garden filled with withered hydrangeas. Wrestling her bags from the car, Katya signed in at the desk, watched by a small, pale woman in a fraying chenille sweater. Then, with relief, she went upstairs and shut the door behind her. She could still hear Julian's voice, lecturing on, and Lily's muttered replies, but they were staying in a room downstairs, well out of earshot, and slowly the sounds faded.

Later, Katya walked down into the town through the October twilight. She had crept through the hallway of the guesthouse and shut the door quietly behind her, in case Lily and Julian overheard and wanted to go with her. She felt a twinge of guilt, but stifled it.

Whitby was crawling with Goths: strolling through the narrow streets in spite of the chill and the rainy air. Anubis Dusk and the Deadmen were playing at the Spa, and Katya slipped into the back after handing over a fiver. And then she was lost for the next hour and twenty minutes, in the shadow-play of music and light.

Coming out, still dazed, into the rain, she had a moment of intense loneliness, just long enough to enjoy, because then she looked up and the others were there. The others, and Damian, thin and nervy and possibly about to become her boyfriend, Katya thought with a rush of hope.

The rest of the evening was snatched up into gossip and chips and pints of snakebite in a nearby pub. Katya was initially too happy to notice what the place was called, but when closing time saw them out on the street once more, she glanced upward and saw that the name of the pub was *The Herring Catch*. Jess' remark floated back into memory and she smiled.

"Walk you back?" Damian asked, and she nodded,

overcome with sudden shyness. They set off up the hill together. Halfway up, reminding herself that she was eighteen now, a grown woman, she reached out and took his hand. It was both cold and clammy; Katya did not mind. They did not say very much. At the door of the guesthouse, he kissed her, rather clumsily, and then he was gone. Slowly, Katya made her way through dripping hydrangeas and up the stairs to her room. She was just easing off her boots when there was a sharp tap at the door.

"It's me," Julian's voice said. He sounded younger and strained. "Is Lily with you?"

"Isn't she with you?" Katya did not want to let him in. She wanted to sit down on the bed and think about Damian.

"No. Can I come in?"

Katya stood in indecision for a moment, then opened the door. Julian seemed very pale, but admittedly it was hard to tell.

"We went to the Disappointed gig at the Metropole. I turned round and she was gone. I've been looking for her ever since."

"I haven't seen her since we got here."

"Where did you go, anyway?" He sounded petulant and accusing.

Katya told him. "She'll probably be back in a bit. I wouldn't worry, honestly."

He seemed inclined to linger, but Katya was too tired. She herded him out of the door and fell into bed.

Net morning, to Katya's relief, Julian was not at breakfast. Somewhat guiltily, she ploughed her way through mushrooms and toast, and examined a flyer for the Bat Conservation Raffle, just in case one of the other residents felt the need to talk to her. No one did. She returned to her room to fetch her coat. Beyond the windows, the sky was a deep, lowering grey.

As she reached the front door, however, her mobile rang. The number shown was Julian's. Katya hesitated, then answered it.

"It's me," Julian said, without preamble. "I'm at the police station."

"Why?" Katya asked, blankly. "What have you done?"

"I haven't done anything!" He sounded rattled. The usual slight, superior drawl was absent. "They found Lily last night. She's dead."

"Dead?" Katya turned, to see her own face looking back at her from the hall mirror. In the underwater dimness of the hallway, her face looked pallid and drowned beneath the heavy make-up. She could see each one of the kohl dots around her eyes, in perfect, unnatural clarity.

"Katya? Are you there?"

"Yes?" It sounded more like a question. "What happened?" The streets had been so slippery, and in high heels... Or perhaps a car... "Was she... run over, or something?"

"She was killed."

"Someone killed her?" His voice seemed to be coming from a very long way away.

"They said I can go. I was with people all evening."

She wondered why he was telling her this, then realised that of course, he would be a suspect, if Lily had been murdered.

"Katya? Can you come to the police station? I don't want to be on my own."

She had to be strong and decisive. "Tell me where it is," she said. Her voice sounded more like a squeak.

Under the neon glow of the station reception, Julian looked even more wan than usual, and scared. He was twisting his long black scarf between his hands.

"Let's get out of here," Katya said. She took his arm and steered him through the doors.

"They might want to talk to you, too. I don't know."

"Did you give them my name?" Katya said.

"I had to." He shot her an uneasy look. "They kept asking if there was anyone else who knew Lily."

"Do they know how she died?" It seemed so unreal, to be having this conversation. It wasn't like this in books, this floating, shocky sensation.

"They said there were marks on her neck. But she hadn't been – you know."

"That means strangling," Katya said in a very small voice.

He glanced at her askance. "Or a bite."

Katya let go of his arm and stared. "A bite? From what?"

He didn't answer. They gaped at one another for a few moments, then Julian turned, abruptly, and began walking slowly down the hill.

The police called Katya once they had reached a tea shop. It was full of Goths and old ladies, mutually ignoring one another save for a few occasional remarks about the rain. Katya made Julian eat a scone. When her phone rang, she nearly dropped it.

They wanted her to come in as soon as she could.

"I can't come back with you," Julian said, staring mutinously out of the window. "I just can't cope with it."

"But I don't want to go on my own," Katya faltered. "And I waited for *you*."

"Well, sorry, but I can't handle it, okay?"

Angry and scared, she rang Damian and he said he would meet her at the station. He was waiting when she got there.

Katya had always thought that it would be rather cool to be questioned by the police, or involved in a murder, but now that it was happening it seemed merely prosaic, upsetting, and at the same time, strange. The room where they questioned her was dingy and smelled of damp dog. The policewoman was kind, not much older than Katya herself, and she took a painstakingly long time to write down the statement. There was no sense that Katya might be a suspect. They just wanted some details, that was all. Then she was allowed to go. She and Damian traipsed back up the hill to the guesthouse and sat in the lounge, drinking endless cups of tea. Katya had brought mint tea bags, since she did not like black tea, and the thin heat of it revived her a little.

That evening, she found herself determined to have a good time. She tried not to think about Lily. It was a horrible thing, but

163

some small secret voice inside her told her that Lily was hard to miss.

They met up with the others at the *Herring Catch*. It wasn't so busy this early in the evening, and they managed to get a window seat. Katya looked out across the expanse of the harbour. The lights from the high streets of the town glittered across the water, fracturing darkness. She thought she glimpsed something moving, out there toward the harbour mouth, and frowning, she craned her neck to see, but it was gone. Perhaps it had been a fishing boat, though she found it hard to believe that anyone would set out on a night like this.

All the talk was about Lily and how she had managed to choose the most appropriate day of the year to die, really. It was Hallowe'en, after all; Samhain, when the dead come back from the other world and the veil between the realms lies thin.

"It's what she would have wanted," Damian said, in wide-eyed earnest.

"Too right," Amy remarked, sourly. "A great big melo-drama."

"That's not very kind," Damian protested.

"No, but it's true." Amy glared around her. "Isn't it?" No one said anything.

The sudden tension, on top of the other events of the day, made Katya uncomfortable.

"Won't be a moment," she muttered, and rose from the table. "Where's the ladies?"

"It's out the back," Amy said, still glaring. Katya made her way through the back door of the pub and found herself in a courtyard: three bare brick walls and a fourth containing a half-open door. Through it, she glimpsed the black waters of the harbour. And again, there was movement across the water: something gliding. Something big. Katya frowned, trying to make sense of it. She could not help but think of bats. She realised that she was shivering: it was freezing, out here in the courtyard. She wrapped her lace– and-velvet arms around herself and sought refuge in the lavatory, lit by a single bulb.

She was trying to coax some water out of the tap when there was a scream from the courtyard. After a frozen moment, she gathered her wits and rushed outside. A girl was crouching in the middle of the courtyard, clutching her throat.

"God!" Katya rushed to her side. The girl was clearly one of the other participants of Goth Weekend, judging from the clothes. "Are you all right?"

"No." The girl was crying. Her hands were sticky with blood. "Something *bit* me."

Katya helped her to her feet and together they stumbled inside. The landlady took one look and phoned what Katya assumed to be a local doctor, then took charge of the injured girl. Katya made her way back to her seat. The floating sense of unreality was back. Everyone was staring.

"What happened?" Amy was shocked out of her bad temper. She put an arm around Katya and guided her into her seat.

"Something bit her," Katya said, in an unsteady echo. "In the neck."

No one said anything. Then, as though a collective decision had been discussed and made, everyone reached for their coats and bags and left the pub.

"Look, I'll see you back up the hill," Bram said.

"Yeah, okay. Thanks." She had no intention of protesting.

That night, she lay staring sleeplessly into the darkness. She thought of vampires, real ones, ones in which, she realised, she did not believe. The Goth scene was no more than role play, a veneer of dark glamour over the banality of everyday life. But what if some people had started taking it too seriously? She knew that such things happened: there were lifestyle vampires in the States, blood drinkers, people who'd had their teeth filed into fangs. She had never met one. She wondered whether Lily had. And thinking back, the person who had told her about the lifestyle vampires had been Julian...

The thunderous knock on the door brought her bolt upright in bed, heart pounding.

"Who is it?"

"It's me."

Warily, Katya opened the door to see Julian standing in the hallway. He looked dishevelled, wide-eyed. He said, "She's going to rise."

"What?"

"Lily. She's going to rise." He made an impatient gesture. "She was bitten last night, and tonight is Samhain. She's coming back. I know it."

"Julian, I don't think –"

But he was off, running down the stairs of the guesthouse. Katya hovered in the doorway, wanting desperately to go back to bed. She heard the bang of the front door. In the end, she could not just leave him. She pulled her clothes over her satin nightdress and followed.

The town was very dark and very quiet. Julian was nowhere to be seen, but as Katya reached the gate, she glimpsed him running along the edge of the cliff in the direction of the whale's jawbone. She thought: *God, if he throws himself off...* She might not like Julian much, but that was an awful thought. It was still raining, a thin cold drizzle, and the grass must be as slippery as ice.

"Julian! Wait!"

He did not look back. Katya charged across the road. The rain was getting heavier and a wind was rising, whipping salt into her face. There was a concrete path running along the cliff and she ran down it, spitting wet hair from her mouth. She could hear the crash and boil of the waves against the rocks. Ahead, she saw Julian stumble.

"Wait!" she cried again.

He struggled to his feet and ran on, but when he reached the whale's jawbone, he doubled up, leaning with one hand on the white, spined arch. Katya could feel a cramp of her own, a tight

166

stitch across her gut. The rain was driving in hard and she could barely see the edge of the cliff now. She slowed and paused, terrified of falling. Above Julian's head, at the joint of the whalebone arch, there was a kind of sparkle of darkness, something that moved and twisted in the air.

"Julian?"

She hurried forward, as quickly as she dared. It came again, darting and swift, and there were more of them now.

She reached the top of the cliff. The jawbone towered above her. She saw straight through it, into a churning mass of spray. But the cliff was high, she should not be able to see the sea – yet there were huge silver forms gleaming within it, leaping, hurtling upward in a blur of scales and teeth. There was an amoebic twist of the edge of the shoal and Julian was gone, falling back without a sound into the wall of water beyond the jawbone. A glistening shape sprang from the shoal to hang in the air before Katya's face. She looked into a cold, gleaming eye, alight with gestalt intelligence. The mouth of the great fish opened in a slow gasp to reveal razor teeth, then closed once more. With a flick of its tail the piscine form was gone, back into the mass, and the shoal shot through the jawbone and streamed down into the town. In wonder, she watched it go. On reaching the harbour it dispersed; she saw silver flickers in the streets, hunting.

At Samhain, the dead return, she thought, but there is nothing to say which dead, nor which part of the natural world, ravaged and over-plundered, might turn the tables on its predators during this one unnatural night of the year. She ran all the way back to the guesthouse and pulled the bedcovers over her head like a child.

In the morning, it was sunny and cold. There was no sign of rain. She dressed in her only pair of jeans, and a red sweater. Avoiding questions from the landlady, she paid her bill with a cheque. This time, she signed it Katy.

Who Pays

Few come through the gate these days, across the sea of night, but I still look after the boat. There has always been someone to take care of the boat; it is the way that things must be done.

I spend my days waiting by the dock, or wandering through the black mirrored halls, though never venturing beyond the Weighing Chamber. Like the boat, the Chamber is little used these days: the great canopics stand empty, their machinery silent and ringed with dust; the scales and their delicate, arcane mechanisms hang in an upset balance, one up, one down. This has always irritated me, but there is nothing I can do to alter it. The base of the scales lies more than a hundred feet above my head, gleaming bronze-black in the light of the single lamp. One day, I suppose, the lamp will finally fail and the Chamber will be plunged into darkness. I used to believe that the Hierith might return if this happened: they are known to be methodical, disliking wastefulness. But over the years I have come to realise that they may never be coming back.

The judging seats are empty now, but I remember when the Hierith used to come and sit in session: Osir, Hadeth, Ise among them. Hadeth was the worst of them: brooding, melancholy, sitting hunched in the judging seat like a scavenger. That one had never agreed with the practice of tokening: it said that it encouraged false ideas among the *amorthai*. Clearly, this was true enough, but Osir would reply that it was a convenient fiction in the absence of any real understanding, and until the *amorthai* gained a reasonable level of conceptual sophistication, the fiction was as good as any.

"Better gods than devils," Osir would add.

"Better neither," Hadeth replied. "We are functionaries,

bureaucrats: it is not our place to be regarded as divine."

"The *amorthai* will realise the truth in time."

"If they are allowed to hang onto comforting stories, they will never realise it. They will remain as First Beings. Do you not remember how you thought, before you disaccreted?"

But Osir said nothing, perhaps recalling the violent nature of that ancient disaccretion.

I was not supposed to be privy to such discussions, but by that time the Hierith had long grown used to treating me as part of the Chamber furniture. I sometimes think that they had forgotten why I was even there: it is hard to judge how the Hierith regarded time. Perhaps they thought I had always been present, perhaps they forgot that I was in their employ. I cannot say. I have visited only one other station, and that was very different. I am told that they all vary, being suited to particular sections of the *amorthai* dimensions.

One of my tasks is to keep the Chamber clean: polishing the black glass surfaces on which the canopics stand, brushing dust from the jars themselves so that they glow lapis blue in the light of the suns beyond the Night Sea. Occasionally, I go to stand before the Sea itself: my bare feet on the galaxy's lip, the spirals of dust and stars uncoiling beneath my feet. And I wonder how it all came into being, whether there was truly intelligence behind it. The Hierith, who after all hold the deepest secrets, claimed not to know. Then I turn from the crimson and gold, the harsh blue of starlight, toward the Chamber, and see myself reflected: a small dark figure against the immensity of the hall, my long, narrow head nodding as though too heavy for my neck, holding a polishing cloth.

I walk back, slowly, the tasks accomplished. But it is not enough. My family – my sister/wife, my daughter/niece -are long since gone across the Night Sea. Many centuries have passed since we all took the pilgrimage boat to Ankhur Ei and stood upon the edge of the sacrificial chasm whilst the larvac disported themselves below. It seems like a different life and, indeed, there are those who would say that this is so. But whenever I look out across the Night Sea, I am grateful: that my family have gone before me, on to a new life and a new time.

This was truth when I wrote it, but today a passenger came.

I was engaged in polishing the embalming coils when the portal gate chimed. The sound rang down the glass corridors, reverberating from stone and synthetic alike. It startled me. I leaped back, to stand shaking on the gleaming floor as the galaxies turned slowly behind the Veil. Then I realised what the sound had been, and dropping the polishing cloth, I hastened toward the portal.

He was lying in the indentation in the middle of the portal, with the disaccretion rods slipping back into the floor. It was, I must confess, something of a relief to see that the old technology was still working. He retained his form well: a tall human, pale haired, dark skinned. He wore a black one-piece covering, halfway between a suit and a robe. I did not recognise his origins, nor his garments, but it was clear that he had been injured. The subsistentiary mechanisms covered him with flickering light, mending his wounds. The disaccretion tokens still lay upon his eyelids, their traceries glowing with their own inner light. I reached down and removed them with the glove, taking care to place them securely in the token pouch. I longed to hasten back and slot them into the oracle's maw, to hear the machinery that powered the boat whir once more into action.

Once the tokens had been taken from his eyelids, and the lacy tracing of subsistentiary modules had begun to fade from his form, he stirred. His eyes fluttered open; he looked up at me and his arm went across his face. He rolled to one side.

"Get away from me!" he cried, the words blurring as the translation archives set to work on the echo. His speech was a language from one of the human worlds.

"Please don't be alarmed," I said. "What is troubling you?"

"For a start, you're a three headed dog!"

I had forgotten that my narrow visage would be reflected in triplicate on either side of the entry portal. It had been a common mistake; in the old days, the passengers and I had often shared a good laugh about it, once they had recovered consciousness.

"I am a being like yourself," I told him, not with strict accuracy, it is true. "See? I stand upright, am humanoid, as you are. I am no monster, no supernatural fiend. I am merely a functionary, here to serve you in your time of disaccretion from the physical plane to the next uncarnation. It is a great honour. You are most welcome here, but be grateful."

"What are you talking about? Am I dead?"

This was always a tricky explanation to make, since I had never managed to grasp precisely what the passengers meant by this word. Earnestly, I sought to provide reassurance.

"You have entered the next stage of your being. You still retain your physical form; but shortly, this will change. As I have said, it is an honour. You have been selected to pass across the Night Sea to the new colonies. Do not worry. You will suffer no pain – disaccretion and embalming are simple enough procedures when the correct processes are applied, and then what remains of you – your essence – will be placed in the boat and sent forth. We have up-to-the minute equipment here." Again, not strictly the case, but I was keen to reassure him. The embalming machinery, when last used, had exhibited a distressing clank that I had been unable to trace.

He huddled against the wall, shaking.

"I am dead. And this is Hell."

"You'll have to forgive me," I told him. "There are many concepts with which I am not really familiar. I –"

"Where are the others?"

"The others? I'm afraid you are the only one to come through the portal in recent times."

"Then perhaps they are alive!" He rose to his feet and began to move about jerkily, stumbling on the smooth floor of the chamber.

"Who do you mean?"

"The others, the cleric-warriors. I am a linguist, travelling on the world of Meth to examine their languages. The convoy was attacked, by cold-men from the mountains. The last thing I remember was going down beneath the wheels... There was a great weight, then pain. But if the others are alive –" He glanced about him, agitated.

"There is no one except yourself. Who put the tokens on your eyelids?"

"What tokens? The Methai have a custom of putting coins on the eyes of the dead – it is ancient, a practice of old Earth, where I come from. There was one of their priests in the closed van with the youngsters – perhaps it was he, believing me to be slain. I do not know." He looked down at his chest, which was heaving, and his face filled with dismay.

I put a gentle hand on his arm but he jerked away.

"Don't be afraid. You will be disaccreted, that is all."

"What does that mean?"

"You will be placed in an embalming canopic. Your physical form will be kept as a record. Your *ka* – the part of you that is unsubstantial – will be put on the boat and travel on to the new colony."

"What 'new colony'?"

Patiently, I said, "A long time ago a race named the Hierith became weary of the division inherent in the mortal form – the difference between the conscious mind, the physical body and the seed, known as the *ka*. They resolved to purge mortal species of this division and so they journeyed among the worlds, granting folk the technology to make the journey here to the gate-station and undergo the necessary processes for disaccretion. Detached from flesh, the person is then enabled to travel on to the new colonies, to the system of Yblis."

He was staring at me in horror. "So you bring people here. Then you kill them and send their ghosts into the void?"

"I am not certain what you mean by some of these terms. It

173

is a great service that the Hierith have provided for the mortal races." I spoke with a fervour that I truly felt. I did not tell him how pleased I was to see a new passenger, to note that the millennia of work put in by the Hierith to assist the lesser species had not entirely gone in vain and was still being used.

The tokens had been widely employed, but gradually the stream of folk coming through the gate had become a trickle, then no more. Osir claimed that they had lost their understanding of their borrowed technology, that they were using it incorrectly, upon folk whose physical form had already started to decay: I do not know if this was true.

"Come," I said, as reassuringly as I could. "It is time for embalming."

The passenger was staring at me, aghast.

"Oh no," he said, simply. He dodged past me. I reached for him with the holding hook, but I was out of practice and he was too quick for me. Next moment, he was running down the passage and out of sight.

I pursued him, but when I reached the Weighing Chamber, there was no sign of him. I prowled around the canopics, listening intently, but heard nothing. It was as though he had vanished.

"Come out!" I cried. "I only want to help you!"

But there was no reply. I was beginning to think that I had imagined him, conjured him forth from boredom and need. Methodically, I searched the rest of the station, seeking my passenger in the subsidiary rooms that the Hierith had used as their own quarters. I had not ventured into this part of the station for many years: the rooms were thick with a kind of sticky dust. A few vestigial remnants of the Hierith remained: Osir's judging hat, crowned with the serpent, sat forlornly on a shelf. And I wondered again why they had never come back, whether the station had been an experiment, now abandoned, or whether they had transgressed in some way and been recalled. That was the problem with being a mere functionary, but then, the Hierith had termed themselves functionaries, too. Perhaps they had simply been recalled and an explanation never given to them.

The passenger was not there. I searched the rest of the station, even checking the boat itself. Its black, glassy walls reflected no sign of movement: the navigation banks hummed when I touched them, like long lost music. The sound comforted me, though I could not have said why. At last, I gave up and went back to the Weighing Chamber, where I crouched before the Veil and looked out onto the Night Sea. When I had first come to the station, Presences used to move across the vast expanse, that were themselves too huge to be seen properly: striding, gliding, my mind refusing to comprehend them. I once summoned the courage to ask Ise if they were what the passengers called 'gods'. Ise replied that she did not know, but that in her private opinion, such phenomena were merely the thoughts of the universe as it conversed with itself. I asked then if these presences might be termed dreams, for the passengers had often spoken about the curious state they called sleep, which I did not suffer from and did not understand. Ise replied, in kindly enough fashion, that perhaps this could be so. But then, Ise was kind: it had been Ise who had searched for the disaccreted physical elements of Osir after his encounter with the Seti, and pieced them back together again. She often laughed about this, saying that this had been when they were young and foolish, and did not comprehend the nature of things.

"Had I known that it would not be worth the effort, I would not have bothered," Ise said, smiling. "For Osir was waiting for me at the station all the while."

This was another station of which Ise spoke, and another gate-keeper. But I digress. Sometimes it comforts me to speak of those of whom I have been fond, though I could not tell you why.

I searched for the passenger for the rest of that day, but I could not find him. It perturbed me, that there might be some corner of the station unknown even to myself. The station possessed no alarms, no means of tracing an individual. I could not recall such a thing ever happening before.

Eventually I abandoned the search and trudged about my daily chores. I took polishing equipment to the Weighing Chamber and began once more to burnish the surface of the first of the great canopics, methodically rubbing until it gleamed and shone. It was as well that I did so, for had the dust remained, I should not have seen my missing passenger creeping up behind me with his fist raised to strike.

I whirled around, but he was already sprawling on the floor. The glassy surface itself had betrayed him, but it betrayed me, also. He scythed about and knocked my feet from under me. Within moments, we were wrestling on the lip of the Veil, stars wheeling beneath us.

"Listen to me!" he was shouting. "You have to listen to me!"

He grasped the polishing cloth and forced it between my jaws. I was amazed by his strength, but then, although I was the larger being, I had never been a warrior and my physical powers were largely untested. Choking, suffocating, I signalled my surrender. At once, he released me. We sat, gasping, on the edge.

"It is all written down," he said, when he had regained his breath.

"Written? What do you mean? What is written?"

"The hieroglyphs on the travelling canopics. Do you not know what they mean?"

"They are numerals, nothing more."

"They are an ancient language of Earth, and the sigils of the dead! Have you never opened one of those jars, to see what it may contain?"

Puzzled, I answered, "But I know what they contain. Mortal remains."

"And the *ka* goes on – I know what you believe. But the lists at the base of the canopics – they contain details of species, of dissection. Do you not understand what this means?"

I gazed at him. He reached out, grasped me by the

functionary's collar and shook me.

"There is no colony! The dead are dead. They stop here. They do not travel on to some better place."

Of course, he was mad. I had to be both cunning and careful.

"What you say is of interest," I told him, cautiously. Then, I had an idea. "Perhaps there is more information on the boat itself. Maybe we should look."

He nodded, at once. "Good idea. I can prove it to you, I am sure. And then you can send me back."

"Back?"

"To Meth. Or even Earth, perhaps?" His eyes were bright.

"Perhaps. We will see."

The boat possessed a disaccretion device of its own, for in the old days, Ise and Osir had occasionally taken it to certain of the worlds, I do not know why. Perhaps there were places that were inaccessible to the tokens. Once the passenger was within the confines of the boat, I planned to shut him into the device and turn it on. The physical remains would then be dealt with automatically – I could put them into a canopic once the dust had settled – and the *ka* would then be liberated, to be taken to its rightful place in the boat and dispatched. This seemed a simple and effective plan.

I led him to the boat, being careful not to turn my back upon him. He said, "How long have you been here, anyway? You spoke of the 'Hierith'. Are there any of them left?"

"I do not know," I told him. "Nor could I tell you how long I have been here. It is many, many years since the Hierith last came to the station, and so a great number of the old customs have gone – there is no judgement now, for example. And I have been here longer yet."

He stared at me and I thought his flat visage displayed dismay. He said, "But – do they pay you? What benefit do you get from all this?"

"My family were among the first to travel the Night Sea," I

177

said. "My sister/wife, my daughter/niece. It was a great honour."

"They killed your family?"

"My family were disaccreted, yes."

He was still staring. "Do you miss them?"

"Of course. But I like to think of them in Yblis, living the disembodied life that was so kindly granted to them. It is only a very few of the disaccreted of this level who have been sent across the Night Sea."

"What happens to everyone else?"

"Their *kas* merge with the greater realms, like water drops into the sea. They do not retain any memories of who or what they were."

"And do you have proof of all this?"

"The Hierith have said so, and that is enough."

"You have believed this for too long, my jackal-headed friend," the passenger said. "Your belief has become atrophied, as hard as stone."

I glanced at him, puzzled. "But it is the truth."

He nodded. "Very well. Show me the boat, then."

We stepped across the fragile arm of the docking mechanism and into the boat itself. The boat is not large – even a full cargo of *kas* does not take up a great deal of space – and curved at both ends. I hoped he would make some comment on its beauty: the black-and-gold gleam of its sides, the glassy floor, but he said nothing. He paused by the consignment of canopics that were kept just inside the door

"You first."

I went backwards through the door of the boat, to keep an eye on him, but he did nothing.

"Are there any inscriptions? Any data banks?"

"The inscriptions are all here." I gestured toward the scroll of symbols that adorned one wall. He stepped forward eagerly and began to read, but he kept glancing at me as he did so. I waited to make my move.

"These are instructions for the operation of the boat, I

think. It is a long-dead language and not easy to read."

"Does it speak of the Hierith?" I was aware of an agitation, deep within. I could not help thinking of them both: my sister/wife and daughter/niece. I had prepared the canopics for them myself. And the Hierith themselves had said that they were functionaries... But my belief in them could not be swayed for long, I found. I thought with determination of Yblis, and grew calm.

The passenger, still keeping a close watch on me, had come to the end of the scroll and was wandering over to the instrument banks.

"Wait," I said. "I would not touch anything –"

– but with a last glance at me, he ran a hand down the instrument panel and grasped the docking release. The boat is designed for immediate power-up. It roared backwards to the end of the docking bay, throwing me to one side, then lurched. The canopics came loose and rolled across the deck. The passenger, too, was fighting for balance. The boat righted itself. I hauled myself upright, but I was too slow. He seized one of the heavy canopics and lifted it. The last thing I remember seeing was my own reflection in the polished jar, coming down upon my head.

The boat is moving. I can feel it, a comforting vibration throughout myself. I cannot see, nor can I hear. The vibration, too, is beginning to fade. I cannot feel my limbs. There is a sensation of lightness, of a lack of weight. I have tried calling out, but I do not seem to have a voice any longer. I think of the Hierith, of their promises. My belief, however, is still weighty, like a stone. I think of Yblis, as all else falls away.

Ikiryoh

Every evening, the kappa would lead the child down the steps of the water-temple to the edges of the lake. The child seemed to like it there, although since she so rarely spoke it was difficult to tell. But it was one of the few times that the child went with the kappa willingly, without the fits of silent shaking or whimpering hysteria, and the kappa took this for a good sign.

On the final step, where the water lapped against the worn stone, the child would stand staring across the lake until the kappa gently drew her down to sit on what remained of the wall. Then they would both watch the slow ripple of the water, disturbed only by the occasional wake left by carp, or one of the big turtles that lived in the depths and only occasionally surfaced. Legend said that they could speak. Sometimes the kappa thought that she detected the glitter of intelligence in a turtle's ebony eye, behind the sour-plum bloom, and she wondered where they had come from, whether they had always been here in the lake, indigenous beasts from early times, or whether they resulted from some later experimentation and had been introduced. If the kappa had been here alone, she might have tried to capture one of the turtles, but she had her hands full enough with the child, the *ikiryoh*.

Now, she looked at the child. The *ikiryoh* sat very_still, face set and closed as though a shadow had fallen across it. She looked like any other human child, the kappa thought: fine brows over dark, slanted eyes, a straight fall of black hair. It was hard to assess her age: perhaps seven or eight, but her growth had probably been hothoused.

When the palace women had brought the child to the kappa, all these questions had been asked, but the kappa had received no satisfactory answers.

"Does she have a name?" the kappa had asked the women. One had merely stared, face flat and blank, suggesting concentration upon some inner programming rather than the scene before her. The other woman, the kappa thought, had a touch of the tiger: a yellow sunlit gaze, unnatural height, a faint stripe to the skin. A typical bodyguard. The kappa took care to keep her manner appropriately subservient.

"She has no name." the tiger-woman said. "She is *ikiryoh*." The word was a growl.

"I am afraid I am very stupid," the kappa said humbly. "I do not know what that means."

"It does not matter," the tiger-woman said. "Look after her, as best you can. You will be paid. You used to be a guardian of children, did you not?"

"Yes, for the one who was -" the kappa hesitated.

"The goddess before I-Nami," the tiger-woman said. "It is all right. You may speak her name. She died in honour."

"I was the court nurse," the kappa said, eyes downward. She did not want the tiger-woman to glimpse the thought like a carp in a pool: *yes, if honour requires that someone should have you poisoned.* "I took care of the growing bags for the goddess Than Geng."

"And one of the goddess Than Geng's children was, of course, I-Nami. Now, the goddess remembers you, and is grateful."

She had me sent here, in the purge after Than Geng's death. I was lucky she did not have me killed. Why then is she asking me to guard her own child? – the kappa wondered, but did not say.

"And this child *is* the goddess I-Nami's?" she queried, just to make sure.

"She is *ikiryoh*," the tiger-woman said. Faced with such truculent conversational circularity, the kappa asked no more questions.

In the days that followed it was impossible not to see that the child was disturbed. Silent for much of the time, the *ikiryoh* was prone to fits, unlike anything the kappa had seen: back-arching episodes in which the child would shout fragmented streams of invective, curses relating to disease and disfigurement, the worst words of all. At other times, she would crouch shuddering in a corner of the temple, eyes wide with horror, staring at nothing. The kappa had learned that attempts at reassurance only made matters worse, resulting in bites and scratches that left little impression upon the kappa's thick skin, but a substantial impression upon her mind. Now, she left the child alone when the fits came and only watched from a dismayed distance, to make sure no lasting harm befell her.

The sun had sunk down behind the creeper trees, but the air was still warm, heavy and humid following the afternoon downpour. Mosquitoes hummed across the water and the kappa's long tongue flickered out to spear them before they could alight on the child's delicate skin. The kappa rose and her reflection shimmered in the green water, a squat toad-being. Obediently, the child rose, too, and reached out to clasp the kappa's webbed hand awkwardly in her own. Together, they climbed the steps to the water-temple.

Next morning, the child was inconsolable. Ignoring the bed of matting and soft woven blankets, she lay on the floor with her face turned to the wall, her mouth open in a soundless wail. The kappa watched, alarmed. Experience had taught her not to interfere, but the child remained in this position for so long, quite rigid, that at last the kappa grew alarmed and switched on the antiscribe to speak to the palace.

It was not the tiger-woman who answered, but the other one, the modified person. The kappa told her what was happening.

"You have no reason to concern yourself," the woman said, serene. "This is to be expected."

"But the child is in grave distress. If there's something that can be done -" The kappa wrung her thick fingers.

"There is nothing. It is normal. She is *ikiryoh*."

"But what should I do?"

"Ignore it." The woman glanced over her shoulder at a sudden commotion. The kappa heard explosions.

"Dear heaven. What's happening?"

The woman looked at her as though the kappa were mad. "Just firecrackers. It's the first day of the new moon."

Out at the water-temple, the kappa often did not bother to keep track of the time, and so she had forgotten that they had now passed into Rain Month and the festival to commemorate I-Nami's Ascension into goddess-hood. Today would be the first day of the festival: it was due to last another three.

"I have matters to attend to," the woman said. "I suggest you do the same."

The screen of the antiscribe faded to black. The kappa went in search of the child and to her immense relief, found her sitting up against the wall, hugging her knees to her chest.

"Are you feeling better?" the kappa asked.

"I'm bored!"

Like any young child. Bored was good, the kappa decided.

"Let's make noodles," she said, and then, because the *ikiryoh's* face was still shadowed, "And then maybe we will go to the festival. How would you like that?"

The kappa was supposed to be confined to the water-temple, but there were no guards or fences, and she was aware of a sudden longing for a change of scene. There would be so many people in the city, and a child and a kappa were so commonplace as to be invisible. They could hitch a ride on a farm cart.

The child's face lit up. "I would like that! When can we go?"

"First, we will have something to eat," the kappa said.

They reached the city toward late afternoon, bouncing in on the back of a truck with great round wheels. The child's eyes grew wide when she saw it.

"That is a strange thing!" she said.

"Surely you have seen such vehicles before?" the kappa asked, puzzled. After all, the child had presumably grown up in the palace and she had been brought to the water-temple in one of I-Nami's skimmers. A vegetable truck seemed ordinary enough.

The child's face crumpled. "I can't remember."

"Well, don't worry about it," the kappa said quickly, not wanting to disquiet her. She held tightly to the child's hand and peered over the top of the boxes, filled with melons and radishes and peppers, with which they were surrounded. The road was a congested mass of hooting trucks, crammed with people, and the occasional private vehicle. The hot air was thick with a gritty dust and the kappa was thankful for the wide hat that she wore, which kept the worst of the heat from her sparsely-haired head. The child sneezed.

"Is it much further?"

"I hope not." But they were turning into Sui-Pla street now, not too far from the centre. The kappa could hear the snap of firecrackers and the rhythmic beat of ceremonial drums, churning out prayers in praise of the goddess.

Goddess, indeed, the kappa thought. *She is only a woman, grown in a bag like everyone else.* These deified elevations did little good in the end. At first, after each new coup, the folk all believed, not so much from credulity as weariness, the hope that now things might finally become better. But each time it was the same: the woman behind the mask would begin to show through, the feet turn to clay, and the masses would grow angry as yet another ruler succumbed to self-indulgence, or apathy, or cruelty. Than Geng had been one of the former sort, and had at least retained the status quo. The kappa knew little about I-Nami, what manner of ruler she had become. She knew better than to ask, because that might betray her as someone who doubted, and for some rulers, that was enough.

Certainly, the people were putting on a good show. Still clasping the *ikiryoh's* hand, the kappa stepped down from the back of the truck and into the crowd.

"Hold tight," she told the child. "Don't let go. I don't want to lose you among all these people."

They watched as a long dragon pranced by, followed by lions made from red-and-gold sparkles. Slippered feet showed beneath. As the sky darkened into aquamarine, fireworks were let off, exploding like stars against the deep-water colour of the heavens. The kappa and the child walked past stalls selling all manner of things: candy and circuit components and dried fruit and flowers. The kappa bought a small, sticky box of candy for the child, who ate it in pleasurable silence. It was good, the kappa thought, to see her behaving so normally, like an ordinary little girl. She pulled gently at the *ikiryoh's* hand.

"Is everything all right?"

The child nodded, then frowned. "What's that?"

The firecracker explosions were doubling in intensity. There was a sudden cacophony of sound. A squadron of tiger-women raced around the corner, wearing ceremonial harness, heads adorned with tall golden hats. They carried pikes, with which they pretended to attack the crowd. The child let out a short, sharp, shriek.

"Hush," the kappa said, her heart sinking. "See? It's only a game."

The child shrank back against her skirts, hand hovering near her mouth. "I don't like them. They are so big."

"It means the goddess is coming," a young woman standing next to the kappa said. She sounded superior: a city girl enlightening the ignorant peasants. "The procession has already begun up in the main square – from there, it will come down here and into Nang Ong."

"Do you hear that?" the kappa said, tightening her grip a little on the child's hand. "You're going to see the goddess." She bent to whisper into the child's ear. "Do you remember her?"

"The goddess?" the child whispered. "What is that?"

The kappa frowned. The tiger-woman had specifically said that the child had come from I-Nami. Maybe the *ikiryoh* simply did not remember. But it raised further questions about her upbringing and age. "You will soon see," the kappa said, feeling inadequate.

Through the taller humans, the kappa could get a glimpse of the start of the procession: a lion-dog, prancing. At first she thought the *kylin* was composed of another set of costumed people, but then she realised that it was real. Its eyes rolled golden, the red tongue lolled. The child's grip on the kappa's hand became painful.

"Don't worry," the kappa said. "See – it is on its lead." The *kylin's* handlers strained behind it, laughing and shouting out to one another as the beast tossed its magnificent mane. Behind them came a litter, borne on the shoulders of four beings that were a little like kappa, but larger and more imposing. Heavy, glossy shells covered their backs. They lumbered along, smiling beneath their load. All of these beings – the turtle bearers, the *kylin*, the tiger-women – all were the genetic property of the palace itself. No one else could breed or own such folk, unlike the commonplace kappa, who had been bred so long ago for menial work in the factories and paddy fields of Malay. The kappa remembered people like this from her own days in the palace; remembered, too, what was said to have taken place behind closed doors for the amusement of the goddess Than Geng and her guests. The kappa had not mourned Than Geng in the slightest, but the rumours were that I-Nami had become worse.

"Our goddess is coming," someone said softly behind her. There were murmurs of approval and excitement. *If only they knew*, thought the kappa. But it had always been the way of things. She looked up at the litter, which was drawing close. The curtains were drawn, and now I-Nami herself was leaning out, waving to the crowd. Her oval face had been painted in the traditional manner: bands of iridescent colour gliding across her skin. Her great dark eyes glowed, outlined in gold. The very air around her seemed perfumed and sparkling. Surprised, the kappa took a step back. Illusion and holographics, nothing more, and yet she had never seen anyone who so resembled a goddess.

"She is so beautiful!" a woman said beside the kappa, clapping her hands in excitement.

"Yes, she is," the kappa said, frowning.

"And she has been so good to us."

"Really?" The kappa turned, seeking the knowing smile, the cynical turn of the mouth, but the woman seemed quite sincere.

"Of course! Now, it is safe to walk the streets at night. She came to my tenement building and walked up the stairs to see it for herself, then ordered the canal to be cleaned. Now we have fresh water and power again. And there is food distribution on every corner for the poor, from subsidised farms. Things are so much better now."

There were murmurs of agreement from the crowd. Startled, the kappa looked down at the child. "Did you hear that?"

But the child's face was a mask of fainting horror. Her eyes had disappeared, rolling back into her head until only a blue-white line was showing, and a thin line of spittle hung from her mouth. She sagged in the kappa's grip. Without hesitating, the kappa picked her up and shoved through the crowd to an empty bench. She laid the child along it. The *ikiryoh* seemed barely conscious, muttering and cursing beneath her breath.

"What's wrong?" the kappa cried, but the child did not reply. The kappa shuffled back to the crowd as fast as she could and tapped a woman on the shoulder. "I need a healer, a doctor – someone!"

The woman turned. "Why, what is wrong?"

"My ward is ill. Maybe the heat – I don't know."

"There is a clinic around the corner in Geng Street, but I should think they'll all be out watching the procession," the woman said.

The kappa thought so too, but she had little choice. What if the child was dying? She picked the *ikiryoh* up and carried her through a gap in the buildings to Geng Street, which was little more than a collection of shacks. I-Nami's benign influence had clearly not penetrated here – or perhaps it had, because the street pump was working and when the kappa touched the button, a stream of clear water gushed out. She wetted the corner of her skirt and dabbed at the child's face, then carried her on to the blue star that signified the clinic.

At first, she thought that the woman had been right and there was no one there. But as she stood peering through the door, she saw a figure in the back regions. She rapped on the glass. A stout woman in red-patterned cloth came forward. Her face soured as she set eyes on the kappa.

"We're closed!"

"Please!" the kappa cried. She gestured to the child in her arms. Muttering, the woman unlocked the door.

"You'd better bring her in. Put her there, on the couch. You're lucky I was here. I forgot my flower petals, to throw. What's wrong with her?"

"I don't know. She suffers from these fits – I don't know what they are."

"You're her nurse?"

"Yes."

"She's very pale," the woman said. "Poor little thing. The healer's out – we have three here, all of them are traditional practitioners. I'll try and call them." She pressed her earlobe between finger and thumb. The kappa saw the gleam of green. "Ma Shen Shi? It's me, I'm at the clinic. There's a little girl who fainted. Can you come?"

It seemed the answer was positive. "Sit down," the woman said. "He'll be here in a bit."

The kappa waited, watching the child. She was whimpering and moaning, fists tightly clenched.

"Has she ever been this bad before?" the woman asked.

"No. She has – episodes." The kappa glanced up as the door opened. A small, elderly man came in, wearing the healer's red, with a cigarette in his mouth.

"Go and throw flower petals," he said to the woman. "And

you, kappa – do something useful with yourself. Make tea. I will examine her."

The woman melted into the warm darkness outside. Reluctantly, the kappa found a kettle behind the reception desk and switched it on, then put balls of tea into three cups, watching the healer as she did so. He examined the child's eyes and ears, stretched out her tongue, knocked sharply on her knees and elbows and checked her pulse. Then he simply sat, with eyes closed and one hand stretched out over the child's prone form. The kappa longed to ask what he was doing, but did not dare interrupt. The child began to pant, a terrible dog-like rasping. Then she howled, until it became a fading wail. The healer opened his eyes.

"What is wrong with her?" the kappa whispered. "Do you know?"

"I know exactly what is wrong with her," the healer said. He came over to the desk and sipped at the tea. "If you can put it like that. She is *ikiryoh*. A fine specimen of the art, too."

The kappa stared at him. "That's what they told me, when they brought her to me. But what is an *ikiryoh?*"

"An *ikiryoh* is something from legend, from the old stories they used to tell in the Nippon archipelago. It is a spirit."

"That little girl is no spirit. She's flesh and blood. She bleeds, she pees, she breathes."

"I am not saying that the legends are literally true," the healer said. "I have only ever seen one *ikiryoh* before, and that was male. In the old tales, they were formed from malice, from ill-will – the projected darkness of the unconscious."

"And now?"

"And now they are children grown to take on the worst aspects of someone – a clone, to carry the dark elements of the self. Emotions, concepts, feelings are extracted from the original and inserted into a blank host. That little girl is the worst of someone else. Do you have any idea who?"

The kappa hesitated. She knew very well who had done such

a thing: I-Nami, the glowing, golden goddess, who had sent her small fractured self to live in the swamp. Then she thought of the woman in the crowd: of the clean canal, the tenement with lights and fresh water. It was enough to make her say, slowly, "No. I do not know."

"Well. It must be someone very wealthy – perhaps they had it done for a favoured child. I've heard of such things. The kid gets into drugs or drink, or there's some genetic damage psychologically, so they have a clone grown to take on that part of the child and send it away. It costs a fortune. It would have been called black magic, once. Now it is black science."

"But what is happening to her now?"

"My guess is that she came close to the original, whose feelings she hosts, and that it's put her under strain. I don't understand quite how these things work – it's very advanced neuro-psychiatry, and as I say, it's rare."

"And the future?"

"I can't tell you that it's a happy one. She is all damage, you see. She has no real emotions of her own, little free will, probably not a great deal of intelligence. You are looking at a person who will grow up to be immensely troubled, who may even harbour appetites and desires that will prove destructive to others."

"And what would happen if the *ikiryoh* died?"

"I'm not sure," the healer said. "but in the legends, if anything happens to the *ikiryoh*, the stored emotions pass back to the person who once possessed them."

"Even if the person does not know that the *ikiryoh* is dead?"

"Even then."

He and the kappa stared at one another.

"I think," the kappa said at last, "That I had better take her home."

Next day, toward evening, the kappa once more sat on the steps of the water-temple. The child was sleeping within. It was very quiet, with only the hum of cicadas in the leaves and the ripple of fish or turtle. The kappa tried to grasp the future: the long years of fits and nightmares, the daily anguish. And once the *ikiryoh* reached puberty, what then? The kappa had seen too much of a goddess' dark desires, back at the temple: desires that seemed to embody a taste for the pain of others. How different had Than Geng been from I-Nami? And yet, I-Nami now was restoring the fortunes of her people: thousands of them...

The kappa looked up at a sudden sound. The child was making her way down the steps to the water. For a moment, the kappa thought: *it would be easy, if I must.* The child's frail limbs, powerless against the thick-muscled arms of the kappa; a few minutes to hold her under the water... It would be quick. And better do it now, while the *ikiryoh* was still a child, than face a struggle with an angry, vicious human adult. But what if the *ikiryoh* had a chance after all, could be remade, not through the aid of an arcane science, but simply through the love of the only family she had?

The kappa stared at the child and thought of murder, and of the goddess' glowing face, and then she sighed.

"Come," she said. "Sit by me," and together in stillness they watched the shadowy golden carp, half-seen beneath the surface of the lake.

The Age of Ice

I was in a tea house in Caud, head bent over the little antiscribe, when the flayed warrior first appeared. Everyone stared at her for a moment, tea glasses suspended halfway to gaping mouths, eyes wide, and then it was as though time began again. The shocked glances slid away, conversation resumed about normal subjects: the depth of last night's snow, the day's horoscopes, the prospect of war. I stared at the data unscrolling across the screen of the 'scribe and tried to pretend that nothing was happening.

That wasn't easy. I was alone in Caud, knowing no one, trying to be unobtrusive. The tea house was close to one of the main gates of the city and was thus filled with travellers, mostly from the Martian north, but some from the more southerly parts of the Crater Plain. I saw no one who looked as though they might be from Winterstrike. I had taken pains to disguise myself: bleaching my hair to the paleness of Caud, lightening my skin a shade or so with pigmentation pills. I had also been careful to come anonymously to the city, travelling in a rented vehicle across the Crater Plain at night, hiring a room in a slum tenement and staying away from any haunt-locks and blacklight devices that might scan my soul engrams and reveal me for what I was: Hestia Memar, a woman of Winterstrike, an enemy.

But now the warrior was here, sitting down in the empty seat opposite mine.

She moved stiffly beneath the confines of her rust-red armour: I could see the interplay of muscles, stripped of the covering of skin. The flesh looked old and dry, as though the warrior had spent a long time out in the cold. The armour that she wore was antique, covered with symbols that I did not recognise. I thought that she must be from the very long ago: the

Rune Memory Wars, perhaps, or the Age of Children, thousands of years before our own Age of Ice. Her eyes were the wan green of winter ice, staring at me from the ruin of her face. Her mouth moved, but no sound emerged. I knew better than to speak to her. I turned away. People were shooting covert glances at me, no doubt wondering why I had been singled out. The attention drawn to me by this red, raw ghost was the last thing I wanted.

I rose, abruptly, and went through the door without looking back. At the end of the street I risked a glance over my shoulder, fearing that the thing had followed me, but the only folk to be seen were a few hooded figures hurrying home before curfew. Hastening around the corner, I jumped onto a crowded rider that was heading in the direction of my slum. I resolved not to return to the tea house: it was too great a risk.

Thus far, I had been successful in staying out of sight. My days were spent in the ruin of the great library of Caud, hunting through what was left of the archives. I was not the only looter, sidling through the fire-blackened racks under the shattered shell of the roof, but we left one another alone and the Matriarchy of Caud had bigger problems to deal with. Their scissor-women did not come to the ruins. Even so, I was as careful as possible, heading out in the dead hours of the afternoon and returning well before twilight and the fall of curfew.

My thoughts dwelt on the warrior as the rider trundled along. I did not know who she was, what she might represent, nor why she had chosen to manifest herself to me. I tried to tell myself that it was an unfortunate coincidence, nothing more. Caud was full of ghosts these days.

Halfway along Gauze Street the rider broke down, spilling passengers out in a discontented mass. We had to wait for the next available service and the schedule was disrupted. I was near the back of the crowd and though I pushed and shoved, I could not get on the next vehicle and had to wait for the one after that. I stood shivering in the snow for almost an hour, looking up at the shuttered faces of the weedwood mansions that lined Gauze

Street. Many of them were derelict, or filled with squatters. I saw the gleam of a lamp within one of them: it looked deceptively welcoming.

By the time I reached the tenement, varying my route through the filthy alleys in case of pursuit, it was close to the curfew gong. I hurried up the grimy stairs and triple-bolted the steel door behind me. I half-expected the flayed warrior to be waiting for me – sitting on the pallet bed, perhaps – but there was no one there. The power was off again, so I lit the lamp and sat down at the antiscribe, hoping that the battery had enough juice left to sustain a call to Winterstrike.

Gennera's voice crackled into the air.

"Anything?"

"No, not yet. I'm still looking." I did not want to tell her about the warrior.

"You have to find it," Gennera said. "The situation's degenerating, we're on the brink. The Caud Matriarchy is out of control."

"You're telling me. The city's a mess. Public transport's breaking down, there are scissor-women everywhere. They seek distraction, to blame all their problems on us rather than on their own incompetence. The news-views whip up the population, night after night."

"And that's why we must have a deterrent."

"If one is to be found, it will be found in the library. What's left of it."

"They've delivered an ultimatum. You saw?"

"I saw. I have three days." There was a growing pressure in my head and I massaged my temples as I spoke into the 'scribe. I felt a tingling on the back of my neck, as though something was watching me. "I have to go. The battery's running down." It could have been true.

"Call me when you can. And be careful." The 'scribe sizzled into closure.

I put a pan of dried noodles over the lamp to warm up, then

drew out the results of the day's research: the documents that were too dirty or damaged to be scanned into the 'scribe. There was little of use. Schematics for ships that had ceased to fly a hundred years before, maps of mines that had long since caved in, old philosophical rants that could have been either empirical or theoretical, impossible to say which. I could find nothing resembling the fragile rumour that had sent me here: the story of a weapon.

"If we had such a weapon, it would be enough," Gennera said. "We'd never need to use it. It would be sufficient that we had it, to keep our enemies in check."

Ordinarily, this would have created disagreement throughout the Matriarchy, purely for the sake of it: Gennera was thought to be too popular in Winterstrike, and was therefore resented. But the situation had become desperate. A conclave was held in secret and they contacted me within the hour.

"They remember what you did in Tharsis," Gennera said. "You were trained out on the Plains, and these days you are the only soul-speaker in Winterstrike. You have a reputation for accomplishing the impossible."

"Tharsis was not impossible, by definition. Only hard. And that was thirteen years ago, Gennera. I'm not as young as I once was, soul-speaker or not."

"That should benefit you all the more," Gennera said.

"If I meet a man-remnant on the Plain, maybe not. My fighting skills aren't what they were."

Even over the 'scribe, I could tell that she was smiling. "You'd probably end up selling it something, Hestia."

But I had not come to Caud to sell, and I was running out of time.

In the morning I returned to the library. I had to dodge down a series of alleyways to avoid a squadron of scissor-women bearing heavy weaponry. These morning patrols were becoming increasingly frequent and there were few people on the streets. I hid in the shadows, waiting until they had passed by.

Occasionally, there was the whirring roar of insect craft overhead: Caud was preparing for war. My words to Gennera rose up and choked me.

I reached the ruin of the library much later than I had hoped. The remains of the blasted roof arched up over the twisted remains of the foremost stacks. The ground was littered with books, still in their round casings. It was like walking along the shores of the Small Sea, when the sand-clams crawl out onto the beaches to mate. I could not help wondering whether the information I sought was even now crunching beneath my boot heel, but these books were surely too recent. If there had been anything among them, the matriarchy of Caud would be making use of it.

No one knew precisely who had attacked the library. The matriarchy blamed Winterstrike, which was absurd. My government had far too great a respect for information. Paranoid talk among the tenements suggested that it had been men-remnants from the mountains, an equally ridiculous claim. Awts and hyenae fought with bone clubs and rocks, not missiles. The most probable explanation was that insurgents had been responsible: Caud had been cracking down on political dissent over the last few years, and this was the likely result. I suspected that the library had not been the primary target. If you studied a map, the matriarchy buildings were on the same trajectory and I was of the opinion that the missile had simply fallen short. But I volunteered this view to no one. I spoke to no one, after all.

Even though this was not my city, I could not stem a sense of loss whenever I laid eyes on the library. Caud, like Winterstrike, Tharsis and the other cities of the Plain, went back thousands of years, and the library was said to contain data scrolls from very early days. And all that information had been obliterated in a single night. It was a loss for us all, not just for Caud.

I made my way as carefully as I could through the wreckage and into the archives. No one else was there and it struck me that this might be a bad sign, a result of the increased presence of the scissor-women on the streets. I began to sift through fire-hazed data scrolls, running the scanning antenna of the 'scribe up each one. In the early days, they had written bottom-to-top and left-to-right, but somewhere around the Age of Children this had changed. I was not sure how much difference, if any, this would make to the antiscribe's pattern-recognition capabilities: hopefully, little enough. I tried to keep an ear out for any interference, but gradually I became absorbed in what I was doing and the world around me receded.

The sound penetrated my consciousness like a beetle in the wall: an insect clicking. Instantly, my awareness snapped back. I was crouched behind one of the stacks, a filmy fragment of documentation in my hand, and there were two scissor-women only a few feet away.

It was impossible to tell if they had seen me, or if they were communicating. Among themselves the scissor-women do not use speech, but converse by means of the patterns of holographic wounds that play across their flesh and armour, a language that is impossible for any not of their ranks to comprehend. I could see the images flickering up and down their legs through the gaps in the stack – raw scratches and gaping mouths, mimicking injuries too severe not to be fatal, fading into scars and then blankness in endless permutation. There was a cold wind across my skin and involuntarily I shivered, causing the scattered documents to rustle. The play of wounds became more agitated. Alarmed, I looked up, to see the ghost of the flayed warrior beckoning at the end of the stack. I hesitated for a moment, weighing ghastliness, then rose silently and crept toward it, setting the 'scribe to closure as I did so in case of scanning devices.

The ghost led me along a further row, into the shadows. The scissor-women presumably conversed and finally left, heading into the eastern wing of the library. I turned to the ghost to give thanks but it had disappeared.

I debated whether to leave, but the situation was too urgent.

Keeping a watch out for the scissor-women, I collected an assortment of documents, switching on the antiscribe at infrequent intervals to avoid detection. There was no sign of the ghost. Eventually, the sky above the ruined shell grew darker and I had to leave. I stowed the handfuls of documentation away in my coat. They rustled like dried leaves. Then I returned to the tenement, to examine them more closely.

The knock on the door came in the early hours of the morning. I sat up in bed, heart pounding. No one good ever knocks at that time of night. The window led nowhere, and in any case was bolted shut behind a grille. I switched on the antiscribe and broadcasted the emergency code, just as there was a flash of ire-palm from the door lock and the door fell forward, blasted off its hinges. The room filled with acrid smoke. I held little hope of fighting my way out, but I swept one of the scissor-women off her feet and tackled the next. But the razor-edged scissors were at my throat within a second and I knew she would not hesitate to kill me. Wounds flickered across her face in a hideous display of silent communication.

"I'll come quietly," I said. I raised my hands.

They said nothing, but picked up the antiscribe and stashed it into a hold-all, then made a thorough search of the room. The woman who held the scissors at my throat looked into my face all the while, unblinking. At last, she gestured. "Come." Her voice was harsh and guttural. I wondered how often she actually spoke. They bound my wrists and led me, stumbling, down the stairs.

As we left the tenement and stepped out into the icy night, I saw the flayed warrior standing in the shadows. The scissor-woman who held the chain at my wrists shoved me forward.

"What are you looking at?"

"Nothing."

She grunted and pushed me on, but as they took me toward the vehicle I stole a glance back and saw that the warrior was gone. It occurred to me that it might have led the scissor-women to me, but then in the library it had helped me, or had seemed to.

I did not understand why it should do either.

They took me to the Mote, the matriarchy's own prison rather than the city catacombs. That suggested they might have identified me, if not as Hestia Memar, then as a citizen of Winterstrike. That they suspected me of something major was evident by the location, and the immediacy and nature of the questioning. Even Caud had abandoned the art of direct torture, but they had other means of persuasion: haunt noise, and drugs. They tried the haunt-tech on me first.

"You will be placed in this room," the doctor on duty explained to me. She sounded quite matter-of-fact. "The blacklight matrix covers the walls. There is no way out. When you are ready to come out, which will be soon, squeeze this alarm." She handed me a small black cube and the scissor-women pushed me through the door.

The Matriarchies keep a tight hold on the more esoteric uses of haunt-tech, but everyone will be familiar with the everyday manifestations: the locks and soul-scans, the weir-wards that guard so many public buildings and private mansions. This chamber was like a magnified version of those wards, conjuring spirits from the psycho-geographical strata of the city's consciousness, bringing them out of the walls and up through the floor. I saw dreadful things: a woman with thorns that pierced every inch of her flesh, a procession of bloated drowned children, vulpen and awts from the high hills with glistening eyes and splinter teeth. But the matriarchy of Caud was accustomed to breaking peasants. I had grown up in a weir-warded house, filled with things that swam through the air of my chamber at night, and I was used to the nauseous burn that accompanied their presence, the sick shiver of the skin. This was worse, but it was only a question of degree. Fighting the urge to vomit, I knelt in a corner, in a meditational control posture, placed the alarm cube in front of me, and looked only at it.

After an hour, my keepers evidently grew tired of waiting. The blacklight matrix sizzled off with a fierce electric odour, like the air after a thunderstorm. From the corner of my eye, I saw things wink out of sight. I was taken from the chamber and placed in a cell. Next, they tried the drugs.

From their point of view, this may have been more successful. I cannot say, since I remember little of what I may or may not have said. Haunt-tech is supposed to terrify the credulous into speaking the truth. The mind-drugs of the matriarchies are crude and bludgeon one into confession, but those confessions are all too frequently unreliable, built on fantasies conjured from the depths of the psyche. When the drug that they had given me began to ebb, I found my captors staring at me, their expressions unreadable. Two were clearly matriarchy personnel, wearing the jade-and-black of Caud. The scissor-women hovered by the door.

"Put her under," one of the matriarchs said. She sounded disgusted. I started to protest, more for the form of it than anything else, and they touched a sleep-pen to my throat. The room fell away around me.

When I came round again, everything was quiet and the lights had been dimmed. I rose, stiffly. My wrists were still bound and the chains had chafed the skin into a raw burn. I peered through the little window set into the door of the cell. One of the scissor-women sat outside. Her armour, and the few inches of exposed skin, were silent, but her eyes were open. She was awake, but not speaking. I could not see if there was anyone else in the room. I knocked on the window. I needed her undivided attention for a few minutes and the only way I could think of to do that was by making a full confession.

"I'll talk," I said, when she came across. "But only to you."

I could see indecision in her face. It was not really a question of how intelligent the scissor-women were; they operated on agendas that were partially programmed, and partly opaque to the rest of us. Her voice came though the grille.

"I am activating the antiscribe," she said. "Speak."

"My name is Aletheria Tole. I am from Tharsis. I assumed

another identity, which was implanted. I came here looking for my sister, who married a woman from Caud many years ago..."

I continued to speak, taking care to modulate the rhythm of my voice so that it became semi-hypnotic. The scissor-women had programming to avoid mind control, but this was something else entirely. As I spoke, I looked into her pale eyes and glimpsed her soul. I drew it out, as I had been taught so many years before on the Plains. It span across the air between us, a darkling glitter. The door was no barrier. I opened my mouth and sucked it in. It lay in my cheek like a lump of ice.

The scissor-woman's face grew slack and blank.

"Step away from the door," I said. She did so. I bent my head to the haunt-lock and released her soul. It fled into the lock, tracing its engrams through the circuit mechanisms, grateful to be free of me. The door swung open; I stepped through and struck the scissor-woman at the base of the skull. She crumpled without a sound. My own 'scribe was sitting on a shelf: they would have copied its contents. I snatched it up and ran through the maze of corridors.

Discovery was soon made. I heard a cry behind me, feet drumming on the ceiling above. I headed downward, reasoning that in these old buildings the best chance of escape lay in the catacombs below. When I reached what I judged to be the lowest level, I ducked into a chamber and flicked on the antiscribe as I ran. I could not get a signal for Winterstrike. But then, turning the corner, I found the flayed warrior before me.

"Where, then?" I said aloud, not expecting her to respond, but once more the ghost beckoned. I followed the rust-red figure through the labyrinth, through tunnels swimming with unknown forms: women with the heads of coyu and aspiths, creatures that might have been men. I ignored the weir-wards, being careful not to touch them. Sometimes the warrior grew faint before me and I was beginning to suspect why this should be. I could hear no signs of pursuit, but that did not mean that none were following. The scissor-women could be deadly in their silence.

At last we came to a door and the warrior halted. In experiment, I closed down the 'scribe and she was no longer there. I put it on again, and she reappeared.

"You're no ghost," I said. She was speaking. There was still no sound, but the words flickered across the screen.

She was not conversing. The words were lists of archived data, skeins of information. I had not been entirely correct. She was not the ghost of a warrior. She was the ghost of the library, the animated form of the cached archives that we had believed to be destroyed, and that the Caud matriarchy, in their ignorance, had not bothered to find.

I knew what I had to do. I hastened past the warrior and pushed open the door, kicking and shoving until the ancient hinges gave way. I stumbled out into a frosty courtyard, before a frozen fountain. The mansion before me was dark, but something shrieked out of the shadows: a weir-form, activated, of a woman with long teeth and trailing hair. She shot past my shoulder and disappeared. I heard an alarm sounding inside the house. But the 'scribe had a broadcasting signal again and that was all that mattered. I called through to Winterstrike, where it was already mid-morning, and downloaded everything into the matriarchy's data store, along with a message. The warrior's face did not change as she slowly vanished. When she was completely gone, I shut down the 'scribe and waited.

The scissor-women were not long in finding me. They took me back to Mote, to a different, smaller cell. I was not interrogated again. Later next day, a stiff-faced cleric appeared in the doorway and announced that I was free to go.

I walked out into a cold afternoon to find the streets thronging with people. There would be no war. The matriarchy had, in its wisdom, come to a compromise and averted catastrophe, or so the women of Caud said, mouths twisting with the sourness of disbelief.

I wondered what Gennera had discovered in the library archives that had given Winterstrike such a lever. It would most likely be a weapon, and I wondered also what I had done, in handing the power over one city across to another, even though it was my own. For governments can change, so swiftly, and benevolence never lasts. But I caught a rider through the gates of Caud all the same, heading for one of the way station towns of the Plain and then for Winterstrike, and did not look behind me.

La Malcontenta

The coldest night of the year in Winterstrike is always the night on which the festival of Ombre is held, or Wintervale if you are young and disdain the older dialects. The Matriarchy knows how to predict these things, how to read the subtle signatures in snowdrift and the length of icicles, the messages formed by the freezing of the breath upon the air, the crackling of the icy skin of the great canals.

In the centre of Winterstrike, Mars' first city, in the middle of the meteorite crater that gave the city its name, stands the fortress: a mass of vitrified stone as white as a bone and as red as a still-beating heart. And at the top of the fortress, at the summit of a tower so high that from it one can see out across the basalt walls to the dim, shimmering slopes of Olympus, stands a woman. She is surrounded by four glass windows. She stands before a brazier and beneath a bell. She wears triple gloves: a thin membrane of weedworm silk, then the tanned leather of vulpen skin, then a pair of woollen mittens knitted by a grandmother. In spite of this, and the spitting coals of the brazier, her hands are still cold.

When the day freezes below a certain point, and the signs are relayed to her, she turns, nearly overthrowing the brazier in her haste, and rushes to the windows. She throws them open, letting in a great gust of cold air which makes the coals crackle, then strikes the bell three times. It rings out, fracturing the cold. The woman, Essegui Harn, runs down the stairs to the warm depths of the tower before the echo has even died. One by one, the coals hiss into silence as the bell note fades.

This takes place shortly before dawn, in the blue light before the sun rises. All Winterstrike can hear the bell, except one woman, and except for one woman, all Winterstrike answers. Women throw aside their counterpanes, rush to the basins to wash, and then, still dressed in their night clothes, run upstairs to the attics of mansions, or to the cellars of community shacks, to retrieve costumes forgotten over the course of the previous year, all six hundred and eighty seven days of it. From chest and boxes, they pull masks depicting the creatures of the Age of Children and the Lost Epoch, the long muzzles of cenulae, or the narrow, lovely faces of demotheas and gaezelles. They try them on, laughing at one another, then falling silent as they stand, masked and suddenly foolish above the thick night-dresses.

By Second Hour the robes, too, have been retrieved: confections of lace and metal, leather and stiffened velvet, scarlet and ochre and amethyst, sea-green and indigo and pearl. Above these, the masks no longer appear silly or sinister, but natural and full of grace. Then the women of Winterstrike set them aside and, frantic throughout the short day, they make sweet dumplings and fire-cakes for the night ahead, impatient for the fall of twilight.

Essegui Harn is in equal haste, rushing back to the mansion of Calmaretto, which lies not far from the fortress. Essegui hurries through the streets, pounding snow into ice under her boots and churning it into powder against the swing of the hem of her heavy coat. She is thinking of the festival, of her friend Vanity, whom she is planning to seduce tonight (or be seduced by, even more hopefully). She is trying not to think about her sister.

When she reaches Calmaretto, she does not hesitate but puts her eye to the haunt-lock. The scanner glows with blacklight, an eldritch sparkle, as the lock reads her soul-engrams through the hollow of her eye. The door opens. Essegui steps through into a maelstrom of festivity.

Both her mothers are shouting at one another, at the servants, and then, without even a pause for breath, at Essegui.

"...there is not enough sugar and only a little haemomon? Why didn't you order more?"

"...Canteley's best dress has a stain, she refuses to wear it even under her robes..."

"And I cannot find the tracing-spoon anywhere!"

Essegui ignores all this. She says, "What about Shorn?"

The silence is immediate and tense. Her mothers stare at Essegui, then at one another. "What about her?"

"You know very well," Essegui says. "You have to let her out. Tonight."

Upstairs, in the windowless heart of Calmaretto, Shorn Harn sits. Her birth name is Leretui, but she has been told that this is no longer her name: she has been shorn of it, and this is the only name she can take from now on. She does not know that it is the day of Ombre, because the sound of the bell rung by her sister has not penetrated the walls of Calmaretto. Nor can she witness the haste and bustle outside in the street, the skaters skimming up and down Canal-the-Less, because she has not been permitted to set foot in a room with windows. She is allowed books, but not writing materials or an antiscribe, in case she finds a way to send a message.

At this thought, Shorn's mouth gives a derisory twist. There would be little point in composing a message, since the one for whom it would be intended cannot read, cannot be taught to read, and is unlikely ever to communicate with someone who can. But Shorn's mothers will not countenance even the slightest possibility that a message might be sent, and thus Shorn is no longer allowed to see her little sister Canteley, as Canteley is young enough to view the scenario as romantic, no matter how many times her mothers have impressed upon her that Shorn is both transgressor and pervert. She is occasionally permitted to see Essegui, since Essegui is of a similar mind to the mothers.

Essegui usually only puts her head around the door once a week, though Shorn finds it difficult to estimate the days. Even so, she is surprised when the door hisses open and Essegui strides through, snow falling in flakes from her outdoor coat.

"Essegui?" Shorn turns her head away and does not rise. "What is it?"

"Ombre falls today. I've told our mothers that you are to be allowed out, when the gongs ring for dusk."

Shorn's mouth falls open and she stares at her sister.

"Out? And they agreed?"

"They hate it. I hate it. But it is your last remaining legal right, ancient custom, and we have no choice."

Shorn says, slowly and disbelieving, "I am to be allowed out? In the mask-and-gown?"

Essegui leans forward, hands on either arm of the chair, and speaks clearly. "Understand this. If you use the mask-and-gown as a cover to flee the city, our mothers will go to the Matriarchy and ask for a squadron of scissor-women to hunt you down. The city will, of course, be closed from dusk onward, and they will know if anyone tries to leave. Or if any*thing* tries to get in."

"I will not try to leave," Shorn whispers. "Where would I go?"

"To that which brought you to this plight?"

Shorn gives a small, hard laugh like a bark. "Where indeed?"

"To the mountains, in winter? You would die of cold before you got half way across the Demnotian Plain. And the mountains, what then? Men-remnants would tear you to pieces and devour you before you had a chance to find it." Essegui grimaces. "Perhaps it would even be one of them. I've heard that all women look alike to them."

Shorn lowers her gaze. There is a moment's silence. "I have told you that I will not try."

"There is a mask waiting for you," Essegui says. She turns on her heel and is gone through the door, leaving it open behind her.

Shorn does not leave the chamber immediately, but stares at the open door. She has been dreaming about this day ever since the evening of her imprisonment, which she now knew to be six hundred and eighty seven days ago. Ombre then was like every other festival, a chance for fun and celebration, supposedly. She had thought no further than a possible assignation with Celvani Morel, an old college friend, recently detached. She wonders now whether she hoped that it would fill the emptiness within. She did not expect to meet what stepped from under the bridge of the Curve.

The open door seems as dark, but Shorn, once more, hesitates for only a moment before stepping through.

The mask is one that she remembers from her childhood: the round, bland face of a crater cat. It is a child's mask: for the last few years, Canteley has been wearing it. Now, however, it is the only one left in the box. Shorn pulls the gown - a muted red-and-black brocade - over her head and then, slowly, puts the mask on. The cat beams at her from the mirror; she looks like a too-tall child, no longer the woman they call the Malcontent. She twitches aside the fold of a sash, but the box is empty. There is no sign of the other mask: the long, narrow head, the colour of polished bone, mosaiced with cracks and fractures. She searches through the draperies, but there is no sign of it. She tells herself that she feels nothing.

As she turns to go downstairs, a gaezelle dances in through the door.

"Tui, is that you? Is it?" The gaezelle flings her arms around Shorn and holds on tight.

"It's me. But don't call me Tui." It sounds as though she's spitting. "That's not my name any more." Canteley has grown over the last months: she is almost as tall as her sister now. Shorn has nearly forgotten the piercing quality of her voice, shrill as a water-whistle. She feels as though an icy mass has lodged deep in her own throat.

"Are you coming? Essegui said our mothers are letting you out for the Wintervale. Is it true? You should run away, Tui. You should try to find it."

"I won't be going away, Canteley," Shorn says, but as she says this she feels as though the walls are falling in on her and she knows that she lies.

"Is it true what they say, that the vulpen steal your soul? That they entrance you so that you can't think of anything else?"

"No, that isn't true," Shorn says, but she is not really sure any more. She takes her sister's hand and leads her through the door.

I won't be going away. But better the devouring mountains than the windowless room. Better the quick, clean cold. She should never have let them shut her in, but she had been too dazed, with grief and bewilderment and incomprehension. Now, she has had time to think, to become as clear as ice. "Canteley, I'll talk to you later." She gives her sister a swift hug. "Go downstairs. I'll join you in a minute." Once her sister has gone, she takes a pair of skates from the wall and stands looking down at the long, curved blades. Then, holding the skates by their laces, she follows her sister down the stairs.

They are all standing in the doorway, staring upward: Essegui, Canteley, and her mothers. It is a moment before Shorn is able to differentiate between the three adults. Essegui stands a little apart, legs braced beneath the intricate folds of the gown. Of the mothers, Thera is the shorter, and so it must be Alleghetta behind the demothea's mask. Shorn looks from one to the other before coming down the stairs. No one speaks. As Shorn reaches the last step, her mothers turn and push open the double doors that lead out onto the steps to the street. Winter fills the hallway. The gongs ring out in the twilight, filling the street and the house with sound. It seems very loud to Shorn, used as she is to the silence of the windowless room.

The mothers grasp Canteley firmly by each hand and pull her through the doors, so decisively that Essegui is the only one who has time to turn back, a flickering twitch of her head in the direction of Shorn. She is wearing a cenulae's mask: a pointed, fragile countenance, painted in green. She will, Shorn thinks, see only the bland cat face smiling back at her. Then Shorn herself runs across the black-and-white mosaic of the hall floor, through the scents of snow and fire-cake and polish, out through the doors and into the street. Then she is standing uncertainly in the snow.

Canal-the-Less, on which Calmaretto stands, is frozen solid and filled with skaters bearing snow-lamps. They weave in and out of one another with insect-skill. Shorn, breath coming in short gasps in the unaccustomed cold, is tempted to take the round cat's face from her own and fling it into the drifts, but she does not. She ties on the skates with trembling hands and lowers herself over the bank of the canal onto the ice. Then she is off, winging down Canal-the-Less toward the culvert that leads to the Grand Channel.

The Channel itself is thronged with skaters, milling about before the start of the procession. Shorn twists this way and that, keeping to the side of the Channel at first, then moving out to where the light is less certain. The great houses that line the Channel are blazing with snow-lamps and torches, mirrored in the ice so that Shorn glides across a glassy, shimmering expanse. She is heading for the Curve and the labyrinth of canals that lead to the Great North Gate.

Behind her, the crowds of skaters fall away. Ahead, she can see a mass of red gowns, the start of the procession, led by the Matriarchs. Her mothers, not quite so elevated, will be just behind, amid their peers. A pair of scissor-women speed by, the raw mouths of holographic wounds displayed across the surface of their armour. They are unmasked. Their faces are as sharp as their blades and Shorn flinches behind the cat-face, until she realises that to them, she is nothing more than a tall child, and not the malcontent of Calmaretto. But she watches them go all the same, then slinks from the Grand Channel and into the maze.

It is much quieter here. The houses along the waterways have already emptied and there are only a few stray women lingering beneath the lamps or the bridges, waiting no doubt for assignations. Shorn keeps her masked head down, speeding toward the Great North Gate.

As she reaches the turning into the stretch of water known as the Curve, she hears a shout go up from the direction of the Grand Channel: the procession has begun. Shorn skates on, though the long months of forced inactivity have taken their toll. Her calves and thighs are burning. She does not want to think of what will befall her if she makes it past the North Gate: the vast expanse of snow covered plain, the mountains beyond. She hopes only that it will be a swift death and that she makes it out of Winterstrike. It will be her revenge on the city and on Calmaretto, to die beyond its walls. She knows that this is not rational, but she left reason by a canal bank, a year before.

In summer, the Curve is lined with cafes and weedwood trees, black-branched, with the yellow flower balls spilling pollen into the water until it lies there as heavy as oil, perfuming the air with a subtle musk. Now, the cafes are cold and closed - all the trade will have moved down the Channel for the night.

Shorn's heart pounds with exertion and memory. It was here, a year ago, on this stretch of the Curve just beyond the thin-arched bridge, that something - some*one*, Shorn corrects herself, angry at her use of Essegui's term - drifted from the darkness to stand as still as snow.

Shorn glides to an involuntary halt. She has replayed this scene over and over in her mind: the figure outlined against the black wall and pale ice, the head swivelling to meet her gaze, the frame shifting under the layers of robes and the sudden realisation that this was not just another reveller, but real: the mild dark eyes set deep in the hollow of the skull, the ivory barbs of its teeth. What she had taken for the curve of skate blades beneath the hem of the robe was its feet. One of the Changed, a vulpen, from the mountains: the genetically-altered remnant of a man.

They are said to tear women limb from limb in vengeance for old woes: the phasing out of the male by Matriarchal geneticists. But this one merely looked at her, and held out its hand. She should have fled; instead, she took its two long fingers in her own. It led her along the Curve, skating alongside with human skill. Nothing else befell her. The vulpen gazed at her as they moved, blinking its mild eyes. It said: *I have been waiting for one such as you.*

And as it spoke, they turned the bend and ran into a squadron of scissor-women. Unlike Shorn, the warriors took only a moment to realise what was before them. They skated forward, scissors snicking. One of them seized Shorn, who cried "No!" and struggled in the warrior's grasp. The other three surrounded the vulpen, who suddenly was springing upward to land on the bank on all fours, blade-feet skidding, casting the disguising robes away to reveal a pale, narrow form, the vertebral tail whipping around. Its erection resembled a bone, and when they saw it, the scissor-women shrieked in fury. Then it was gone, into the snowy night.

They took Shorn back to Calmaretto, on a chain, and sat with her until her family returned, laughing and exhausted, at dawn.

Remembering this now, Shorn is moved to wonder if any of it was even real. It seems long ago and far away - and then it is as though she has stepped sideways into her own memory, for the figure of a vulpen once more skates from beneath the arch. It holds out its hands, but does not attempt to touch her. Shorn skates with it, back along the Curve in a haze and a dream, flying through the winter dark, until they are once more out onto the Grand Channel.

The procession has passed. Circling, whirling, Shorn and the vulpen dance out to the middle of the Grand Channel and now Shorn is beginning to understand that this is, after all, nothing more than a woman in a mask, just as she is. Thoughts of flight, of dying beyond Winterstrike, skate through her head and are gone, leaving loss and yearning behind.

She lets the woman in the vulpen's mask lead her back to Calmaretto. As they step through the door, the woman pulls off the mask and Shorn sees that it is Essegui.

"I could not let you go," Essegui says, and Shorn, exhausted, merely nods. Essegui leads her up the stairs to the windowless room and closes the door behind her.

In the morning, Winterstrike is quiet. Mask ribbons litter the ice and the snow is trodden into filth. Essegui, waking late, head ringing with explanations that she will have to make to Vanity, goes to the heart of the house and opens the door of the windowless room.

Shorn sits where her sister left her, upright, the cat's face beaming.

"Shorn?" her sister says. There is no reply. Essegui goes haltingly forward and touches her sister's shoulder, thinking that she sleeps. But the brocade gown is stiff and unyielding, moulded in the form of a woman's figure. Essegui tugs at the cat's mask, but it will not budge. It remains fixed, staring sightlessly across the windowless room, and slowly Essegui steps away, and once more closes the door.

Dusking

You don't go dusking when the moon is dark, everyone knows that. Too many things waiting in the shadows, coming to cling to your little light, coming to bite and snap. But when the moon is full or new, that's the time to go dusking, and that's when you find all the young couples out in the parks and on the downs, dressed in their Sunday best, carrying candles in a globe of glass, chasing spirits under the oaks.

We didn't have such practices in Greenwich. It was too close to the river, but when my parents died and I was sent to live with my aunt in Blackheath, it was all the rage. One could buy trapping globes in the local market, in a variety of pleasing colours. I remember that in the year of my arrival at my aunt's, blue was very popular, but then it was during the summer and, as the winter months drew on, the blue globes were put away and red ones took their place.

I was too young to go dusking, my aunt said. I begged and pleaded, but she refused, and took to locking me into my bedchamber early in the evening, with a supply of improving literature. My aunt was devout, fervently so, and she disapproved of dusking; it encouraged the Others, she said, and that would never do. Perhaps if I had been a boy, she might have relented.

Of course, the more she disapproved, the wilder I was to do it. I used to lean out of my bedchamber window holding a jam jar with a candle in it, but I never attracted anything larger than moths. Only on one evening, close to the autumn equinox, did something else come close to the flame. I saw it only briefly, because it veered away into the eaves on seeing my face reflected in the light: a small, pinched thing, the colour of dead leaves, with little sharp hands. I often wonder what would have happened if I had caught it. You're supposed to let them go before sun up, but plenty of people forget and find a leaf in the bottom of the globe in the morning, or a bundle of twigs.

This was not the only restriction placed upon me by my aunt. Education was frowned upon for girls, particularly any interest in the developing sciences. I was not to go to school, although she instructed me in Bible study at home. I was to learn needlework, and the basics of the culinary arts, and household management. I grew increasingly frustrated and resentful as the years went by. I remembered what I had learned in my mother's house, but I could do nothing with it: I had no books here, nor access to them.

We only spoke of it once. I'd burned a saucepan, again. My aunt had not been pleased.

"If you would just apply yourself to the *rudiments*, Emily…"

I drew myself up. She was a short woman, and I was no taller, but I pretended. "I," I said, "have *Skills*."

My aunt looked me straight in the eye. "I," she replied, "am well aware of *that*."

Clearly, they were yet another thing of which she Disapproved.

And so I began to plan. I despised the necessity; I found it tedious. But until I had reached my majority, this sort of thing had to be done.

Then, when I was sixteen and some way along with the planning, a young man asked me to go dusking. Chaperoned, of course, by a friend of my aunt's – the young man's mother, in fact. Tristan was eminently suitable, my aunt considered, and I think she was hoping that he might offer for my hand and thus relieve her of the responsibility of myself. I was young, true, but better marry me off as soon as possible and find a more appropriate channel for those skills I'd mentioned… There was a belief in those days that marriage, and all that it involved, could tame those wild and latent powers that occasionally afflict young ladies.

This wasn't a view to which I subscribed. But I thought I should like to go dusking, all the same.

Green globes were very fashionable that year. Autumn was sliding into winter; it was the end of October, and London had been touched by the edge of the great storms that had swept so much of the north and west. Wild nights, with the trees lashing against the windowpane, a thundering rain whipping even the sluggish Thames into a froth. I loved this weather, but it was clear that Tristan was deeply concerned about my health, that I might catch a chill.

"You are so *pale*, Emily. Perhaps it's just that your hair is so very fair. But I worry that this weather will be too much for you."

I could have told him not to fuss. I'd never had a day's sickness in my life – not a genuine one, anyway. Instead I lowered my eyelashes and murmured that it was so kind of him to worry. I could feel my aunt watching me as I did so; it's sad not to be trusted by your closest relatives. My plans took a little hop forward.

"But I have a thick velvet cloak, Tristan, proof against even the harshest winter chill. And I think I – I should like to venture out. If you're quite sure it's safe, of course."

Thoughts of the woods, of bone and blood and the wet black earth, the wind ripping through the trees... I didn't know where these thoughts came from, but they were occupying more and more of my attention. I felt my aunt's gaze sharpen like an icicle, as though she could see into those thoughts. I lowered my head still further and gave a little *I-must-be-brave* sigh. Tristan put out a hand, as if to reassure me, but the icicle stare drove it back.

"I shall be quite sure to protect you, Emily. I – I'd do anything." He must have realised that he'd said enough after that, because he grew pink and flustered. I gazed at him admiringly, all the same, and the pinkness increased.

"I should be pleased to see you settled, Emily," my aunt said, stiffly, after Tristan had made a blushing farewell. I'd learned by now not to argue: it was pointless. Instead, I nodded.

"I should like a home of my own, aunty." This was quite true; I didn't have to say what sort of a home, after all.

"Perhaps I have misjudged you," my aunt said, but not as if she believed it. "I suppose you can't help your ancestry, after all. Your poor mother –"

I dabbed my eyes with a lace handkerchief and I think that helped, too.

Upstairs, in my own chamber, I looked out at the weather hissing across the heath, the gaslights blurring the city beyond.

Her mother disappeared, you know.

It broke her father's heart. He didn't live long after that.

I'd heard the whole story by now, delivered in whispers behind the parlour door. My aunt had never liked my mother, I think, but I didn't know why. To my knowledge, Mama had never actually *done* anything; she was always so meek and mild, at least until she'd vanished. Run off with another man, my aunt had said, still whispering. But I didn't think that was true. And she'd looked so much like me: the same fair hair, almost white, the green eyes that in some lights took on an odd chestnut tinge, nearly red... My mother had been considered a beauty.

It is my opinion that my aunt thought that I had not shown enough proper mourning at my father's death. Children are frequently stupid; I should have made a better job of it.

Now, there was Tristan to weave into my plan. But what I'd failed to consider was that events cause plans to change.

It rained solidly for a week, which meant that there could be no dusking anyway. The Others won't come out when it pours, although I've seen them at the edges of storms, flashing in the darkness like snatches of lightning. On the Friday night, however, the sky cleared over and a thin new moon rose over the heath. Tristan, still flustered, presented himself and his mother on the doorstep at six thirty in the evening. I waited modestly on the stairs, clutching my new globe, a stout jade-green affair with a night-light smouldering within.

"Emily? I thought, if you wish – ah, I see you are ready. It is quite chilly, we must make sure you wrap up warmly."

My cloak was green as well: the colour of forests, with an enveloping hood. I liked the hood, it hid my expression at convenient moments. And I liked the greenness, which matched my eyes.

Watched like a hawk by my aunt, and with Tristan's mother promising to have me safely back by nine, I took his arm demurely and we stepped out onto the heath.

The lights of London blazed beyond and I felt a small strange pull, not to the lights themselves, I thought, but to what they represented: the freedom. If I had my way, I'd run across the heath and down towards the river, and then through the streets and beyond to the northern moors, and – I blinked.

"Are you quite well, Emily?"

"I think so, Tristan. You're right, it *is* a little chilly."

We weren't the only ones dusking. There were a number of other young couples out with globes, and on the other side of the heath a girl was chasing a little light with a series of squeaks, like an excited mouse. I sighed. I supposed I'd have to behave in a similar fashion.

Tristan's mother parked herself on a nearby seat in a complacent manner. I was slightly surprised by this: I would not have thought that I was all that marvellous a catch, but then I reminded myself that the only side of me she'd seen had been the frail young thing, and besides, there was that rather large inheritance to consider... My aunt might not have seen fit to point out my shortcomings, hoping as she was to be rid of me.

However, it seemed to please Tristan. He showed me how to hold my globe up to the new moon, how to weave it to and fro in order to attract anything that might be passing. I held my tongue and allowed myself to be shown; it was possible, I found, to treat it as a game.

"And don't be frightened if anything comes close," he instructed me. "They're just – just like butterflies, or moths."

Moths with sharp teeth, I thought, and pointed fingers, but I giggled in a vacuous manner and this seemed to please Tristan. I held up my globe, moving it clumsily from side to side, and permitted Tristan to show me once more how it was done. He looked at me as my gloved hands were enclosed fleetingly within his own, but I affected not to notice. Over on the bench, his mother coughed, and he dropped his hands. I saw the new moon through the green wall of the globe, distorted, like a smile on its side.

And then something huge and bee-like was humming and buzzing around me.

"Look!" Tristan cried, very excited. "You've nearly got one!"

Of course I had. I'd known that I would, without knowing how I knew. Earth and roots and something whistling up into the darkness – the thing that was hissing around the globe sheared away, towards shadow.

"Nearly!" Tristan was still marvelling. "I don't think I've ever seen one so close before."

I'd taken careful note, of the long wings, as lacy as a dragonfly's, the pinched countenance, human-like, but only as far as mockery, the sharp nails, black as thorns.

"There's another one!" Together, briefly united in purpose, we ran across the heath, ignoring the sudden agitation of shuffling from Tristan's mother on the bench. Scarves fluttering, my cloak billowing out behind me, our flying feet – but we could not catch it. The little light, dim as blue gas, danced and tumbled ahead of us, heading for the fringe of woodland that lay at the far end of the heath. It disappeared within and Tristan caught my arm as I was about to go after it.

"Better not go in there, please, Emily," he pleaded and I pretended to be breathless.

"Why, I hardly knew where I was," I told him. It was almost true, but not for the reason he supposed.

"I must not tire you out. Perhaps we should go back…"

I did not want to go back. I wanted to go on, into the black shadowed woods, into the city to slip along the riverside in the light of the smiling moon. But instead, reason took hold and I nodded, feigning exhaustion, and let myself droop. We walked slowly back, with Tristan talking – I think – about his studies, and parted company on the doorstep.

Later that night, I woke. I thought at first that something was tapping on the windowpane, a branch in the rising wind, but then I saw the flickering light. I got out of bed and went to the window. It was perhaps the length of my hand, scratching its nails down the glass. The moon was just visible behind, low above the city and almost swallowed by a bank of cloud.

I did not hesitate for more than a moment. I was too curious. I opened the window and let it in.

Like moths... it fluttered around the room, now high, now low, until coming to hover near my face. I did not like having it so close to me. The eyes were a dim burning gold; I looked for a sign of reason, but found none, or at least, not as we would know the word. Its mouth opened and I saw pointed teeth. It did not speak. Instead, a hand shot out. Too late, I stumbled back, but I felt the minute tear of its nail across my eye. There was a blinding pain, which lasted for a second: I think I cried out and then pressed my hand to my mouth. I did not want my aunt bursting into the room, demanding explanations.

And I could *see*, as if a little rent had been torn in the fabric of the world. The moon, again sailing through cloud but this time not coming out again, fading to a circlet of dark above the garden of the house: I knew this was my aunt's garden, because I could see the back wall, the long skeins of ivy. Someone was standing underneath the ivy, statue-still, looking out, as if carved from a block of night.

I knew I had to go to this person. Not now, but when the moon was dark, when you are not supposed to go dusking, when you might meet something you cannot catch. Nor was I to meet it here, but in the patch of woodland on the edge of Blackheath. And in the presence of it, even foretold, even half there, I bowed my head. I felt something hot and wet run down my cheek, like a

221

tear.

The rent closed and the window banged in the wind. I was left with a stinging eye and a memory of a shape in the night, and the knowledge of what it wanted.

I knew that I must choose my time carefully, that I must reel him in. The shadow was waiting. So I feigned illness, sent word to Tristan that I had caught a cold on the heath, was not feeling my best. My aunt watched me, not believing at first, but I let myself droop and drift and grow even paler, and I think she finally allowed herself to acknowledge that there was something wrong with me. It might even have been true. I stayed huddled beneath the covers, listening to the rain on the window and the wind in the trees, dreaming of forests and the endless moor, the stars above me and the world below. I did not know where these dreams came from, only that they were a part of me and, in all of them, I saw those flickering lights.

When I rose, I sat staring out of the window, at the thin sliver of an old moon. It did not look to be smiling now.

Next day, I told my aunt that I felt better. I also allowed myself to appear despondent, saying that Tristan must think me terribly foolish. I moped so successfully that my aunt eventually offered to allow me to convey a message to him, via his mother.

I asked him to meet me in the parlour. He came several minutes early, so I kept him waiting until the appointed time.

When I went downstairs I apologised as prettily as I could to Tristan. This time, his mother had not accompanied him: it seemed that she, too, was suffering from a chill.

"I'm afraid I have a dreadfully weak constitution," I murmured.

"I don't think girls should be too robust," Tristan declared. "All those women wanting to be nurses, for example – it's not ladylike."

I put a hand to my throat. "I should hate to be a nurse," I said. Well, that was true enough. "But I do feel much stronger. I was wondering if –?"

"Perhaps just a stroll?" Tristan suggested. "It is not the time for dusking, you see."

He paused expectantly, perhaps anticipating an argument, but I meekly agreed.

"If you wrap up well…" His tone was solicitous, but there was the faintest note of hectoring beneath it and I repressed a smile. So with all marriages, I thought. Father knows best. And surely that was why my mother had run.

My aunt agreed to let me go. I thought that she was probably tired of the sight of me, although she told me that she would be watching from the parlour window.

She would be watching, but would she be able to see? The sky was clear now, so a glance through a gap in the curtains told me, but I could smell the rain in the air, its promise seeping under the door and through the cracks in the windowpane, overpowering the musty potpourri scent of the parlour.

"I should not want to be too late," I faltered.

And that was true, too.

So we walked out onto the heath, Tristan and I, just as we had done a little while before, but this time I held no globe in my hand. The stars were visible across the city, a burning river that mirrored the river below, but of course there was no moon.

I took Tristan's arm, shyly, and pretended to let him guide me across the heath, but in reality, it was I who was guiding him: exclaiming over a moth, feigning interest in a dropped glove. Soon we were near the grove of trees that lay at the edge of the heath.

I could feel the presence waiting. It was very strong and the smell of iron surrounded it. At that moment, I understood why the Others are said to hate iron: it is a blasphemy to them, for it mimics the scent of blood and yet is metal, a made-thing.

A gust of wind scoured across the grass, stirring the trees. Tristan glanced away and I took the opportunity to snatch at my hat and throw it beyond the bushes.

"Oh!" I clutched my hair. "My hat! The wind caught it, how silly!"

And letting go of his arm, I dashed into the woodland.

"Emily! Come back!"

But I did not. I ran on. I do not think I could have stopped even if it had been expedient to do so; I was too consumed with the thrill of running, like a fire in my blood. I could hear him crashing through the undergrowth behind me.

"I can't find my hat!" I cried over my shoulder.

"Emily, you must come back!"

The presencewas ahead of me. I could feel it, waiting. And then the hidden moon sailed out and I could see, in the dark that the moon cast.

Someone was standing in the glade. Huge, hunched, a mass of shoulder and neck. I saw the antlers rearing up from its brow and the glitter of a golden eye. The figure stood upright, much taller than a man, and it wore a cloak of leaves. The iron smell was very strong and the ground was moist beneath my feet.

I began to speak.

"I have brought what you asked for."

But the voice wasn't mine. It drowned mine out. Very slowly, I looked around. Tristan stood behind me, holding out a green glass globe. And from the corner of my bewildered eye, I saw the horned thing step forward.

I do not know what they plan to do with me, only that they are pleased. My mother escaped, they explained to me, ran from both the human world and the Other, and that sort of thing will never do. So they have the next best; they have me, her daughter.

I should have remembered that shy girls and stammering boys might, sometimes, be motivated by the same things.

It's comfortable enough here. There is a velvet couch, a small table, rugs. Food is delivered three times a day and is always the same, sugary, and satisfying for a short while. But when I glance at my surroundings, from the corner of my eye, I see that the velvet couch is really a pile of rushes, and the rugs are leaves. The walls, however, are constant: green glass, green as the grass upon the heath, or the leaves of the forest, or a watching eye.

A Glass of Shadow

"A glass of shadow, *por favore*," I said to the hovering waiter. My Italian wasn't up to much these days: a schoolboy legacy of a handful of words. But I remembered drinking wine here in Venice for the first time, at the age of sixteen, daring under the disapproving eye of my stepmother. My aunt – my father's sister – had been the one who had bought me the wine, and she was more indulgent.

"The boy has to start somewhere, Margaret," she remarked. "Would you prefer him to be down the pub swigging scrumpy with the local yokels?"

I kept quiet. My cider-drinking days had begun rather more furtively than my wine-drinking ones, a couple of years before in a succession of garden sheds, riverbanks and friend's bedrooms in the villages of Somerset. Wine, I discovered now, was not much like cider. This tasted of summer. I said so.

"Very good," my aunt Cass said, with amused surprise. "What else can you taste?"

My stepmother's lips compressed even further, like a letterbox slamming shut.

"Flowers," I said. "It tastes like flowers. What did you say it was called?"

Cass laughed. "I didn't. It's actually a Cabernet Sauvignon, but what I asked for in the local slang was a glass of shade. They call it that because you need to keep wine in the shade."

"Not at the moment," my stepmother said with a rare flash of wryness. We looked out across the frosty expanse of St Mark's. Even at lunchtime, under the prancing footsteps of Carnival attendees, there was still a cold glitter on the old stones. Across the square, the wavering line of the opposite roof was white with a scatter of snow. I was enthralled by the masked women in their galleon dresses, the men in clasped shoes and tricorn hats, the secret faces behind the masks. I felt the wine go straight to my head in a fizzing rush. Reaching for the complimentary glass of water, I took a long, steadying sip. It was my first time abroad. My stepmother had not wanted to bring me, nor, I think, had any real wish to see her sister in law. But my aunt and my father had insisted and so here we were, in this beautiful, sinister city, with my stepmother patently failing to enjoy herself. My aunt Cass, however, was literally at home. She was an aspiring artist – actually rather an indifferent one, I realized later – who had led a rackety life across Paris, Greece and finally ended up here in Venice. She rented a small studio equipped with a lavatory and a gas ring. The studio backed onto a narrow, apparently nameless canal that, according to my aunt, was a sewer in summer.

Sitting in Florian's once more, twenty five years later, I remembered that first time with remarkable clarity. My stepmother was dead and Aunt Cass was living in Hastings on the south coast of England, also in a studio, still painting. I thought of her with affection and bewilderment. I did not know why I had come back to Venice, and carnival, only that I'd seen a cheap deal in the paper on the day my redundancy money had come through, and that Julia and I had always planned to come here at this time of year, and never had.

Now, Julia had been gone for six weeks, timing her departure with Duncan, or whatever the bastard's name was, for two days before Christmas. I hadn't spoken to her since then. My emails went unanswered, and her cellphone was switched off. I only knew that she'd gone to New York from mutual friends. Everyone said that her behaviour was appalling, that I was better off without her. Of course it didn't help. She was a bitch and I missed her.

The waiter, a tall, supercilious man with barred eyebrows and a heavy 5 o'clock shadow, eventually brought my wine. The staff of Florian's always looked to me as though they ought to be waiting on cruise ships. But as he put the wine down on the table, on its elegant silver tray, someone in the next seat caught him by his white sleeve.

"He doesn't want that," I thought the stranger said. "He wants a glass of shadow."

I looked at the interrupter. He was a dark-skinned man, perhaps in his twenties. His hair was pulled back into a mass of dreadlocks and his eyes, behind a half-mask shaped like a plague doctor's protective beak, were amber. He wore a ragged velvet coat, bundled up even in the warmth of Florian's, and on his hands were fingerless leather mittens. One cuff was hanging off.

"You speak English?" I said.

He smiled. "A little. Enough."

"The waiter brought me what I asked for," I told him. The waiter shrugged, drifting away to serve other customers.

"I know. It's what you wanted, but not what you need. Well, it is here now. Drink it. But I can show you something better."

"Oh yes?" Vaguely, I thought it might be some sort of pick-up. Perhaps money might be involved, or drugs. The stranger didn't look like a vagrant – Florian's would never have let him in through the door, for a start, but he wasn't exactly respectable, either.

"This place – it's too new for what you need," my new friend said. It was my turn to smile.

"It's been here since 1720. Says so on the menu."

A gesture of contempt. "That's what I said. Too new. There are much older bars in Venice, you know."

"I'm sure," I said politely. He might, of course, simply be mad. Or telling the truth about these ancient bars – but I had no intention of visiting any of them, certainly not with him. He gave me a piercing amber glance from behind the bony beak of the mask.

"You're here because of a woman, aren't you? Because you think you're failing." His English was better than he'd claimed, and that made me suspicious. But my head hummed with the truth of what he'd just said.

"Is it that obvious?" I murmured.

I could feel the sharp gaze, strong as whisky. "If you know what to look for. And you stink of her, of what she did to you. I can see her standing by your shoulder. Tall, pale blue eyes, blonde hair that's pulled too tight."

"Yes, that's her." I felt as though he was sipping at my will, leaving me slack and deflated.

"And she left you, right? Cruelly, without a real ending."

"She ran off to America with one of her company's partners."

"You're well rid of her."

"Yeah, that's what everyone said."

"But she's still in your head, stuck like something between your teeth. You're rid of her and yet she's still there."

Miserably, I nodded. "It's not as though I haven't tried," I said.

He snorted. "Of course you tried. But she was a shadow-stealer. It's written all over you. She made you weak, and now you need to get your shadow back. I can help you."

He rose to his feet. Somehow, I thought he'd be taller. I paid for my barely-touched wine and followed him into the thin winter sunlight.

"Where are we going?" I asked.

"You'll see," he said over his shoulder. "But don't expect to be able to find it again without me. It's known to only a few people, this place."

"So how do you know about it?" I asked. "You're not Venetian, are you?"

"No. I am from the north of Africa."

"Algerian? Moroccan?"

He smiled again. "Something like that. I came to Venice a long time ago. I haven't left it since. I only discovered this place because of a woman, as you will."

"One who left you?"

"One who found me." He did not say more, but led me into the maze of streets at the back of St Mark's Square.

Venice is not a big city, but it seemed to me that we walked for hours, crossing many small bridges but without a glimpse of the Grand Canal or the lagoon. The tourist shops selling masks and stationary, the expensive designer emporia and the tavernas gradually gave way to more practical shop fronts: greengrocers and ironmongers, and then bolted shutters and flaking plaster. The February sunlight dimmed, turning the upper storeys above the alleyways to a deep, fleshy rose. From the throngs around St Mark's, we passed very few people and of those, all were masked: sometimes in the ornate Carnival costumes – elaborate wigs, crinolines decked with roses, towering veiled hats – but increasingly passers-by wore plain white masks that covered the whole face, as austere and fragile as eggshells, and night-soft velvet capes. I glanced up once and saw a slender crescent moon handing over the small square: next moment, it was swallowed in a wisp of cloud. I remembered that I still did not know my companion's name. He turned to me, and in the dying light, his eyes were gold. He said, "We're nearly there."

"We've been walking for so long," I heard myself say, like a fretful child.

"Not so long. Considering."

"Considering what?" I asked, but he had already turned away and was striding down a narrow passage. It led to a dead end: I saw his hand raised to the wall and a door swung open. He stepped through, and I followed.

As the door closed behind me, I saw that we were standing in a garden. I'd glimpsed some of these walled courtyards before, filled with cypress and the winter stumps of vines, or matted palms. But this garden was in full summer tumult: roses tumbled down the ancient brick walls, terracotta tubs were full of geraniums, and hyacinths were growing in the shadows of the cypress. The garden was bordered by three walls: at the back lay a small canal. Lamps cast a dance of light across the water and a boat was gliding in. I caught sight of a shrouded figure crouching in its pointed prow, and then my companion was hustling me inside.

"Everything's growing so well," I said fatuously. "But it's still so cold."

Teeth flashed bone white as he grinned. "It's not so cold, here." And indeed, the garden had been full of Mediterranean warmth, even though there had been no sign of a brazier.

It was too dark inside for me to see where we were. I was aware of people moving around me. A yellow lamp shone and I saw two little faces beneath it: a golden sun and a silver moon. Then the light was abruptly snuffed out and we were in shadow once more. There was a strong, bitter smell, like scorched earth.

"Where are we going?" I asked.

"Down into the depths," a voice replied, and it was not the voice of my companion, but a woman's.

"Who are you?" I said, pulling back, and the light flared up again. I saw a coy masked face above a seventeenth century gown. Her hair was elaborately coiled and coiffed with roses. Her gown, too, was the colour of a wild rose but as my eyes adjusted to the light I saw that what I had thought to be a necklace of rubies was in fact a delicate tracery of blood, like the scratches made by rose thorns. She held up a feathered fan to hide the mask and held out a crooked finger, beckoning me forward.

"Come. Don't be afraid. No one's going to hurt you." Her voice was faintly mocking and it was this that made me step forward. I let her lead me through an arched doorway.

There was a party beyond. A group of men turned to me as I walked through the arch and all their masks were my face, a perfect facsimile, frozen in expressions of surprise or grief or desire.

"What the hell?" I glanced at my companion and her face had changed, too: she wore Julia's face, stiff with contempt. I could see where each blonde hair of her eyebrows had been painted in. I reached out in rage, but she danced away and was gone behind the arch. I span to face the men, but they too were gone.

I blundered through the room, convinced that this was nothing more than some cruel trick. I even suspected Julia of being behind it. Dimly, I was aware that I was not thinking rationally, but it didn't matter. Another arch, and I was out on a little dock.

The garden must have been on the other side of the building, but the dock, too, was wreathed in roses on a trellis of wicker withies. The gondola was waiting, with the shadowy figure at its prow. It motioned for me to get in.

"No!" I spat, and turned to go back in and face my tormentors, but behind me there was only a bare brick wall, weathered with age. I could see no sign that any door had ever existed there. The roses crowded me, pushing, until I was forced to step into the gondola. The figure hefted a pole and we set off.

"Wait," I cried. "Where are we going?"

"Why, to get your shadow back," the voice said. This time, I could not tell whether it was male or female. The tone was light, and sounded young, but when the figure next spoke, it did so in an old person's quaver. "This will be a long voyage. Make yourself comfortable."

This was not like one of the ornate tourist gondolas. It was painted black, but made of thin strips of wood, woven and latticed together. It looked altogether too fragile to be transporting the pair of us. The winged lion of Venice rose in gilt at the far end of the boat and the lion's eyes glinted, as though the thing was alive. Frustrated, I watched as the town slid by: old walls, hidden gardens, secret doors, passages that led nowhere. I kept looking for somewhere to jump off, but the canal was too wide and I didn't fancy my chances in the sewage-contaminated water. So I stayed put, and gradually we left the town behind.

It's hard to say when I noticed the change. One minute we had been passing a huge empty palace, plaster peeling away like leprosy, the upper rooms silent and brooding behind a row of columns, and the next there were only ranks of willows, trailing their white fingery branches in the water.

"Where are we?" I thought we must have somehow crossed the lagoon and headed up a river estuary. My knowledge of the geography of Venice was very limited.

"We are in her world, now."

"What? Whose world?"

"The lady Cardea."

"Who?"

"You don't know her. She left when the new ones came. But those who need her can still find her." It was a young voice again, young and strong and filled with hope.

"Cardea? I've never heard of her."

"She was a goddess once. And is, again and again."

The gondola glided beside the willows. I looked down into the green water and could see nothing in its depths. Then I looked up and saw it.

Protruding perhaps twelve feet out of the water, it was made of wicker withes, the willow gleaming a little in the moonlight. It was shaped like a curved shell, a slender cowrie of wicker, and at first I thought it was empty. Then I saw the head sticking out of the mouth of the wicker shell, a misshapen lump, tilted to one side. The flesh had long since started to rot: the eyes were blank hollows, the hair a tangled mass, wet with riverweed. The mouth gaped open and as I stared, appalled, it gave out a long exhalation like a sigh.

"It's breathing!"

"The soul breathes."

"Its soul is trapped in there?"

"Until the head fully rots, yes. This is an offering, to Her."

I began to shake, cold and clammy as willow in the wind. "Is that what will happen to me?"

"Not to you," said a voice from the bank. "To her, if you will it."

I looked round. My golden-eyed companion was standing

amongst the willows on the bank. His mask was gone, he stood bare-faced, holding a staff. "I told you. You have a chance to get your shadow back. And take revenge."

"Revenge?"

"On your wife. That's what you want, isn't it?"

I became aware that we were not alone. The gondolier was crouching in the prow of the craft, head bent. Behind me, I felt something huge. Power brushed past me. I forced myself to look around.

She filled the sky. Her brow was crowned with wicker withes, her eyes were golden and dreaming as moons. She was not looking at me, but I knew that she knew I was there. She held a sheaf of grain in one hand, and the grains were stars.

"Lady," my companion whispered, and I heard the deference in his voice. Myself, I was not able to utter a sound. He said to me, "She is here to witness the sacrifice. It is your choice to make."

"Sacrifice?" I did not think I had spoken aloud and it surprised me.

"Your wife. Ask, and a basket will be prepared for her."

"You'll bring her *here*?"

"An easy task. Here to this twilight world, where your shadow will be torn from her, and returned to you. And then she will be sewn into the basket and in time, she will die, as her soul rots alongside her body."

The goddess bent her head and an awful anticipation filled the air, causing the willows to rustle and creak. But I heard myself say, "I will not."

I think I surprised him. "Will not? You want revenge, don't you?"

"Yes, but not like this." I don't know where I found the strength to say it, with Cardea at my back, but I spoke all the same. "Not like this. Something human, something small. Not a living death, in an underworld."

"Not even if you are forced to stay in her place?" my

companion said softly.

I felt myself grow colder. My hands were trembling and I knit them together, lacing my fingers. I could not have stood up, so I remained on my knees. I thought of Julia and what she had done to me, the heart she had ripped out. All the betrayals: somehow, I knew that Duncan had not been the first. But I was an adult. Women had left me before, and I had left them. And we survived and carried on, hurting, but still we carried on and eventually it was for the best. I would not be looking for another Julia. But that did not mean I wished her dead.

"I went with you of my free will," I said and it stung to say it. "I won't bring someone else here, even if she is a bitch from hell. I won't do it."

"Well, then," my companion said softly. He turned to the willows. "You were right, beloved."

My aunt Cass stepped out from behind the leaves. Not old, as when I had last seen her, but young and flame-haired and dressed in red. A priestess, I thought to myself. She was smiling.

"I told you."

The gondola bumped gently against the bank and she reached out. I took her hand and she pulled me to my feet. But I was still shaking.

"Don't worry," she said. "It's not for you."

"But he said -"

"She tests Her priests. And she tests them hard. This will not be the first, if you choose to go on."

"Her priests?"

"She is the lady of loss and change."

The golden-eyed man stepped forward. "You are to be my replacement, if you decide to stay. Remain in Venice, look for others like yourself. Show them the old places, help them face their own choices. You will be trained as a priest."

I looked at him. "And you?"

"I?" He smiled at my aunt. "I will be moving on."

I thought of what I had to go back to, of what I had lost. It seemed to me that I could no longer see her face so clearly. The golden-eyed man was holding out a glass, filled with shadows.

"Your choice," he said. And I reached out and drank it.

Books by Liz Williams

Detective Inspector Chen
Snake Agent (2005)
The Demon and the City (2006)
Precious Dragon (2007)
The Shadow Pavilion (2008)
The Iron Khan (2010)
Morningstar (coming soon, 2012)

Darkland
Darkland (2006)
Bloodmind (2007)

Novels
The Ghost Sister (2001)
Empire of Bones (2002)
The Poison Master (2002)
Nine Layers of Sky (2003)
Banner of Souls (2004)
Winterstrike (2008)
Worldsoul – Book 1 (coming soon, 2012)

Collections
Banquet of the Lords of Night (2004)
A Glass of Shadow (2011)

Fantastical Autobiographical
Diary of a Witchcraft Shop (with Trevor Jones) (Autumn 2011)

Nestling in the idyllic Somerset countryside, overlooked by Britain's most famous Tor, steeped in both myth and history, and host to one of the world's most popular music festivals, Glastonbury is a village quite unlike any other.

The spiritual and the curious, the enlightened and the strange, the weird and the wonderful: all manner of folk feel drawn to Glastonbury for all manner of reasons. Many find their way into a delightfully quirky treasure trove of a shop run by Trevor Jones and Liz Williams, who now open its door and bid you enter their world. You will be enchanted, you will be amused and amazed, but, most of all, please be welcome…

Coming Soon from NewCon Press

Diary of a Witchcraft Shop

By Trevor Jones and Liz Williams

In 2005, fantasy and SF author extraordinaire Liz Williams took the plunge, moving from her beloved Brighton to Glastonbury to live with her partner, Trevor Jones. Trevor ran a witchcraft shop. Liz's life would never be the same again…

"When you find yourself on a London platform shouting into your mobile, 'We haven't got enough demons! Do you want me to order some more?' as folk quietly edge away from you – you know you're running a witchcraft shop."

Entertaining, enlightening, hilarious and unpredictable
Look for *Diary of a Witchcraft Shop* Autumn 2011

Fables from the Fountain

Edited by Ian Whates

A volume of all original stories written as homage to Arthur C. Clarke's classic *Tales from the White Hart*, featuring many of today's top genre writers, including **Neil Gaiman, Charles Stross, Stephen Baxter, James Lovegrove, Liz Williams, Adam Roberts, Eric Brown, Ian Watson, Peter Crowther**, and **David Langford.**

The Fountain, a traditional London pub situated in Holborn, just off Chancery Lane, where Michael, the landlord, serves excellent real ales and dodgy ploughman's, ably assisted by barmaids Sally and Bogna.

The Fountain, in whose Paradise bar a group of friends: scientists, writers and genre fans, meet regularly on a Tuesday night to swap anecdotes, reveal wondrous events from their past, tell tall tales, talk of classified invention and, maybe, just *maybe*, save the world…

Available now from the NewCon Press website,

A5 paperback edition, plus
A special dust-jacketed hardback edition signed by all the authors on two bespoke signing pages. Limited to just 200 individually numbered copies.

www.newconpress.co.uk